Madame Eve's 1 Night Stand Holiday Anthology

Santa, Cutie by Cerise DeLand

He Came Upon a Midnight Clear by Desiree Holt

This Endris Night by D.L. Jackson

All She Wants for Christmas is Her Dom by Stacey Kennedy

I'll be Mated for Christmas by Rebecca Royce

Her First White Christmas by Liia Ann White

Silent Night's Seduction by Clarissa Yip

Decadent Publishing Company

www.decadentpublishing.com

This is an original publication of Decadent Publishing. These stories are a collection of fiction and any similarity to actual persons or events is purely coincidental.

Decadent Publishing Company, LLC
P.O. Box 407
Klawock, AK 99925
www.decadentpublishing.com

Madame Eve's 1 Night Stand Holiday Anthology

Cover design by Fantasia Frog and Cribley Designs
ISBN: 978-1-61333-107-1

Santa, Cutie

by

Cerise DeLand

Chapter One

"Santa, honey," Susanna Corrigan muttered to herself as the tiny private jet bounced through clouds and began their stomach-churning descent from thirty thousand feet. "I hope you know what you're doing."

Castle Alaska might not be the North Pole, but it was definitely not the place she'd hoped to go when she'd filled out the application last summer for 1Night Stand. She'd hoped for a hook-up with a great guy in one of Castillo Resorts' famed locations like Hawaii. Tahiti. Heck, she'd even dreamt of Casablanca! But *Alaska?* "Not even close."

Someplace hot would've been nice, but ice? Not my idea of fun. Never was.

She shivered and clutched her coat collar higher. *The things I do for love.* Or in this case, a mind-blowing night with a man who wanted only pleasure. No ties. No promises. No complications.

And to get that, I'm here to spend six days cuddled up by a fire. She got a mental image of herself wearing one of those ugly furry hats with fat earflaps and layers of reeeeeally bulky sweaters and coats, hiking boots, and sporting a red nose.

Like Rudolf. She chuckled and shot a look out her window.

Whoops. *Wrong move.* She gulped as the bush plane dropped through clouds to pass gorgeous snow-capped mountains that glistened in the eerie northern light of midday. She murmured in gratitude that the pilot was taking them quickly down to the frozen ground. *Nope. Make that...water. Oh, boy.* She dug her nails into the plush armrests.

"Is that—?" She managed to catch the eye of the male passenger across the aisle from her and pointed downward. "Is that the ocean?"

"Yes, but an inlet." The man assured her with a nod. "I've visited here before. So not to worry, the pilot is an expert at landing."

"Swell."

But amazingly, it was. Grand. Fast. Efficient. Smooth. *And I didn't toss my cookies!*

"Thank you," she told the pilot as she extended her hand to help her down the ramp and the two steps to the waiting van. "I enjoyed the landing."

"Good, Ms. Corrigan. Glad you made it for this morning's flight."

"Me, too. The eight inches of snow in Portland yesterday stopped everyone. Especially my rickety old Volvo. But now, I'm ready to get inside the lodge and get warm."

"Then might I suggest you go for a swim in the heated pool in the recreation wing and indulge yourself with a massage at the spa?"

She grinned at him. Clearly, Madame Eve, the owner of 1Night Stand, had provided excellent accommodations, even in the wilds of Alaska. "I will. Anything special you suggest for lunch?"

"Beef bourguignon. And hot chocolate."

"Love it. Thanks. Sorry to have been a Nervous Nelly."

Gil Santana promised himself one more lap before he treated himself to lunch and for a chaser, a snifter of Armagnac. He extended his arm in the pool, ready to push off once more, but his eyes snagged on movement at the far doors. His gaze glued to the perfect vision that walked through them and his mouth fell open.

Through the ladies' spa entrance came a female who took his breath away. The way she walked. Like a queen. The way she pushed back her shoulder-length hair into a ponytail and rubbed her hands together in glee like a kid eager to jump in the creek on a hot summer day. She was, undoubtedly, the most beautiful woman he'd seen here at the resort or in fact, anywhere.

Even in Hollywood.

Hey, Santana, that is the plan, man. You're here to find a woman who isn't like the aggressive types in Los Angeles. So what if this one strikes you as....

Luscious.

He blinked. She strolled to a lounge chair and inched out of her flip-flops.

Five-five or so. Red hair. Lush, wavy hair the color of merlot. Never-from-a-bottle, intoxicating red hair. Oval face. Dark eyes. *Damn! What color?*

She looked around. Didn't spot him, thank goodness. Then she smiled to herself. Padded over to the shallow end, stuck her toes in the water, and grinned.

He swallowed hard and didn't make a move. He wanted to enjoy her. She shook back her hair and pulled at the bottom of her suit. Snapped it beneath the crease of her gorgeous, firm ass and took the steps down slowly into the water. She was quite incredibly lovely.

Quite incredibly *built.*

Madre Mia. With breasts. Half moons. Nipples pebbled beneath the white spandex of her conservative, one-piece suit. Hips like God should give all women. And thighs. Trim. Knees. Cute. Long, long, *long* legs.

Down boy. His cock did not obey. And Gil had to agree with the big guy. This woman was worth the salute.

Stop it, Santana. You act like a drooling teenager.

Yeah, but, wow, did he hope she was his for this 1Night Stand thing.

How could she be?

Yeah, true.

She looks exactly like the type you don't want. She looks like a wannabe movie star who'll do anything to get a part. Including wearing a sign, Casting Couches R Us.

He'd written his request on his questionnaire. *No actresses.* In Hollywood for nearly ten years, he had left Tinseltown last fall for Oregon and a post as a professor in a college fine arts department. If the day job was fulfilling, teaching kids about the history of cinema, he got as big a kick from his "night" job putting together his own independent film company. And he had decided to apply at 1Night Stand for a night of pleasure on a recommendation from a scriptwriter. The man had done one and not only had a great time with the woman they chose for him, but continued the relationship after their fun-filled night.

Gil frowned. He didn't hope for happily-ever-after. He was perhaps too jaded for that. But he did believe it was possible to have a brief affair and value it for what it was. Short. Hot. Creative. And memorable.

Then something hit him right between the eyes.

Chapter Two

"Oh, oh!" Susanna floundered, stunned she'd hit solid flesh. She treaded water and set eyes on the human she'd barged into. "Oh, no! I am so sorry." And as she wiped droplets from her eyes and got a good look at the man she'd clobbered, she slowly sank beneath the surface.

"Hey, hey!" Big hands grabbed her arms and pulled her up against a sweet, hard wall of dark-haired man. Blue-eyed, black-haired *aroused* man. "Don't drown!"

How about in those eyes? She blinked, snapped her mouth shut, and tried to sound less like the idiot who had plowed into him. "I am so very sorry. I was doing the backstroke and not watching where I was going. Did I hurt you?"

"Not at all." His cobalt blue gaze danced all over her face, while he held her close and her legs tangled with his.

"But you have a red mark on your forehead," she noted, as she tried to get some decent distance between his body and her own.

"My bull's eye. Draws only beautiful redheads." His mouth widened in a grin.

His wide, generous mouth and big, straight white teeth made her wonder how he tasted. His breath smelled minty. Her head spun while one of her legs found no purchase, except around his left hip. *Damn, how forward is this? How much of an airhead are you, Corrigan?* "Do all redheads hit you?"

"No, only you."

She stopped fighting him then. The voice killed her. Like a booming storm at sea, it rumbled in his chest and rolled right into her own. Thrilled her insides. Heated her nipples. Flooded her pussy. Made her want to press closer to that long piece of steel that stood rigidly against her belly.

"Gil Santana," he introduced himself as he seemed to drink in all the features of her face. "I've been here for two days. Still unattached. And you?"

"I should have been here yesterday, but got here only a few hours ago. I hate the cold. Had to get warm."

"I'd say it's hot in here now." His voice, his big, deep, bass voice, dropped another octave to illustrate how scorching he thought the pool was.

She gulped, put a hand to his delightfully muscular and furry chest then wiggled her brows. "A little too hot for folks who've just met."

"I can correct that." He punctuated his offer with a little hug. "Have you had lunch?"

"I did," she said as she wrapped her arms around his neck, largely because it was him or leaving his embrace to grab the side of the pool. "This is awfully embarrassing, don't you think? Let me take hold of the—"

"Come sit with me while I have lunch then," he offered, ignoring her plea. "I'll wait for you while you finish your swim. I'll buy you a drink."

"Dessert."

"A woman who eats dessert! Done!"

She grinned at him, realizing she was stroking her fingers over the sculpted power of the nape of his neck. "You know only skinny women?"

"Let's say I've known too many. I like a woman who takes what she wants."

Somehow the way he said those words as he watched her mouth and pressed her so close her nipples drilled into his chest, made her pussy clench with need. "That's me," she managed on a whisper. "Old enough, hopefully wise enough to say what I want and reach for it. Including chocolate." *And you. Would I be wise if I reached for you?*

He inhaled; his eyes narrowed and examined her own.

With that searing blue glance, she might have moved, pushed the fabric of her swimsuit to one side, and guided his thick hard cock into her needy channel. "This is not wise."

"You don't believe in the value of lust at first sight? Neither do I." His gravelly bedroom voice said how badly he wanted to be inside her. "So, we're going to do lunch."

"And dessert."

"Anything you want." He swirled her around so she could grasp the concrete edge. "Ten minutes? In the restaurant with the view of the mountains?"

"Fifteen minutes. I need time to...you know, get ready. I'm all wet."

The way he threw back his head to laugh at her words shocked her and then shook her to the core, even as she knew she blushed like a virgin bride.

"I know you're wet, honey. I'm a mess myself."

His self-criticism tickled her. Men with looks usually had no humor. They were too self-impressed to bother cultivating any wit. So she let her eyes admire the big masculine beauty of his very honed body as he jumped up to the ledge and stood peering down at her, his cock bulging enticingly in his bright blue Speedo.

"A very impressive, hot mess, Mr. Santana."

He winked at her. "Takes one to know one, lady." Then he turned and walked away, leaving her to lick her lips over the sight of his broad back, his tight buns, and the long, lean legs that she'd been so fortunate as to wrap her own around.

"Santa, honey, do I get to do that again?" *And at what cost, if I'm destined for a one-night stand with another man?*

She would force herself to go down into the main dining room for dinner! She hadn't gone to meet Gil Santana for lunch. Nervous that she might start a relationship she knew she couldn't finish, she had remained in her room.

Now, donning one of her own designs, a cocktail dress of sapphire silk, she tied up the corset that cupped her breasts and smoothed the waterfall of fabric that fell to her knees. Then she frowned into the full-length mirror in her suite.

Oh, hell, Suzie. Get out of here and go look for the man you are supposed to be with. Or hope for the message that will tell you tonight's your night. And his name is...Joe Smith!

She stuck her tongue out at herself, picked up her purse, slung the tiny strap over her shoulder, and strode to her door.

But riding down in the elevator, she brooded.

Never out of her room all afternoon, she accused herself of being every kind of chicken, wimp, and nut case. What was wrong with her? Couldn't she have lunch with a man without thinking about jumping his bones? Couldn't she get to know him? Couldn't she just take what came her way?

That was what life was, right? Fate, fortune, serendipity! The things that happened on the way to careful plans. So what if Gil Santana was attractive? So damn attractive she could have crawled right up on his thighs and let him fill her up, take her high and hard and enjoy the moment. That was what she was here for.

She moved over as the elevator stopped and more guests got in.

She was a mess, all right. Gil had been right. Was she so horny she thought the nearest man was the best thing that ever happened to her?

No. That was not the woman she was. She had never fallen into bed with a man if she hadn't felt anything for him. And Gil Santana had appealed to more than her libido. Though just why that was, she couldn't quite say.

In any case, she was here to spend a few days with one man whom someone else had selected for her. A man meant for her. By specific inclination and detail.

So why would she screw that up for a few minutes in the

company of someone else?

She had ethics. She had a good opinion of herself. And coming to a place—okay, coming to Alaska—for a Christmas holiday was meant to be a fun-filled time. No ties. No commitments. Her career should consume all her time and leave no room for a lover. That's what she had promised herself. Her one-night stand would be only that. A temporary affair. A passing fancy.

Even if your one-night stand might be Gil Santana?

"Yes, even if," she said, and the couple next to her gazed at her as if she were a little mad. She shot them a wan smile.

Thank God, the elevator doors swished open and she watched all the others exit.

She inhaled. N*o time like the present to be brave. And I am hungry.*

She wandered down the hall toward the main lobby. Tons of people, mostly couples, were standing, talking, laughing. *Oh, hell. Your prince had better come find you soon!*

In the meantime? Dinner! Food!

She pivoted toward the wing where, according to the map of the resort, the French restaurant was. Tonight, she'd relish some escargot and a good Bordeaux.

"*Bon Soir, Monsieur,*" she greeted the *maitre d'*. "Table for one, please."

He frowned at her. "*Jeer suis desole, Mademoiselle.* I have nothing for another hour or so. Would you like to wait in the bar?"

"No, *merci.*" Drinking, especially drinking alone, was not her scene.

"Perhaps the ballroom then? Take this ringer. It will vibrate when I have a table."

"What's going on in the ballroom?" She turned toward the music that sounded more like a waltz than disco.

"Tonight we have a band that plays hit songs from famous Broadway shows and movies."

"Really? Okay, that's where I'll be!"

"Your ringer, *Mademoiselle.* And your name, please?"

"Yes, yes." She told him, tucked the pager in her purse, and hurried off to the entrance to the ballroom. There up on a dais was a full orchestra with violins and trumpets, bass fiddles, guitars, the works. This was heaven!

Her mother and father had been wardrobe mistress and warder for one of the oldest, finest Broadway theaters. She'd learned her own trade, most of her sewing techniques from them. After her college graduation when she told them she wanted to design for the theater, they were overjoyed. Even if she had never fulfilled their expectations to serve Broadway productions herself, they assured her they adored her and that she must always do what her heart said was right. Being wardrobe mistress and draper at a resort in Las Vegas for six years had allowed her to cut her teeth in the industry. Now that she had her new job as costume designer for the Ashcroft, Oregon Shakespeare Festival, she knew her mom and dad smiled down on her from heaven. And she herself was smiling now as the orchestra ended the waltz from "The King and I" and started a number from one of Fred Astaire and Ginger Rogers' famous flicks.

A hand came to land around her waist—and hug her close. As if she knew how well his body molded to hers in this position, as in the pool, she knew she needn't feel alarm. Oh, my. She *knew* the man beside her was no other but Gil Santana.

Every inch of him—plane to plane, curve for curve—seemed meant for her. His heat warmed her every cell. His scents of cardamom and citrus filled her nostrils and swam in her head. She closed her eyes, as red-hot lava of desire burst over her, melting her mind and sinking her against him.

"I saw only you even here in this crowd." His resonant voice flowed over her like tropical sunshine. "I love the dress you almost have on."

She chuckled, but dared not look up at him because she hadn't calmed her raging heart just yet. "I designed it."

"It suits you. The color. The cut. The silk shows every man in the room how stunning your body is." His breath was near her ear. Mint again. Seducing her. Thrilling her. "I missed you at lunch."

"I decided not to come." She met his gaze with her own bold

one. "I'm here to meet someone."

His face went lax with despair. "An arranged meeting?"

She swallowed hard on the truth. "Yes. A one—"

"A one-night stand?" The hope in his voice caught her by surprise.

"Yes," she acknowledged with trepidation he'd think her a loser or an opportunist to have to go to Alaska to meet a stranger for a grand, if brief, affair.

"So then," he declared in a tone so mellow she knew he understood her challenge, "you didn't come to lunch because you were afraid?"

"Conflicted."

"I know." He buried his lips in the crown of her hair and hugged her closer. "I am, too. You see that's why I'm here, as well."

"You *are?*" The urge to hug him back made her quiver with the expectation that he had met no one else yet whom he liked better and no one yet whom he *should* like better. "So...you haven't gotten any instructions yet?"

"None. Any for you?" he persisted.

She felt like she'd burst with joy. "I'm thrilled to say no."

"Well, then." He took her hand so gently, she thought he might think her made of glass. "Let's face the music and dance."

Breaking into a grin, recognizing the title of the song and the problem they both faced, she let him lead her out to the polished floor. From the back, in a dark suit, he looked so smart, so debonair, she wanted to email Madame Eve and tell her she'd found her man. *This man.*

He turned and faced her.

Her heart did stop this time. He was so stunning, she could barely think of a thing to say. Logic rose up and she blessed her meager brain cells for it. "How do I know you can dance, Mr. Santana?"

"You won't until you've danced with me at least a dozen or more times." He pulled her toward him and now, at last, she let herself feast on the man in her arms.

The man in the pool with cobalt blue eyes and wet black hair had been a sleek, charming creature. This man was more. Dry. Combed. Polished. Dressed. He was every tall, dark, handsome icon stage and film had devised. Dashing. But dangerous. He was Laurence Olivier, Cary Grant. A hint of James Bond with Hispanic machismo, thick black lashes, and a powerful frame. More than all of that, he was real, here, virile, and warm beneath her fingers, and for now, hers. She couldn't get over how arresting he was. His forehead was high. His cheeks carved. His jaw square. A dimple, a smidgen there to the left. And then there was his mouth.

She licked her lips.

His mouth. Generous and firm. Oh, sin had never looked so irresistible.

"Darling," he told her in a thread of sound, "we're here to dance. Neither of us will last longer than two measures if you keep looking at me like that."

"I love the scenery." Her clear conviction belied the raging desire she felt in her bones.

His expression softened as he wrapped her closer. "Fox trot."

At his command, she burst out laughing but had absolutely not one moment to think as he swept her away to do just that. And. Oh. My. God. Was he good.

She had a helluva time keeping up, but she got into the swing of it so much that other couples left the floor to watch them. Blushing, proud, counting on years of her father's lessons and ballet and some kind of grace to get her through, she watched Gil's face and felt his body lead her, take her, compel her to the most fascinating use of it she'd had with a man ever.

And as the music died, she was thrilled. Sad. Hating the end of it.

"God, you are wonderful." He crushed her against him and picked her up to swing her around while those near them applauded.

"Again?" She hugged him close in glee. "Can we do that again?" She leaned back, cupped his movie-idol face in her hands, and beseeched him. "I haven't done that in years. So many men have no idea how to dance."

He arched a wicked dark brow and nodded toward the orchestra. "I will do anything you want. Dancing for a start. To this? Do you...do *this?*"

"Tango?" She wanted to kiss him! Absurd delight swept up her spine. "You *tango?*"

He put one hand on her waist and lifted her other hand high in the proper position. His eyes adored her own, then caressed her lips. "I hope we don't split your dress."

"Promise."

"God save me," he murmured and then took her, possessed her, and as the sultry music decreed, he made love to her in front of a hundred people or more. He commanded the floor and she followed him. He seduced her with his rhythm, his agility, the power of his arms, and the strength of his legs. She reveled in his dexterity, his drama. Like the tormented affair within the music, she played her part as the temperamental woman. She taunted him, rejected him, and he caught her back, refusing to give her up, demanding she surrender to the attraction that bound them both. Consumed them and made them one body, one mind, one soul.

Even as the music died, she stood in his arms, flush to his body, all his as she had never been with any other partner on a dance floor. Or off.

The applause this time was thunderous. Even the orchestra members joined in.

"Dinner." Gil took her arm, seemingly unable to look at her for more than a second. "We need conversation, something to do with our hands. A table between us."

Chapter Three

Her big baby doll eyes were gray.

Gray as a summer storm. Gray as charcoal. Dewy like summer rain on flower petals. Gil had finally gotten a good look at them as she smiled up at him when they danced. He hadn't wanted to stop looking at them.

But if he hadn't, he would have crashed them both into ten other couples and never had the chance to charm her or please her.

He led her from the ballroom, knowing he'd better hurry to put some space between them before he carried her off like a caveman and made love to her like one.

She suggested the French restaurant, blessedly close, with a table for two available now.

Gil asked the *maitre d'* for a quiet corner. In a sumptuous leather semi-circular banquette, he slid in beside her but stayed well away. The two of them had touched enough of each other in their two brief encounters. Gil thought for sure if he got any nearer her sweet supple body again tonight, he'd go up in flames.

And you've got to get hold of your mind here, Santana. There is no real reason on earth to feel so bound to her if you know nothing about her. *Talk, dammit.*

"Do you like seafood?" he asked her, trying to be a good boy, keep his hands to himself and peruse the menu.

"I do. Anything at all. Except eel."

He winced. "Not my favorite, either. How about for appetizer, half a dozen oysters?"

"Great, with a chaser of escargot? To split, of course."

He glanced up at the waiter. "So it is."

As the man left them alone, Gil fought for a way to open a neutral topic, something to take them from the simmering desire that pounded in his blood. Shocked he couldn't find anything at once, he satisfied himself with examining her hands. Long fingers. Short nails that were her own, nothing fake. Clear polish. Small wrists. A bit of a tan on that flawless skin, despite the season. His eyes, poor willful things, couldn't seem to stop on the way to her shoulders...and the tops of her breasts.

She shifted. "Gil Santana, it is get to know each other time."

Recognizing her discomfort at his forwardness, he covered her hands with one of his own. "I'm sorry. I'm not being a gentleman."

"I like you as you are, though." She swallowed, then met his gaze dead on. "And if you look at me like a hungry wolf, I'm bad enough to say, I like it. But I'm not used to it."

"You must live near blind men."

Falling back in her seat, she hooted in laughter and waved a hand about. "There! You see? You tickle me."

He nodded. "I can see by the way you look at me."

"How's that?" she whispered.

"Like you can't ever stop."

Her mouth formed a perfect little O.

Wild to strip her and take her right here on this table in front of these very nice people, he knew he'd better dial back the dialogue to acceptable dining room conversation. His brows rose by silly little increments. "You do more than tickle me. My funny bone is—" He stopped short, realizing despite his good intentions, he was about to say something risqué and he didn't want to frighten this lovely creature and make her run from him.

"Ah." She tipped her head. "Shorter than other bones, perhaps?"

He barked in laughter. "Honey, you are definitely such a

surprise!"

"So are you," she said in that smooth contralto that put him in mind of whiskey-voiced jazz chanteuses. "I don't usually click with men I meet. Not at first."

"I can't understand why not."

She shrugged, taking her time to form her words. "I don't do chit-chat. I work too hard. All work and no play makes me a dull girl. I don't do a lot of parties or the bar scene, and I prefer my own company to poor company."

"Agreed. And what do you do?"

She swept her hands down her bodice. "I'm a designer."

"Professionally?" This time when he examined the way the sapphire corset hugged her full, creamy breasts and the silk smoothed over her ribs to a small waist and flared over her thighs, he was appreciating the artistry as well as the delicious woman inside it. "You are talented. In the ballroom when you said you designed it, I thought you meant you sewed it. I owe you an apology. It is quite stunning. The corsetry looks...expert."

"Thank you. I am. An expert, that is. On Elizabethan period attire. I make tons of corsets or rather, now, my draper sizes them and my seamstresses fit and sew them. And did you know your mouth is hanging open?"

He snapped it shut and grinned at her. "No, I did not. But thank you for that. I hate flies. And for whom do you design all these wonderful garments?"

Her smile went wide and showed the pride she took in her work. "I was appointed costume designer to the Ashcroft, Oregon Shakespeare Festival this past September and my first season's costumes will appear in this summer's plays."

"Ashcroft." *How far is that from Portland?* "And have you always done period clothing? Designs, I mean?"

"Yes. My last job was in Las Vegas."

Rambling on, she told him the name of the resort where she had worked as the wardrobe mistress. It was a five-star getaway he had visited often with producers and investors for various film projects. A place where for years, he could have found her within minutes. So close. And yet so far.

She had come to a stop, confused by his silence and maybe even the dumb look on his face. “What’s the matter?”

“I’m sorry. I’m being stupid here. You see, I’ve been there so often. I could have seen you. Met you. Who knows? We could have—”

“Gotten to know each other sooner?” Compassion glistened in her soft gray eyes. “Life doesn’t work like that, does it?”

“No,” he said, hearing some ineffable sadness in her tone and wondering about the cause. “Sometimes it has to work in odd ways.”

“In its own time.” She squeezed his hand and let go to put hers in her lap. “I’m thrilled to be with you here now.”

What had he just said that made her withdraw from him physically? Frowning, he sat back. At once, he knew. “You don’t have affairs, do you?”

Her eyes on him, she shook her head. “No.”

He reached across to tip up her chin. “I don’t, either. Not worth it.”

Tiny tears dotted her lashes. “I am not a nun.”

“God, honey, I hope not! I’m not a monk.”

“I applied for a one-night stand because I wanted to be close to someone if only for a few hours. Someone who might understand me without all the trappings of introductions and movie dates and....”

“I understand. That’s why I’m here, too.”

The waiter appeared and they sat back, watching him uncork the bottle, offer Gil a little wine to taste, then pour it for both of them.

Cutting the icy silence, Gil raised his glass toward her. “To the two people who never took vows of celibacy.”

She feigned a horrified grimace, but he could see she was still uneasy. Dying to change that, he asked, “How do you like the wine?”

“Love it.”

Another waiter hovered over them with their oysters and

escargot.

"What do you think? Look good?" Gil asked of their appetizers after the man departed. Still looking for daylight in a dark atmosphere.

Surveying their hors d'oeurvres, she got a comically dreamy look on her face and then rolled her eyes at him. "They look absolutely delectable."

Like you. "Shall we?" He lifted his fish fork.

She raised hers, then put it down. "Because I don't have affairs, doesn't mean I don't want to."

His gaze dropped to her lips as he said, "I think we should text Madame Eve and tell her she's been terrific but we've found our own partners for our one-night stand."

As if she saw a pot of gold at the end of a rainbow, she straightened and stared him in the eye. "You're right."

The urge to kiss her welled up in him like volcanic rock. "We can't go on like this.

"How can this feel so right if you and I are not meant—?"

"Sir?" Their waiter appeared at Gil's side and bowed slightly. "Mister Santana, is that correct?"

Gil shot a look from the waiter's face to his hands where he held an envelope. *Oh, no, not now. Not this. If that's what I think it is, I can't go through with this agreement.*

"Yes, I am he." Gil put out his hand. Best to get on with contacting Eve. "Give it to me." His head pounded with fear.

"Gil?"

Tearing into the envelope, he paused to look into pleading gray eyes.

"Gil, listen to me. Whatever that note says, we'll get through it."

"I know we will. It has to be you."

"Open it."

He tore at the edges. "Hell. From Madame Eve, all right." He read it once. Twice. The letters swam before his eyes. Just when things were getting good. Great. Unbelievably wonderful.

Wait!

He stared at the redhead next to him who had come to mean laughter and warmth and shared values to him. Her face was tight with tension. "What's your name?"

Her fine red brows knit together.

"You never told me your name, honey. What is it?"

"Susanna Corrigan."

Groaning, he crushed the paper in his hands and struggled out of the damn booth, then signaled their waiter. "All this and two steaks, medium rare, my room, 342. And a bottle of Brunello. Chocolate something for dessert."

Susanna had turned her head to one side. Clearly, she was not listening but sliding to her side of the leather seat. But as she was about to stand, he stepped toward her and pulled her to her feet. "Susanna Corrigan, I do believe you were meant for me."

Stunned, her lovely gray eyes devoured his own. "You're serious."

"No doubt about it. You belong to me. You knew it, so did I, long before I got that."

She held back, mouthing soundless objection. "But...if you got yours, where's mine?"

He braced his feet and looked her squarely in the eye. "Maybe they couldn't find you."

Sunshine broke over her face. Her eyes twinkled and her nose wrinkled. Her lips spread wide in glee. "We found each other."

As they hurried from the dining room through the corridor toward the hall, the only part of him she dared touch was his hand. Warm and strong, he gripped her as they took the empty elevator up the three floors and down the long, endless hall to his room. As he extracted his key card from his trouser pocket and unlocked the door, Susanna tried to catch her breath and steal some reason from the overwhelming desire to strip him of his clothes the minute they had any privacy.

As he pulled her inside, Susanna backed up against the wall

and heard him turn the security lock. In the dim light, she examined the stark contrasts of the hollows and planes of his facial features. He was so devastatingly handsome, she had to press her thighs together to quell the need to have him inside her in the next second.

His breath heavy and hot, he lifted her chin. "You are the most beautiful woman I have ever met. I don't want to rush you, but I think I'll die if I can't have you soon."

Quivering from head to toe at his declaration, she put her fingertips to his lips. "I feel the same, but I don't want it over *too* soon."

He pressed tiny kisses to her fingers, laughing. "You can't believe there will be only one time."

"Oh, no. Not merely once with you, Mister Santana." She brushed her breasts against his chest, loving the friction of her silk dress against his wool coat. "We'll be craven. Exhausted. And oh so happy when we're done."

His indigo eyes narrowed on hers. "We might never be done."

Once more, she stilled his movement and his words with her fingertips to his mouth. "I can't bank on that. You shouldn't either." *If I cared too much for you and lost you, I would dissolve into a crazy mess. I can't let that happen. Can't.*

Wrapping his arms around her, he drew her close. "For now. Let's live for now."

She pushed him back a bit and smoothed the collar of his crisp blue shirt and the expensive silk of his navy and gold tie. Then she began to undo it. "Let me take the measure of the man then, shall I?"

"You'll undress me?" He cocked a brow at her as her hands got busy.

"For each piece, I'll tell you a fact about me."

"I get it." His fingers bit into her wrists. "So we won't be strangers when we make love?"

She nodded, proud of his prescience. "Exactly."

"Deal but when I'm naked, I undress you."

She tipped her head and wiggled her brows at him. "You'd like that?"

"*Like?*" He held his arms out to his sides as she sank her palms against his broad chest and smoothed his suit coat from his shoulders. "Lady, no such word exists for me where you're concerned."

"Passion," she crooned as she undid the buttons of his shirt and tugged it from his trousers to land on the floor with his other clothes. "I might become addicted to your passion."

"The tie, the coat, the shirt now are gone," he said with a tight jaw. "Three facts, baby, before you move on."

"I was born in Manhattan, lived there even for college, and hated Vegas. Oh, *Gil....*" She skimmed her palms up over his six-pack to his sculpted shoulder blades and down his long, corded, heavily veined arms. "Gil, you are a beautiful animal. All sinew and muscle. I'd say you are...um...a forty-two in the chest." She tried to circle her fingers around the bulge of his triceps. "Maybe twenty inches here. You'd make a very hunky Othello, you know. Or a dashing Henry the Fifth."

Tracing the arc of her cheekbones, he got a funny gleam in his eyes. "When you touch me, I feel more like the Incredible Hulk."

She nestled her lips to the hollow of his throat and rubbed her nose against his fragrant skin. "Not you. You're too fine a man for that. And I love the way you smell. The citrus. The way you dance. *You.* Everything about you."

Shoving a leg between hers, he pushed her back to the wall and with two thumbs raised her chin. His cobalt eyes swam with dangerous lights. "You'd. Better. Hurry. Here."

She chuckled, letting the satisfaction in her gaze tell him she was putty in his hands. "I've never known a man so interested in me."

"Good." And then he kissed her—like a man claims the woman he cannot live without, like a caveman needs a mate, like flowers crave sunshine. He broke away, dragging air into his lungs. "I'll work to make sure you never know another man as desperate to have you."

He kissed her again, his lips this time supple and coaxing,

insistent and lingering, sweet then wild, demanding surrender until she felt her core swell to near exploding, until her thong soaked for the hundredth time tonight in need of him. Until she wanted only to undo his fly and have him high up inside her.

He groaned, then broke the kiss. She was dazed as he pushed away and took her hands to place them on his belt. With a flick of her fingers, she unhooked the buckle and slid it from his waist. Facts were the furthest things from her mind and so she told him a simple one. “I’m thirty-one.”

He placed her fingers on his waistband button. “And what’s your favorite song?”

Floating with this dreamy man so close, she let her head fall back so she could better admire his taut features. *The hungry wolf*, she mused and smiled. “Anything that I’m dancing to with you.”

He clamped his hand over hers and led her to undo the button. At once, his trousers hit the floor.

Susanna caught her breath, not daring to look down, not needing to in order to know that he was fully erect, and that even standing up, like in the pool, he would fit her. Precisely. Deeply. “Gil,” she sighed his name, her eyes closing, overcome with the need and the awe-inspiring power of his nearness.

Some part of her knew that he stepped out of his shoes and bent to remove his socks while she seemed suspended in air, lolling against the wall.

“My turn,” he announced.

Licking her lips, she wound her arms around his shoulders. “Kiss me again.”

She felt his chest heave with a small chuckle while he put his hands to the clasp of her necklace and slipped her earrings from her lobes.

“In a minute, I’m going to kiss you until you don’t know your name.”

“Oh. Make. My. Day,” she taunted him. “But first. Three facts for the jewelry.”

He tweaked her nose, then bent to place the items on the side table. When he came back to her, he settled her hips against his, so closely, so precisely that she moaned.

"I grew up along the border in South Texas. Went to school in New York City. At the University."

When she opened her mouth in surprise, he gave her a winsome look. "Chance. Timing. Our chance, our time is now. Besides, did you go to NYU, too?"

She shook her head. "No. Parsons."

He hugged her a little. "See? Not our time or place. Besides, I'm older than you."

Feeling the rightness of this meeting with every passing moment, she grinned. "Not too much older."

"Six years." He brushed an index finger around the outline of her lips. "By the time you were a freshman, I was long gone."

"Where did you go?" she asked, knowing she sounded forlorn, betting he had been as fascinating as a young man as he was an older one in his prime.

"London." He put his lips to her forehead. "Ever been there?"

"No."

"I'll take you there," he promised her. "But now, this second, I'm here...."

"Wanting me," she whispered, complimented, thrilled, impatiently digging her fingers into his flesh.

"Wanting you," he confirmed, his gaze dropping to the corset even as his long, lean fingers picked up the ends of the laces and pulled the bow loose. Then, with shaking hands, he hooked two fingers inside her lacings and left the front of the corset gaping. Seeing the edges of her nipples become visible above the dark silk, she felt her skin pebble, contract, and heat. He tugged once more and the corset fell completely away, sagging to her waist.

In ragged Spanish, he said something she knew spoke of molten need. He watched her for long, sultry seconds, drinking in the sight of her exposed breasts. At once, his fingers circled her waist, sought a zipper and found it, then yanked it down. Her skirt drooped, taking the whole garment down to catch on her hipbones. In one smooth whoosh, his hands pushed the silk to the floor and then the fiery satin of his skin met hers, from chest to belly, thighs to thighs. His cock was a blazing brand to her stomach and she moved, softly mewling her hunger for him. His fingers delved beneath the waistband of her thong while he demanded, "Look at me."

Clinging to his arms as if she clung to a life raft in a hurricane, she could barely see him in the haze of her longing.

"You are going to remove my briefs and I'm going to tell you one fact more. Then I'll take this scrap of material off you and you will tell me one thing about you. After that, the only sounds you'll hear will be me loving you. The way this was meant to be."

Hands trembling, she skimmed her palms over his hips and down to his waistband. In one determined move, she undressed him completely. Naked, he pressed against her and she swayed, her eyes taking in the incendiary hunger in his own eyes. "Tell me my fact," she urged, empty, lost as she had always been before this moment and this man captured her desire.

"I teach the history of film at a college in Portland. Portland, Oregon."

"Oh Gil, so close," she gushed, choking on a laugh, thrilled he might be so near to her in her every day life, shoving aside the fear that she might want to invest emotion in him after tonight. *That's tomorrow's problem to solve.* "I'm a real pushover for you tall, dark, handsome movie types."

Snorting, he slid her silk thong from her hips and she shimmied to let it fall to the floor. He stepped back, his nostrils flaring at the sight of her naked, in her heels, her scrap of blue silk, soaking wet as it was, around her ankles. With two lithe moves, she stepped out of her heels. Bending, he picked her up in his arms like she weighed nothing. As he strode past the suite's living room and into the bedroom, he grinned at her and laid her down on the king size mattress. And in a voice vaguely reminiscent of a suave Cary Grant type, he asked her, "Tell me then, why didn't any smart, tall, dark guy snap you up long ago?"

"I've only ever dated blond guys."

Standing over her at the side of the bed, he ran one big hand down her naked, needy body from throat to cleavage to tummy to pussy to cup her wet heat there. Two of his thick fingers slid along her seam, found her opening, and delved inside. His voice was rough, shaky as he asked, “Why do you think that is?”

Hearing the sound of her readiness for him, catching her bottom lip between her teeth and undulating to give him better access, she felt crazy longing in every nerve ending. “I was waiting for a perfect hero.”

At the compliment, he sucked in a breath and caught her gaze. “I make no claim to perfect, Susanna. But God, do I want to be your hero.”

Chapter Four

She reached up to pull him down to her, the sight of his tender expression, the feel of his rough satin skin on hers a ravishing fulfillment. Tangling her legs with his, she bound him close. His sensuous dark blue eyes caressed her own for a long second. Then his mouth captured hers.

His lips were sure and strong, mating with hers, melding with hers, demanding more and more of her. She groaned, arching up into his embrace, pleading with her body for his.

His tongue plunged inside her mouth, sweeping and exploring, while his big, heavy body crushed her into the plush mattress. One hand to the side of her throat, he kissed the line of her jaw. "Christ, you are everything I wanted."

She swallowed hard on the lovely words, his meaning more precious to her than any she'd heard from other men. *Why is that?* she asked herself, but abandoned rational thought to tell him her own truth. "I asked Santa for a thrilling man. You're so much more."

Like a dark angel, Gil smiled slowly, then blessed her throat and her shoulder with his ravenous kisses. Up on one elbow, he cupped one of her big breasts and with a dexterous thumb, circled her nipple. Her body, ripe for anything this man had in mind, shivered in delight. His mouth came down and his lips surrounded the point, laved her and licked her. Then he caught her between his teeth to nip her and make her buck right up into his waiting arms.

"Susanna," he murmured her name over and over as he nibbled his way to her other breast and her other starving, straining, hot nipple that he savored as lavishly as he had the first.

She drove her hands into his hair, spread her thighs, and felt him drop between them. His legs were long, furry, and hot. She whimpered, wanting, "More, more, everything."

"I know, baby, I know." His voice a rasp, a wreck.

She drove her hand down his torso to his cock. Sweet heaven, was he long and broad. She thumbed his crown, the pre-cum of his need thick and warm. "Oh, you are so happy to see me," she husked using the Mae West line to please him.

He clamped a hand over her own and levered himself up to look down into her face. "I want this good for you. Slow and—"

"You don't want to kill me here, do you, Santana?"

He blinked at her bossy tone. Then he broke into a grin. "No, ma'am."

"Save slow and whatever for later, or I could die of neglect. And you wouldn't want me unhappy."

"I aim to please."

She rubbed her thumb over the helmet of his very impressive cock and nestled it at the entrance to her hopelessly wet, throbbing core. "Aim right here."

"Ah, darlin'," he growled, giving her the first hint he might have a latent Texas drawl. Then he edged her fingers aside to trace her seam and sink inside her pussy. "I am gonna thrill us both 'til we can't walk, but I need a condom. You know I do. So let me do this my way. Let me." He punctuated his pleas with tiny kisses while his skillful fingers toyed with her drenched folds and pinched her swollen clit.

She shuddered in ecstasy, lying back, letting him play inside her. "Gil." She called his name, oblivious to everything except her pulsing need for his cock inside her and his talent for making her tremble and want and beg.

"Mindless is the way I want you, honey," he gruffed as he

pinned her to the bed and slid down to lift her thighs around his shoulders. Then in the dim light, he looked at her for a long, tormenting time. "My redhead. My pretty, wet redhead. Love your landing strip, baby. You are so lovely here. Like the rest of you."

Never had she been so thoroughly examined by a lover. Never had she really ever wanted to be. But never had she delighted in the raunchy high of it, nor found beauty in the look on a man's face as he admired her pussy. Her fingers plucked at his shoulders. "Gil, I need you."

But he ignored her beseeching, and instead parted her slick lips, finding the tender button of her clit and fastening his sweet mouth on her so that she burrowed her thrashing head into the pillows and keened like a well-loved cat.

"I knew you'd be gorgeous here." He scooped his fingers inside her channel and withdrew. "I knew you'd be sweet and juicy."

"Just for you," she managed, then licked her lips as she watched him suck her cream from his fingertips.

"Want a taste?"

Eager, she nodded.

Grinning, he delved inside her pussy once more to gather another sample of her desire for him. "What do you think?"

She took his fingers into her mouth and rolled her tongue around them. "Delicious. Like you."

His eyes narrowed in on her mouth as he withdrew his fingers, caught her against him and seized her lips in a ravening kiss.

She clamped her legs around him, then pressed at his chest. "Condom." She fought for sanity and breath. "Now."

He pushed away, but even as he went, he tormented her with kisses to her throat and one begging breast. "Condom," he muttered and looked about the bedroom, a hand raking his hair as if he couldn't remember quite where he'd put the damn things. Then he snapped his fingers and ordered her, "Go nowhere."

"Like I'd go anywhere without you," she mused as he rose and turned back for a second to grin at her.

"Got that right, babe." Then he padded off to the bathroom

and came back like his skin was on fire, holding up a string of five packets. "Got 'em."

She grabbed his wrist as he tore one off. "I want to use all of them."

He stared at her, her meaning dawning on him with salacious joy. "Your wish is my command." Then, his gaze in hers, he unwrapped the foil and in a few flicks of his hand, had himself dressed for the party. He nestled close.

She opened her thighs, craving him now deep inside her.

Taking his cock in hand, he placed himself at the entrance to her core and drove ever so slowly inside her.

And God was he *huge*.

She caught her breath, her mind spinning away, her hands urging his hips closer and closer.

"Baby, you are so tight."

"Mmmm. You are so big."

He pulled out.

"No!" She gasped. "Don't leave."

"Never. Let me...." He eased inside her again, stretching her wide and making her undulate to grab more of him, all of him. *Oh, geez.* As much of him as she could take.

Scooping his hands under her ass, he lifted her and dropped more securely into her scorching flesh.

She arched upward, taking even more of his long, luscious cock, hearing how creamy she was for him. Then she did something she had long forgotten, but wanted to do for him now. She used the strong muscles of her cunt to hug him tightly to her and claim him as her own.

Panting, he dropped his forehead to her chest. "God, baby. You are talented."

"You think?" she teased and caressed him again.

"Ugh!" He rocked into her, once, twice, and set up a rhythm that had her flowing with him, the tip of his massive cock hitting the top of her core and rubbing her G-spot, filling her up with so much man that she bared her teeth and let him take her. His friction, the way he seized her pussy, her mind filled her up with only the need to follow him up to a ledge and jump off. The throbbing fulfillment in her cunt spread to her legs, her arms, her heart, and she clutched him as she saw electric stars of raw sexual delight.

He slammed into her, eyes closed, rocking in his own release and falling over her, exhausted and replete.

The sound of them dragging in breaths filled the silent room. He nestled his lips against her throat. She skimmed her nails along the rigid power of his spine.

Rolling to his side, he let his cock slide out while he curled her close to him. "You are incomparable."

She let out a laugh, then looked up at him. "Santa did a great job for me. I'm grateful I got a Santana in my stocking."

He arched a brow. "Not just in your stocking."

The two of them burst out laughing.

"And am I the luckiest girl at the North Pole." She swept a hand out to denote the room, the hotel, and the cold Alaska night.

"I'll take the tag for luckiest man in the world."

"You are the sweetest man, that's for sure," she told him, ready to confess how much his company and his gentle loving meant to her. More than she had asked for. *More than you wanted when you applied for this one-night stand.* She opened her mouth to begin to tell him when a rap came at the door.

"That must be our dinner." He dropped a quick kiss to her lips, rummaged in his closet to don the fluffy white hotel robe, and headed for the hallway door.

Saved by the bell.

Why say anything at all about not wanting more than a one-night affair? The whole concept of 1Night Stand was that the connection be temporary, the pairing compatible but not with any demands for future commitments.

It wouldn't be fair not to tell him I can't handle a love affair.

But isn't that what this has become?

Gil signed the receipt and showed the waiter to the door. On the way past the bathroom, he rolled off his condom and put it in the trashcan, then headed back toward Susanna.

As he rounded the corner, he stopped, struck by the picture of the ravishing redhead with the svelte body and gossamer skin. Up on one elbow, she frowned down at the sheets. She was an artist's study of a female, fresh from making love, her heavy breasts rosy from his kisses, her large nipples puckered, and the frothy hair of her pussy making his cock twitch with excitement. She was the most gorgeous woman, inside and out. Funny, endearing, smart and *oh, by the way, thanks Madame Eve. The lady in question and I have another link in common. She's in the entertainment industry.*

A beauty. A wit. Skilled. And a breathtaking lover.

But the expression on her face told him she was perplexed.

"What's the matter, honey?" he asked, jamming his hands in his pockets, promising himself not to touch her unless he could make her happy again. "Did I do something wrong? Forget something?"

Surprised he had been looking at her from across the room, she blinked and met his gaze with frankness. Oh, yes, that was another fact he loved about her. She was real.

Her sensuous gray gaze still locked on his, she rose like a nymph from the sea out of that big, broad bed and strolled toward him. His cock appreciated every sinuous ripple of her muscles, every sway of her luscious breasts, every swirl of her long red hair.

She came and stood right up against him, her hands shoving aside the robe and pushing it to the carpet so that they stood once more, chest to breasts, stomach to stomach, cock to pussy. "No, Gil. You've done everything right."

He lifted her chin with a thumb and forefinger. "Susanna." He said her name, urging her to share with him whatever disturbed her.

But she cupped his jaw and kissed him with the sweetest persuasion. "You're perfect, Gil. I could not have hoped for anyone better. You dance like Fred Astaire."

He hooted as she pressed kisses down his throat and his sternum only to sink to her knees and use her lush lips on his navel, his hipbone and finally, dear God, his cock. "I'm only as good as my partner, Ginger."

She cupped his balls, rolled them in gentle fingers, then licked the semi-turgid length of his cock. "Think we make love like Bogart and Bacall?"

"Ha!" He nearly shouted as she took him fully in her mouth and sucked him deliciously hard. "Jesus. If we don't have it down yet, I want to practice."

"Me, too. All you have to do is whistle, honey," she said in imitation of the Bacall line to Bogie, "and I'll be there."

He braced his feet apart, put one hand behind him to the wall and one in her hair as she primed him like a well-practiced lover. His cock was going to fall off if she made him any harder. "Darlin', listen to me. I want to fuck you again and you can't—"

With a pop, she let him go, and he groaned. "Can't suck you off?" Like a kid denied a treat, she rubbed her nose into the hollow above his inner thigh. "Why not?" She sounded like she'd weep if he stopped her. Hell, he'd weep if she didn't put her talented mouth around him again.

"I have no fucking idea, babe. Do want you want."

"Oh, Gil Santana, I do want to give you a Christmas gift."

He gulped, a noisy sound of giant frustration. "Yeah. Give it all to me."

She let her head fall back, her mouth open, her eyes twinkling at him. "Wow. A man after my heart."

"Get busy, babe. I'm after more than that."

She licked him and laved him, sucked him and stroked him until he thought he'd howl like a banshee. And when his sight left him and he knew he'd soon be done for, she took him so deep inside her mouth, he could have sworn she'd swallowed all of him. He let loose, his scalding cum spurting down her throat, and she groaned as she kept caressing him and swallowing.

Backed up against the wall, both his hands in her jumbled tresses, he came to with her nuzzling his groin. With shaking hands, he took hold of her underarms and pulled her up to him.

Lifting her face, he wiped a few glistening drops of cum from her lower lip and led her to bed. Wrapping her tightly against him, he buried his lips in her hair. "No one has ever done that for me before."

She seemed to hide her face in his throat, sweetly shy at her own success of swallowing all he had to give. "Really?"

"Really."

"I'd think you'd have so many women after you, ready to do anything to have you, keep you."

Too many for all the wrong reasons. "I never *wanted* anyone to do that for me. Not until now."

She raised her head, her eyes shining with pride. "Really?"

He nodded.

"I've never done that before."

It was his turn to rear back in surprise. "Then I'd say you've got talent."

"For the right man."

"Bogart." He hugged her close, grinning to himself.

"Bogart, honey," she called him, sounding a bit brazen suddenly. "This Bacall is starving. Shall we eat?"

She bounded from the bed, naked and natural and so damn appealing he wanted to sit there and look at her.

"What's the matter, Bogie?" she teased as she ogled his lax penis. "Too tired to eat?"

He threatened her with a tight look. "You want me to gain my strength back so that I have energy enough for you."

Teasing, she plunked her hands on her hips and tapped a toe at him. "And what's wrong with wanting to be loved like it'll never end, huh?"

He stood up and ran his hands right down the front of her pretty breasts to her sopping wet pussy. "Where you're concerned? Nothing. I hope I live long enough to satisfy you."

An odd light sparked in her eyes. It lasted only a second, but it had her stepping away from him toward the living room and their dinner.

He followed her, her lover now, her very enchanted lover. Her very inquisitive and apprehensive mate.

As she took the dome off one of the dishes, he caught her hand. "No more prevarications. Tell me what bothers you."

"I said that about wanting to be loved like it would never end."

"And?"

Like a shot, she straightened up, put the dome down on the cart and stared at him. "I know that caring like that requires an equal and opposite kind of love." She tried to escape his grasp.

A knot tightening in his gut, he wouldn't let her go. "And?"

"I don't want to love like that."

She might have knocked him over with a feather. They'd been so natural together. So free. What had he misunderstood? What had he not perceived? He gaped at her.

"I want too much else to be anyone's lover."

Feeling like she'd knifed him in the heart, he dropped her hand and crossed his arms. "Like what?"

His challenge had her lifting her head, sticking to her guns, looking like a brave kid facing a firing squad. "I want a great career. Shakespeare is fine for now. But I want Broadway. I want Hollywood. I want my own salon, my own line of clothing for stage and screen. I want name recognition and—"

Right. He knew what she wanted. "Fame. An Oscar. Your name on the credits."

He knew his spine had stiffened. His jaw had clenched. Funny thing, even the tender heart he was discovering he might have here with her seemed to have dissolved in a thousand poison words. Those were the very words he'd heard from the women who had crowded his life for the past nine years. The starlets crazy to get him in a room. The ones who chased him on the sets or into a café. Those whom his own boss demanded he "cultivate." *Hell.*

Susanna was no starlet. No actress. But she wanted similar markers of success in a savagely competitive business—name recognition, in print, on credit rolls, along with the awards that came with talent and skill and years of apprenticeship.

"I want the same thing," he told her now because it was

probably the one fact missing from their introduction to each other. The one thing they had no time to say when they had been so enchanted by the other they could barely breathe.

Her brows knit. She stepped backward. "What do you mean?"

"I teach history of the movies right now, Susanna, but for the past fifteen years I've been the assistant director to a few different men you may have heard of."

"Like who?" she asked tenuously.

He named two Brits he'd begun with in London and the one tyrant for whom he'd slaved in Hollywood most recently.

She put a hand to her chest. "My god. Gil, they are such...artists. So well renowned. With Oscars."

"Yeah. And I paid my dues. Learned what I needed to. Met enough investors and creative types to fill me up to here." He sliced a hand across his throat.

Her eyes widened at the nasty implication. "What happened? Why did you—?"

"Leave? Because it was time. I'd learned enough. I'd seen enough. I'd put up with enough phonies and wannabe's. Enough also-rans and never-beens. I'm starting my own production company. Next summer, in Portland, I begin shooting my first independent film."

"Oh, sweetie," she whispered, beaming with pride for him, and took a step forward. But she halted, looking dazed and sad that she shouldn't try to approach him. "Gil, that's wonderful."

"I want my own life, my own career, my way. No pressures from people I don't respect or like. The ability to say no to a man or a woman who thinks they can influence me in any way that I don't want to be."

His vitriol had her nodding. "I see," she said on a thread of sound. "I want you to know I would never do that to you. To anyone. I'm not like that."

Yeah. That's what I thought. But now, who's this other Susanna? The one who doesn't want to risk love because of her career.

"I want my success on my own merit, Gil."

"Thanks for clarifying that," he bit off, yet he felt like he'd turned to stone. She had seemed like everything he'd always wanted, and yet this one small part of her...turned out to be a big part. The professional part. The hungry, aggressive part that made people unprincipled. He couldn't bear to know she was like that.

He found himself staring at the blank wall. She was walking around him, picking up her clothes, escaping to the bathroom and shutting the door.

He found his robe in a heap on the floor.

When she came out, she faced him with a tenuous smile and moist gray eyes. "I loved tonight. I'll always remember how unbelievably wonderful you are."

What could he say to her? *Sure? Thanks? Me, too?*

He watched her let herself out and close the door behind her.

He hadn't felt so alone, so miserable, so damned bereft in all his life. "Merry Christmas, Santana. Hell, it's only another night of the year, right?"

Chapter Five

Susanna walked the floor that night so much she thought there ought to be a hole in the carpet. The letter from Madame Eve that she'd found slipped under the door in her suite this morning sat on the dresser. As the digital clock clicked over to five, Susanna picked it up once more to re-read the last few sentences.

"*Gilbert Santana matches you in so many ways. In temperament. In professional attitudes and aspirations. I have great hopes that your one-night stand with him will be one of the most fulfilling nights of your life.*"

"It was until I botched it!" *Brusque, afraid to care too much for him—and then lose him, I destroyed him. I saw his despair in his eyes.*

"Why couldn't I be blunt? Tell him the whole story?" she kept asking herself like an idiot who knows the answer but can't form the words. "If I told him the whole thing, it might not have gotten all out of proportion, out of whack. I am not that crazy, driven career woman who declared I'd do anything to get where I wanted to be!"

That was not who she was. But she lit on the professional need to illustrate her deeper problem. Hurt, he had matched her words with his own experience of nutty broads who would do anything or say anything to get ahead.

She went to the window and hit the remote to draw the drapes. The sun wasn't up. Did it ever come up here in the North Pole?

But she had adored being with him. And she had not revealed to him the whole story. But she should try…if he'd allow her to explain. She owed it to him to try.

Her stomach growled.

Okay, Corrigan. Courage. Food. And an apology to a man who deserves one.

Twenty minutes later, she walked down the hall to Room 342 and saw that the room service waiter had hovered a few rooms down as she had ordered, until she could arrive.

"Thank you," she murmured, signed the check, and tried to smile. "Wish me luck."

"At this hour of the morning, ma'am, you bet!" He walked off.

She pulled down her sweater, licked her lips, and raised her hand to knock on Gil's door.

It fell open before she could make contact. And there he stood, hair wet from a shower, eyes as bleary as hers, dressed in sweats…and confused. "What? What are you doing here?"

She couldn't find words and flapped her arms, helpless.

He pulled her forward.

Suddenly she was in his room against the same wall where he'd made love to her only hours ago. She wanted his hands on her again. But she forced out her jumbled thoughts. "My…my cart. Breakfast. I ordered for us," she explained, pointing outside. "A peace offering."

"I see," he said, and reached out to roll the cart inside. Then he closed the door. "What are you doing here?"

She shifted from one foot to the other. "I came to apologize. To…to say I'm sorry and let me…let me explain." She blinked back the tears that sprang to her eyes.

He opened his palm. Inside were her two earrings and her necklace. She had forgotten them in her rush to leave. "I was coming to you. To apologize. Explain. To talk."

"Oh, Gil." She swiped at tears that threatened to blossom and roll down her cheeks. "I'm so glad. I want us to be friends."

"I don't."

"What?"

"I don't want to be friends with you, sweetheart. I want to be lovers. Talk to me. Tell me whatever it is and I'll tell you my story, too. We'll be even."

"I signed up for 1Night Stand because I wanted to be close to someone...again. Not a permanent lover, but someone to enjoy and laugh with. I needed that for a few hours because, you see, I lost my sister, my only sibling, last July. A long illness, terrible and sad. She was my friend. My best friend. And that was a few months after our mother died. So, it's been a rough year for me."

Now she was looking at him through the mist of fat tears. "I've told myself for months that I ought to be fulfilled with the new post at the Shakespeare. That all that work is enough. That it's good for me to want all that fame and glory I ran on about here to you. But I don't really believe it. I don't, Gil. I sold myself a bill of goods that I needed a grand career to fill up my hours and my loneliness."

She gulped hard but two tears rolled down her cheeks. "I'm sorry. I didn't want to be a wuss here. I wanted to be bright and positive."

"You are, sweetheart. Ninety-nine percent of the time!" She smiled at him for that.

He would have kissed her then, but she put her fingers to his mouth. "Oh, Gil. Let me tell you. Let me...finish. I never found a man I cared deeply about. Not in all my life. But I thought when I heard about 1Night Stand and Madame Eve that maybe I could take it for what it was worth. One night. A few hours with a great man. And when I learned that I was invited for the holidays, I snapped up the chance because I...I would have been all alone this Christmas." She clamped a hand over her mouth at the sob that escaped her.

He cradled her close, his lips in her hair. "Darlin', you are not alone this Christmas. You are here with me."

She snuggled nearer. "I want to be with you and be happy."

"Look at me." He wiped her tears from her cheeks. "I'll do my damnedest to make you warm and safe and happy. I'm so sorry, honey. I was hurt and crazy with it. I went off on you like a jerk, ascribing qualities to you that I had no right to. Things that were ridiculous given how I knew in my heart you weren't any of those things."

She smoothed the fabric of his sweats. "Oh, but I am some of those things where you are concerned. I'm selfish. I want you for myself."

He grinned. "I want it no other way."

"And I'll be a jealous wretch if any woman ever puts her hands on you."

"You show her, babe. I'm yours."

"Are you? Can we be? Together for this week?"

"And why not come visit me in Portland for New Year's? I have a second bedroom, if you would prefer to use it. No ties. Unless you want."

She kissed his dimple. "You are charming, Santana, but I do want the hot bed with the tall, dark, handsome hero."

"He's trying to be a better man for you."

"He doesn't have to try. He already is. I came here not wanting to care. Not wanting to risk loving and losing. But you changed that for me. I do care for you. More than care for you."

A wistful look in his eyes, he pushed a few strands of hair from her cheeks. "I won't hurt you, honey. I won't go away. And I won't fly off the handle again, either. We'll go as slowly as you want, Susanna, but I know where we're going together."

She hugged him, desperate to show him how she loved him. "Would you say you and I are meant for more than one night together?"

"Gable and Colbert?" He pulled back to ask her.

She threw her arms around his shoulders. "It happened in one night for them. Why not for you and me?"

"I haven't felt so right with anyone, ever," he admitted.

"Life is not like the movies. This reality of ours is better."

"I want to make ours better all the time. More talk, no misunderstandings."

"We have Santa to thank. And his helper, Eve. She got us right."

"Very." He agreed as he hooked his fingers in the bottom of her sweater and took it up and off to land on the floor.

"So are you going to kiss me?" she demanded, hooking one leg around his hips.

"I'm thinking about it," he whispered as he unsnapped her bra and caressed her breasts. "You do need kissing badly. 'That's what's wrong with you. You should be kissed often and by someone who knows how.'"

She loved how he remembered Rhett's line to Scarlett. But these words were meant only for her. "You know how."

"You bet I do. Only me. And I'll be kissing you for a long, long time to come."

~About the Author~

What's a gal to do if she hails from D.C., lives now deep in the heart of Texas, travels often everywhere, and adores Paris, Florence, London, Tokyo and all points east and west?

Ah.

She becomes an author who can write about those romantic places. And for readers who crave spies, pirates, bodyguards and gutsy women of all periods, then she is the author they crave for smoldering erotic encounters and captivating love affairs!

Her name? Cerise DeLand.

What's more is that Cerise is the award-winning author of 18 print novels of mystery, mainstream and romance with St. Martin's Press, Pocket Books and Kensington. Her books have been best sellers and Featured Selections of The Mystery Guild, Doubleday and Rhapsody Book clubs.

Busy lady. Happy writer.

www.cerisedeland.com

He Came Upon a Midnight Clear

by

Desiree Holt

Chapter One

Cody Alvarez turned up the collar of his sheepskin-lined rancher's jacket against the biting cold of a Seattle winter. Someone had been waiting for him when he exited his Southwest flight from San Antonio at SeaTac and delivered him to a one story metal building. Now, he had to wait until he got the go-ahead to board the private Castillo Resorts plane waiting on the tarmac to take him to his final destination.

Someplace very cold, the instructions said. *Bring warm clothes. And a tuxedo.*

What the hell?

But he reminded himself he'd agreed to the adventure, knowing it could be his best—maybe his only—chance. Uncle Cesar hadn't given him much choice. The terms of the will were very clear—engaged by New Year's Day or Rancho Alvarez would be sold. And Cody could not let that happen. He wanted that ranch more than anything. His parents had been unhappy that rather than follow them into their law practice, he'd opted for Texas A&M and studied both agribusiness and animal husbandry. But they saw how he thrived on it.

Pushing open the door to the private air terminal, he stepped gratefully into the blast of warm air.

"We're just waiting for the other passenger to join us," the man behind the small counter told him.

"No problem."

"I'm Carl, by the way. And there's fresh coffee on the table over by the wall."

"Thanks."

Cody poured some of the steaming liquid into a thick mug, carried it to one of the chairs and sat down, stretching his legs out. With his free hand he pulled two pieces of paper from his jacket pocket. The attorney had handed over the first one, from Uncle Cesar, at the reading of the will.

Cody,

You are like a son to me. The son I wish I'd had. All those summers you spent here on the ranch showed me what a natural rancher you are. I know that your dream is to own your own spread. You've spent the last ten years squirreling away every cent toward that. So many times I wanted to tell you what I had in mind, but I liked watching your determination.

Now I am gone and Rancho Alvarez will be yours, as it should be, under one condition. You work too hard and enjoy life too little. My greatest sorrow is that I never married and had children. Rancho Alvarez needs a family. So I give you until New Years Day to find a wife and become engaged. Otherwise I have left instructions for the ranch to be sold.

Take some time for this, Cody. The rewards will be great.

Uncle Cesar

Cody folded the paper. That had been eight months ago, eight long months that he spent working the ranch, learning how to be the boss. Not much time for socializing. The attorney called right after Thanksgiving to remind him time would soon run out. If he hadn't mistyped a web address one time and found Madame Evangeline's 1Night Stand matchmaking service, he would really be screwed.

God, wouldn't his friends laugh their asses off if they knew that Cody Alvarez, the hero in many a female wet dream, had to resort to what amounted to a dating agency to find a wife. Worse, he had to meet someone, dance around his situation for a week before he got to spend the night with her and convince her that she should marry him.

Yeah, right.

The second piece of paper, folded into a small square, he'd memorized.

Cody,

Thank you for contacting my service for this important moment in your life. You have been chosen for a variety of reasons to attend the special Christmas Ball Week at Castillo Lodge in Alaska. During that week you will meet your one-night stand, and if things go well, you will attend the Christmas Ball together. It is my hopeful expectation that by then you will have news to share.

Your companion is a delightful young woman who has just completed some major changes in her life. I think the two of you will be well suited to each other. At some point during the week you will be handed an envelope with the final arrangements for your one-night stand. You will not be disappointed.

Joyeux Noel.

Madame Evangeline

No description, no details other than her age, thirty-two, and Cody would find her physically pleasing. He hoped she'd at least be someone he could carry on a conversation with and tolerate in bed. She must have some kind of problem if she needed to resort to retaining the services of INight Stand?

Get real, Alvarez. Isn't that the pot calling the kettle black?

But his curiosity piqued at the absence of other information. The form he filled out asked very specific questions which he assumed created the profile given to the other person. Well, damn. The service had a great reputation. He'd checked it out. He had to trust that Madame Eve knew what the hell she was doing.

The door opened, letting in a rush of cold air, the stiff wind practically blowing the woman inside. Cody studied her from beneath the brim of his Stetson. He wasn't great with guessing height but he guessed five-six in the heels of the high leather boots she wore. Dark blonde hair fell like ripples of silk to match the color of the fur coat she had clutched around her.

She looked around, spotted Cody, then Carl. "I, um, think I'm the person you're waiting for," she said in a tentative voice.

Oh, great. A nervous Nellie. I hope she doesn't turn out to be the one on my menu. I'll never be able to tell her what I need.

"I'll let the pilot know we're all set, then," Carl told her, coming out from behind the counter. "The driver put your luggage on the plane so we'll be set to go in a minute."

"Thank you."

Her voice was soft and musical and tickled Cody's senses.

No. You have a plan in place, dumbass. Stick to it.

Madame Eve assured him the woman would know the score. His only challenge? Convincing her to make the right choice.

"Coffee's over there," he said in a gruff voice, nodding.

"What?" She jumped like a startled bird. "Oh, no thanks." Even her smile was tentative. "I think I'm coffee'd out."

The door opened and Carl stuck his head in. "All set, folks."

Cody pushed himself out of the chair and headed out of the terminal, waiting for his traveling companion to precede him. The wind hadn't abated at all and the cold clawed at him like a tiger. He watched the woman pull her coat even tighter as she battled her way to the short drop-down stairway. The pilot, standing at its foot, held out a hand to help her up into the plane. Cody was right on her heels as they entered the cabin.

He didn't know what he expected in the small plane, but not the obvious luxury that greeted him. The little cabin boasted four comfortable leather loungers in slate gray, each with a small table attached to it. They were arranged in a circle, all facing each other but it was obvious from their construction they could be swiveled in any direction for privacy and locked in place. Thick carpet in a slightly darker shade of gray than the chairs covered the floor and padded the walls of the plane.

"Please, sit where you like," a voice said behind him.

Cody turned to see the pilot, a tall woman comfortably dressed in woolen slacks and a sweater with the Castillo Resorts logo on it.

"I'm Katherine." She flashed a friendly grin. "Pilot, navigator and cabin attendant."

Cody smiled back and shook her hand. "Cody Alvarez."

Katherine looked at the woman. "You must be Miss Morris."

She nodded. "Libby."

"Anything I can get for either of you before we take off? Coffee? Water? Wine?"

They both shook their heads.

"Well, then, take your seats. Enjoy the flight." She entered the cockpit and closed the door.

Cody peeled out of his rancher's jacket and tossed it on one seat before buckling himself into the one next to it. Libby shrugged her coat off and his jaw nearly dropped as he saw the figure now revealed. The red dress of some soft material clung to lush curves in all the right places, draping over full breasts, hips and thighs. She settled herself carefully in the other empty seat, directly opposite him, fastened her seat belt and made an obvious effort to relax. Her graceful hands were folded in her lap and he might have thought she was good to go if he hadn't noticed the extremely white knuckles.

"Nervous flier?" he asked.

She hesitated then nodded. Once. A jerky movement of her head. "I haven't flown a whole lot. And small planes seem a lot scarier."

"Maybe you should have taken the glass of wine," he suggested.

"No." Her full lips curved in a tiny smile. "I'd probably just throw it up and that would put a real damper on the rest of the trip for you."

"You, too," he pointed out. He couldn't stop staring at her face with its expressive hazel eyes, thick lashes and elegant bone structure.

She frowned. "Is my makeup smeared or something?

"What?" Her question startled him.

Her tongue peeked out to wet her lips in a nervous gesture and

Cody instantly grew hard.

Great! Just great!

"You're looking at me so strangely, I thought maybe my face was a mess or I had dirt on it. Or something."

"Oh. No. Sorry. Just my bad manners. You look fine."

Fine. What a completely inadequate word to describe her. She looks...enticing. Erotic. Intoxicating. Madame Evangeline, I hope the woman you've chosen for me comes even close to this one.

"So, are you from Texas?" she asked.

The plane began its taxi to the runway and Cody guessed she was trying to distract herself. Fortunately, the thick padding on the cabin walls made conversation easier than expected over the noise of the engine.

One corner of Cody's mouth kicked up in a grin. "What gave me away?"

She looked at his feet. "The boots. I guess there are cowboys in other states, but Texas usually comes to mind first."

He looked at the custom-made Lucchese boots on his feet. He'd dished out a bundle for them, his first custom pair ever, but he wanted to "put his best foot forward" at this *Invitation Only* shindig where he hoped to secure his future. He still didn't know how the hell he'd been chosen out of the pile. Maybe Madame Evangeline liked the Stetson in his photo.

"You got the Texas part right. But the boots I wear at home don't bear much relationship to these. I usually have on work boots."

"So you're a rancher?"

"Got it in one."

The plane had paused for a moment, but at that moment the engine noise grew louder as they readied for takeoff. Looking at the bundle of nerves sitting across from him Cody couldn't help himself. He reached over and put one of his large hands over both of hers.

Zap!

He almost jerked away at the sizzle of heat that flowed

between them. He could tell she felt the same thing by the way her eyes widened and her hands tightened even more.What the hell was that all about?

He forced his voice to remain a calm, even tenor. "Take off is always louder in a small plane. Nothing to worry about."

Like he had all the experience in the world. Two trips to a cattlemen's convention in a small plane didn't exactly make him an expert on them. But the desire to soothe her frazzled nerves struck him unexpectedly. And it gave him an excuse to keep his hand over hers.

Cool it, Alvarez. You already have a date you'll be meeting sometime this week and so does she.

Oh yeah? the devil in his head asked. *Does that mean you can't fool around a little on the side?*

But that wasn't his style and he knew it. He had a very strong code of honor, instilled by his parents and Uncle Cesar. But at least he could enjoy her company while the opportunity presented itself.

He rubbed his thumb over her knuckles as the plane launched itself from the runway, hoping it soothed her because soothing definitely didn't describe what touching her did to him. To the contrary, his cock stayed so hard he wondered if it would break through the fabric of his pants and point itself directly at her.

When they were in the air and leveled off, she relaxed fractionally and he forced himself to remove his hand, although he hated to break the contact. She took in a deep breath and let it out slowly.

"Well." Her voice was still a little shaky. "So we're in the air."

"No pulling the wool over your eyes," he chuckled.

Her blush was as charming as the rest of her. "I'm not usually such a ninny. It's just...."

"I know. You haven't flown much. It's okay."

When she uncrossed and recrossed her legs, the hem of the dress rode up on her thigh and Cody caught a glimpse of a tempting, dimpled knee and a plump thigh. He loved women who had some meat on their bones. Something to hold onto.

Something soft in bed. He never figured out why half the women in the world starved themselves to death when men really wanted luxuriance rather than skin and bones.

"So," he began, mostly to distract himself from her sensuous body and electrifying presence, "Are you heading to the lodge for something special or just a vacation?"

She blushed a rosy color that made her that much more appealing. "I'm...um...that is, I'm a special invited guest. Part of a package," she added hastily.

"1Night Stand?" *Now why did I have to ask her that?*

The blush deepened. "Well...um...yes."

He winked to ease her embarrassment. "Me, too. So how did you happen to find Madame Eve?"

She wet her lips again, her delicate tongue teasing him as it smoothed over her flesh. "A woman at a place where I...spent some time recently told everyone about it. One of her friends found it and used it and ended up marrying the man she met. It just sounded...exciting."

Exciting. God, let's hope so. At least enough to hook me up with a woman who can get me out of my predicament.

"I'm guessing you haven't had much excitement in your life?"

She sighed heavily. "Sad to say that's the truth."

Cody frowned. "I can't imagine a woman as beautiful and appealing as you are lacking for excitement for very long."

There went that blush again. "You–you think I'm beautiful?"

Didn't she know that? Or was she playing a game? He hated games.

"Have you looked in a mirror lately?" he asked. "If so, you'd better take another look because you're missing something."

Libby knew that damn blush was staining her cheeks again, but this cowboy seemed to be able to push her buttons. Flip her switches. The whole time his hand covered hers, electricity crackled through her. He was absolutely gorgeous, with his golden skin, thick black hair that just reached the collar of his shirt, lean muscled body and long legs. His eyes were darker than onyx, mysterious, and his face was defined by high cheekbones and a square jaw. His romantic Hispanic heritage was very obvious. She could imagine him like the vaqueros of old astride his horse, riding the range, rounding up cattle.

Stop it, you romantic fool. You're lucky if he gives you a second look.

But the desire for a second look from someone had landed her on this trip. Winning fifty thousand dollars in the state lottery had been a shocking windfall. When her best friend, Elaine, convinced her to use the unexpected winnings to change her life, she recklessly took the plunge. She even quit her job as a legal assistant, a pleasant position, but not what she'd planned to do with the rest of her life. She was being careful with her money and after this little trip she could begin job hunting again.

She didn't bother to tell mouthwatering Cody Alvarez that her "vacation" consisted of several weeks at a spa where she trimmed off excess pounds, exercised her way into shape—what a torture of the damned *that* had been—worked with a nutritionist to create a meal plan, and let the stylists do something with her hair and makeup. The day she left the spa, she looked in the mirror, hardly able to believe that the woman who'd walked in as frumpy, overweight Olive Morris now left as sexy—well, almost—Libby.

And with an invitation to an exclusive 1Night Stand Christmas Week at an undisclosed location.

Bring warm clothes and a fancy ball gown. That's all the final email said.

Great. What if I end up in the frozen tundra of Siberia? No, not glamorous enough. Stop second-guessing yourself, Libby.

She wasn't sure whether to curse the woman who'd told her about it or thank her. But she'd never done anything this daring in her life. Ever. And if the man Madame Evangeline had paired her with turned out to be anywhere near as sexy as Cody, it would definitely be worth it.

She thought of the first email she received.

You have been chosen to receive an invitation to our exclusive

Christmas Week at a property owned by Castillo Resorts and Hotels. Travel arrangements and further instructions will be sent to you shortly. I have a particular man in mind for you. I think you two will suit each other well.

Joyeux Noel

Madame Evangeline

But while the instructions that followed were specific, they omitted any mention of the name of the man she was paired with or anything about him. On the one hand, she was excited to know she'd be spending one of the nights with a completely unknown man. One who carried none of her past images in his brain. One who hadn't been one of the pity dates her girlfriends had fixed her up with.

She'd never be model thin. She just wasn't built for it. But she'd trimmed off a lot of excess poundage and worked to tone the rest of it. Oh, she had to keep up with the program. When your body tended to be beyond Rubenesque, it took a lot of work to keep it in shape. But she had incentives now. And if the week ahead and her one-night stand worked out the way she hoped, she'd have a lot more excitement in her future.

If she had any worries at all, they revolved around the concern that she'd turn out to be a dud in bed. She had limited experience. She just hoped whoever the man she paired up with would be patient with her and appreciate her naiveté rather than be turned off by it.

"I can almost hear your brain burnin'," Cody said in his warm, slow drawl. "Some mighty heavy thoughts in there. Care to share them?"

Not really.

She shrugged. "Oh, you know. Just thinking to the week ahead. Wondering what our destination is. What the people will be like. You know. Who...."

"Who your partner will be?"

Oh, he nailed that one.

"Yes. I'd been told that Madame Evangeline always sent each

party a complete profile on the other."

"I thought so, too. But when I emailed her about it, she said this was a little different. They specifically chose the folks to invite for the week and decided to add an element of mystery."

Libby fiddled with the fabric of her dress. "I hope that means this is a lucky thing."

When he didn't say anything she looked over at his face. The slow smile that curved his lips sent flashes of heat through her body, hardening her nipples and dampening the crotch of her bikini panties. She had a sudden urge to see him naked, every inch of him, and knew that damn blush was turning her cheeks red again.

"Penny for your thoughts." His voice was edged with humor.

Not even for a hundred pennies.

"Just, you know, still thinking about this week."

"I hope you'll at least let me buy you a drink."

Her eyes widened. "You want to buy me a drink? But...but...but you're already committed to someone. Just as I am."

He shrugged his powerful shoulders. "Not until later in the week. No law against us having a friendly drink before then. Right?"

He wants to have a drink with me!

"Oh, um, right. Of course."

"So, tell me, Libby Morris. What do you do when you're not flying off somewhere in a private plane?"

"At the moment I'm between jobs. But," she hastily added, "I have some interesting prospects. Why don't you tell me about your ranch?"

They fell into an easy, uncomplicated conversation. Libby had a feeling he had things he held back just as she did, but his stories were entertaining and he made her relax. Not think about flying.

When the pilot's voice came through the cabin speakers it actually startled her. "We're getting ready to land, folks. Make sure you're buckled in."

Libby was more than grateful when Cody closed one of his

hands over both of hers that were again clenched tightly in her lap. She did her level best to ignore the powerful chemistry that came out of nowhere to envelop them. Looking up at him from beneath her lashes, she saw by the heat in his eyes that he felt it, too. She certainly hoped that whoever she was paired up with set off the same sparks in her.

At last the plane touched down, but the landing felt different to her. In scant moments the pilot emerged from the cockpit and opened the cabin door, releasing the foldout stairs. Cody waited until Libby had put her coat on then guided her to the opening. She was startled to realize they weren't on land and the stairs led to a dock.

"We landed on the ice?"

The pilot chuckled. "This is an amphibious plane, made to take off and land on either tarmac or water. And ice. Works great for these trips from Seattle."

It was cold, but to Libby it was the kind that made her feel glad to be alive.When she looked up at the sky it was a black velvet mantle over the earth, with stars embedded in it that glittered like diamonds.

A man in heavy pants and a fur-lined parka stood on the dock, holding a hand out to help her.

He grinned at the look on her face. "I'll be taking you to your final destination, the Castillo Lodge. Welcome to Castle, Alaska."

Chapter Two

Cody stood to one side of the lobby of Castillo Lodge. Activity and noise filled the area, with people in colorful winter clothes standing or sitting in small groups, laughing and chatting. He clutched the coffee in the take-out cup he'd just bought at the coffee shop, taking in the scene. As jittery as his nerves were, he probably should have ordered decaf.

Day Three. I hope I find out who I'm paired up with soon.

His gaze lit briefly on the huge magnificent Christmas tree in its place of honor on the planked floor. Lights twinkling and decorations sparkling, it reached upward to the raftered roof. Christmas carols played continuously over a built-in sound system. Members of the staff, decked out in Santa caps, bustled around making sure the guests were taken care of.

Automatically his gaze raked the lobby searching for Libby. He'd looked for her since their arrival, remembering that drink he promised and actually looking forward to it. But the very few times he'd seen her, she was hurrying from one place to another, always by herself. That struck him as odd. Never mind that he himself had put out an invisible *Keep Away* sign. But a woman as appealing as Libby should have been the object of a lot of attention.

Or had she already hooked up with her date? Well, then, why wasn't he with her?

Which is none of my damn business and I have other things to worry about.

Not much for winter sports, he'd been hard pressed to find things to occupy himself. He was on his cell so often to his ranch foreman, the man threatened to have his service cancelled. The waiting and the edge of expectation played havoc with his nerves. He only wished someone would identify his date, they could hook up and he could make his pitch. The week was drawing to a close and his deadline hovered like the Ghost of Christmas Past.

As if to give him a little jog, his cell phone rang. Caller ID popped up the name of Uncle Cesar's attorney, the only person with whom he'd shared this crazy plan. His ranch hands thought he'd left for a much-needed vacation.

Swallowing his irritation, he pushed talk. "I'm working on it," he said by way of greeting.

"Good morning to you," Emilio Macias said. "Nice to hear you sounding so chipper."

"Yeah, right," he snorted. "Listen, like I said. I'm working on it. The plan's still in place."

"Only a few days until the new year," the attorney reminded him.

"I got it. Okay? It will be taken care of."

Cody heard the sigh across the connection.

"I feel badly for you, *hermano,*" Emilio said. "But I'm obligated to abide by the terms of the will. And there is a buyer lurking in the wings."

"Yeah? Well, he can lurk all he wants, but he's not getting his mitts on Rancho Alvarez. Period. I'll get back to you."

Angrily, he snapped the phone shut and shoved it into his pocket.

"I'm sorry to see you looking so unhappy," a soft voice near his elbow said.

Cody whirled and came face to face with Libby Morris herself. She was in red again, this time wearing a sweater draped lovingly over breasts he suddenly itched to get his hands on. Black slacks fell casually over her hips in a way that made his mouth water. Her full lips, painted a glistening red, looked so tempting he had to restrain himself from rubbing his thumb over them.

Holy shit, Alvarez! Get a hold of yourself.

"Hi." He backed up a half step.

"Hi to you, too. That must have been a bad phone call you received." She wet her lower lip with her tongue.

Cody's cock hardened.

Great. Maybe I can hide behind a chair.

"Uh...oh, right. Phone call. Just business."

She cocked her head. "You're supposed to be on vacation," she pointed out. "I haven't even seen you at any of the activities."

"Yeah, well." He shrugged. "I'm not much for skiing or snowshoeing." He gave a dry chuckle. "Or community doings."

In point of fact, he'd actually spent most of his time people-watching at different locations in the lodge, trying to figure out who his "date" might be. Wondering when he would find out. The whole situation frustrated him and as Emilio had so craftily pointed out, his deadline loomed right around the corner. And now he had something else to disturb him—his body's wholly unexpected reaction to Libby Morris, who gave every appearance of a fragile flower about to come into full bloom. He'd give anything to know her story.

"How about you?" he asked. "You doing the activities thing?"

She laughed. "I gave it a try, but I think my middle name is uncoordinated. You can only fall down so many times before you figure out you weren't cut out for something. I'm on to sightseeing."

He raised an eyebrow. "Really? What can there possibly be to see?"

"Oh!" Her hazel eyes lit up. "The village is really quaint and you can take the tour of the mountain trails and—"

"Stop." He held up a hand, laughing in spite of himself. "It sounds great, but I'm not a sightseeing type of person."

She tilted her head. "Really? What kind of person *are* you?"

"A rancher. One hundred percent." He drank some of his coffee, made a face at the now-cool liquid. "Running a ranch is more than a full time operation."

"But surely you do something for fun." She smiled. "All work and that kind of thing, you know."

He shrugged and changed the subject. "Have you met your date yet? Had your one-night stand?"

He didn't know why he asked except the thought of her in bed with someone else suddenly made him tighten with anger.

And what's that all about?

The smile disappeared. "No, not yet. I wonder what they're waiting for? Christmas is almost here." She looked up at him. "How about you?"

"Same thing. Listen," he said on impulse. "We're both still unattached, so to speak. How about having dinner with me tonight?" When she hesitated he added, "There's nothing in the rules against it. Nothing that says we can't socialize with other guests. How about it?" He tried on what he hoped was an appealing look. "I'd really like it if you said yes."

Her smile returned and hit him like a wave of sunshine. "Okay. Sure. That would be nice."

"Seven o'clock? In the restaurant? I'll make reservations."

"Seven is fine. I look forward to it."

So did Cody, but for the life of him he couldn't figure out why he'd done it. What if he got the message that tonight was the night? That would be incredibly awkward. But he had no intention of cancelling unless he had to. Maybe if his prearranged coupling didn't work out....

Forget it. She's spoken for. Besides, I can't afford for this not to work out. At least I can have an enjoyable meal. And maybe probe the mystery of Libby Morris.

"This is nice." Libby smoothed the napkin in her lap and picked up her wine glass.

She'd had a real attack of nerves getting ready for dinner. She didn't know how to make small talk, didn't have a lot of witty things to say. And even after the weeks at the spa, her figure still had plenty of flaws. So why did this gorgeous man want to have dinner with her when he probably could have had his pick of the women still unattached?

Then she remembered her goal. A new life. Excitement. Dinner with Mr. Sexy. Why not? Besides, when she ran into him in the lobby earlier, just the sight of him made her body sizzle, her nipples peak and tiny tremors race through her cunt. So what was the harm in it?

Right?

One corner of Cody's mouth tipped up in a grin. "I think so, too. But I'd like to think it's a little more exciting than 'nice.'"

A funny little feeling swirled in her stomach. Yes, it was much more than "nice" but she didn't know exactly how to tell him without sounding too forward. God, could she be any more socially clumsy?

While she tried to form words, he leaned across the table and took her free hand in his. "Libby, if something's bothering you, just let it out. I asked you to dinner because I like the way you look and I like talking to you. But if I make you nervous, I'd like to know about it."

She lowered her eyes, looking at their joined hands. Such a strong hand, with fingers so lean and capable-looking. She felt the callouses from hours of ranch work.

"I'm not very good at this," she said, slowly.

He grinned. "At eating dinner?"

She shook her head, still not looking at him. "At...small talk. Dating. Things like this." Her cheeks felt so hot she thought they must match her lipstick.

"Libby?" Cody's voice barely penetrated the fog of embarrassment. And he still had her hand. "Libby, look at me."

Reluctantly, she raised her eyes.

"I'm going to order us each another drink and then I'd be interested to find out why someone as beautiful and sexy as you has trouble in a social situation like this. Surely you must be beating the men off with a stick."

She made herself breathe evenly. She might as well tell him. They'd never see each other again and maybe he could give her some moral support. Besides, he made her feel comfortable, something her assigned date might not do.

The waiter cleared their dessert dishes, brought another glass of wine for her and bourbon on the rocks for Cody. He touched his glass to hers.

"To us. Two people enjoying a *nice* dinner."

She laughed at that and swallowed some wine.

"Now. Let's have it. What's got you skittish as a newborn calf?"

"You'll laugh at me."

He smiled. "Darlin', the last thing I'll do is laugh. I promise."

She took another gulp of wine. "Well, they say it's easier to tell things to a stranger."

"Oh, but we're not strangers," he protested. "Are we? We spent all that time on the plane together, right? But Libby, it's still all right to talk to me."

She drained her wine glass and held it out. "C-Could I have another drink? Please?"

Cody laughed. "Yes, but then I'm cutting you off. I don't want anyone to accuse me of getting you drunk and taking advantage of you."

Her breath caught in her throat. "I...you...."

He signaled for the waiter then picked up her hand again. She wished he'd never drop it. It felt so good and secure.

"Breathe," he teased gently. "It's okay. Just relax. If you don't want to say anything you don't have to."

"I've been fat and frumpy and boring all my life," she blurted out then wished she could dive under the table. When he didn't say anything, she made herself look up and saw him staring at her. "What?"

He cleared his throat. "Libby. I have to say that those are three words I would never associate with you."

The waiter brought their drinks and she paused long enough to sip some of hers. "That's because you didn't know me. Even now I have a long way to go."

"For what?" He sounded astonished.

"For, you know. To look like everyone else."

"Why the hell would you want that? You're perfect the way you are."

She snorted. "Oh, sure. That's nice of you to say, but you don't have to be polite. I just spent two months at a spa to get to this point." He hadn't stopped staring at her. "That's why I booked this thing through 1Night Stand." Her face heated again. "I wanted an exciting, erotic night like my girlfriends talk about. An adventure. You know. Hot sex."

Oh, God, maybe the floor will just open up and swallow me.

Cody downed his bourbon in two swallows and signaled the waiter for the check.

"Finish your wine. We're getting out of here."

"What? Where? Why?" She couldn't figure out what was happening. "Did I say something wrong?"

Of course I did. Now he wants to dump me as fast as he can.

"No. Something right. I want to take you someplace a little more private than this. The first thing I'm going to do is kiss that mouth that's been driving me crazy since we met in Seattle. Then I'm going to explain to you why men—at least this man—don't necessarily want a woman who's been around everyone's block and who is so skinny their bones clank when they try to make love."

Before she could pull her thoughts together he'd signed the check, helped her out of the chair, and hustled her through the lobby. He took her hand and pulled her down the hallway where there were some private party rooms, trying each door until he found one that opened. Inside he slammed the door shut, backed her up against it, cupped her cheeks with his palms and brought his mouth to hers.

Libby had certainly been kissed before. She'd at least passed the shy virgin stage. Not that any sex she'd experienced had been something to write home about. But other kisses compared to this about as much as a match compared to a volcanic explosion. His mouth was soft on hers at first, lips brushing lips, his hands holding her head in place for him. Then his tongue swept over her bottom lip and without thinking, she opened for him. And the explosion became an earthquake of epic proportions.

His tongue singed every inch of her mouth, licking and touching, burning her with his heat. His tongue glided over hers, coaxing it into an erotic dance. Her breasts felt heavy and the pulse in her cunt was beating like a jungle drum. She lost all sense of time and place, nothing existing except her and this man and their mouths fused together. The kiss went on for so long she forgot to breathe. Forgot anything except this.

He moved his body closer to hers, his lean, muscular body with its very thick erection pressing against her, hot and hard.

One of his hands slipped down and found its way under her sweater. Then his fingers were sliding up her rib cage and grazing the side of one breast. He closed over it as he eased his mouth to the side, trailing kisses along her jawbone and down her neck.

"Cody?" she breathed, her heart beating a mile a minute.

"Mm hmm?" He still showered kisses everywhere, his hand squeezing her breast, his thumb chafing her nipple through the satin of her bra.

"What are we doing here?"

"If I have to explain it then you really *have* led a sheltered life." His voice sounded strangled.

"I mean I know what we're *doing*. But—"

He continued to tease her nipple while his other hand stroked her cheek. "I've wanted to do this since you took off your coat on the plane and I got a look at this very tempting body of yours."

"Tempting? Really?" Libby wished there was light so she could see his face.

"Oh, yeah." He brushed his mouth over hers. "Tempting, mouthwatering and a whole lot of other adjectives I can't even think of because right now my brain is so scrambled."

He took the kiss even deeper this time, his tongue hotter, his touch on her breast even more exquisite. When he tore his mouth away, her entire body thrummed with need and she wasn't sure her legs would hold her much longer.

"Libby?" His mouth was at her ear, her tongue tracing circles that made her shiver.

"Um?"

"Come to my room with me. Please?"

What? Go to his room?

"B-But what about our dates? Our one-night stands?"

"Nobody's hooked us up with them yet, and there wasn't anything against being with other guests." He nipped her ear lobe. "Please, darlin'. I want you so badly I can hardly stand it." Another nip. "You said you wanted an adventure, Libby. Have one with me. Please?"

No one had ever desired her like this. Or turned her on so much. For a moment she thought about saying no, but the devil in her brain said, *Dummy. Do it. Now.*

"O-Okay."

His hands tightened on her. "That's a yes? For real?"

"You'd better hurry before I change my mind."

Libby didn't think even a minute passed before they were in the elevator, up to the third floor and in Cody's room. He flicked the switch by the door, turning on the two lamps on either side of the bed.

"Wait," he said, tugging her over to the side of the bed. "Don't move."

Libby trembled with a mixture of need and anxiety, but she stood where she was while Cody raced into the bathroom and returned holding a small box. He slapped it down on the nightstand.

"So I don't have to go looking at an inconvenient time. Now." He stood in front of her, his eyes looking directly into hers. "I'm so hard I could hammer fence posts, but I want to take my time, darlin'. I want to enjoy this."

Cody had to force himself to go slow when he really wanted to rip Libby's clothes off, toss her down on the bed and bury himself in her luscious body. But she deserved more than that and he wanted to savor every moment. Very slowly he raised the hem of her sweater, tugging it up and over her head. He swallowed a gasp when he saw the swell of her full breasts barely contained by the insubstantial satin of her bright red bra, the same color as her sweater. He ran the tip of one finger over her creamy skin, back and forth, the feel of her so soft and full.

"C-Could you maybe turn down the lamp?" she asked again, making a move to cross her arms over her breasts.

"No, I could not. I want to see every gorgeous inch of you." *Man, that's an understatement.*

"But I'm...I'm not...."

He hated the look on her face and wanted to punch out every man who'd ever put it there. "Libby, I don't care who or what you were before you got on that plane, but right now you are the most gorgeous women I've ever seen. The kind of woman I dream about at night. So from now on there's one rule." He touched the tip of her nose. "No apologizing for yourself. Okay?"

"But—"

"No buts. This is your adventure. Okay? Say it."

"O-Okay."

"Good."

Reaching behind her, he opened the clasp and removed her bra, tossing it onto a nearby chair. The sight of her naked breasts took his breath away. They were so full and round, her nipples so dark and rosy. He took each of them between thumb and forefinger, pinching them lightly before taking first one then the other into his mouth. He sucked each one thoroughly, tightening his lips around it, grazing it with his teeth and then soothing it with his tongue. Each bud puckered and swelled beneath his touch, the feel of them heating his blood and kicking up his pulse.

Libby stood exactly where he'd placed her, hands gripping his upper arms to anchor herself. He took the time to lick the swell of her breasts and trail his tongue through the valley between them. Then he kissed the hollow of her throat where her pulse hammered like that of a wild mare. When he licked the slender column of her neck, her breathing ratcheted up a notch.

Before he could lose it altogether, he dropped his hands to her slacks, unfastened the button, and lowered the zipper. Kneeling in front of her, he pushed the fabric down to her ankles, revealing a thong that matched her bra. It barely covered what he could tell immediately was a carefully waxed and trimmed pussy.

Oh, sweet Jesus.

His hands shook slightly as he helped her out of her shoes and brushed away the puddle of fabric her slacks collapsed into. Then very slowly, like unwrapping a gift, he tugged down the thong, eyes fastened hungrily on the beautiful little cunt it revealed. Yup. Waxed, with just a thin line of hair running down each lip. *Holy shit!* He didn't know where to look first—her nicely rounded, little tummy, her warm thighs, or the sweet pussy right in front of his face.

With his thumbs he opened her labia and stared at the slick, pink flesh. He wondered if he drooled, but how could that be possible when his mouth felt dry as dust? Giving in to temptation, he drew the tip of his tongue the entire length of her slit, down and back up again, pausing only to swirl around the bud of her clit. She tasted so sweet and the scent of her arousal drove him crazy.

"Ohhhhh."

The sound whispered from her mouth, sweeping through him like electricity. Her fingers dug into his shoulders as her body trembled beneath his touch. Rising to his feet, he yanked the covers back and placed her carefully on the bed, his eyes never leaving her as he made quick work of his boots and clothing. Then he was on the bed, kneeling between her thighs, spreading them wide to accommodate him and feasting on her pussy again.

Libby was so responsive. Every lick of his tongue, every brush of his breath across her skin brought more of the little whimpers of pleasure from her. He opened her to him, thrusting his tongue inside and rasping her clit with his thumb again and again.

She poured into his mouth, her juices flowing while her pussy contracted around his tongue, as he drank from her. When her body tensed as her orgasm drove up through her, he moved his hands to her hips, holding her tightly, working her as the ripples increased and finally, the shudders tore through her, convulsing her. The whimpers became one long, low moan, vibrating from her throat.

He rode her through it, lapping and sucking until she lay limp and trembling in his hands. Then, when he was at the point of exploding himself, he rose to his knees, fished a condom from the box, rolled it on and lifted her with his hands beneath her buttocks.

"I've been thinking about this all night," he told her in a hoarse voice.

Cody wanted to drive into her, but worried about hurting her. He knew she'd be wet and relaxed from her climax, but he'd discovered just how tight she was. He entered her carefully, in one long, slow glide. When he was fully inside her, his balls touching the curve of her ass, he drew in a deep breath and let it out slowly.

Holy shit!

Her sweet, sweet cunt was so snug around him, hot and tight. He looked down at Libby spread out beneath him, her skin flushed a rosy pink from her climax, her nipples a deep rose, her lips kiss-swollen and her eyes heavy-lidded. Cody knew for sure he'd died and gone to heaven.

"Hold your breasts for me, Libby," he rasped out. "Do it. Please."

Hesitantly at first then more boldly, she cupped her breasts and lifted them toward him.

"Good." He swallowed. Hard. "Hold on, darlin'. I'm taking us on the ride of our lives."

Bracing his hands on either side of her, he moved, thrusting in and out of her, slow at first to let her adjust to the feel of him then faster and harder, his balls slapping against her with each plunge. He hung onto the frayed edges of his control as long as he could, trying to give her time to be fully aroused again. Finally, he moved one hand between them to find her clit and rubbed it in rhythm with his strokes in and out of her.

Just at the point where he was sure he couldn't hold onto it any longer, she pulsed around him. One final push and he took them both over the cliff, falling into space, bodies shuddering in the intensity of the shared orgasm.

Libby's hands fell away from her breasts to her sides and Cody collapsed forward, barely catching himself on his forearms. His chest heaved and his heart threatened to hammer out of his chest. The only sound in the room was the rough in and out sawing of breath as they tried to gather themselves.

When he could move without falling down, Cody eased from her body and headed into the bathroom to dispose of the condom. Libby was in exactly same position he'd left her except one arm lay across her eyes. He slipped into bed next to her, sliding one arm beneath her head to cradle her and uncovered her eyes.

"Libby? Libby, look at me, darlin'."

When she opened her eyes he saw so many things reflected in them, but at least none of them were regret. He didn't think he could have stood that. But one of the things he did see was the same depth of emotion that was roiling inside of him. Maybe he hardly knew much about her, but he knew one very important thing. They clicked. Silently. On every level. They might have some very serious talking to do in the morning. Because he sure planned to keep her in his bed until then.

Chapter Three

Libby lay comfortably in Cody's arms, loving the feel of them around her. Lying like that, cuddled together, they talked at length. Cody shared his situation with her, stressing both his deadline and how much the ranch meant to him. Libby told him about growing up heavy, getting heavier, winning the lottery and using the money to give herself a new start in life.

"So you're basically footloose and free right now?" Cody asked.

"Absolutely. I don't even know what I'm going to do next. But I'm good financially for a while so I'm going to take my time."

As they talked, he worked his magic on her, playing with her nipples, skimming his hand along her tummy, toying with her clit over and over until she'd become so aroused she wanted him again.

He kissed the edge of her ear and nibbled the lobe. "I know this is how we got here, but right now I sure do wish I hadn't already made this commitment with 1Night Stand," he grumbled. "And that you hadn't, either."

"Why?" She turned to look at him.

"Because I think we've got something really good here, darlin'. Even in this short of a time I'd have no hesitation about putting a ring on your finger."

Her heart tripped and stuttered. He wanted her. And not just for quick sex. "But you just met me. What if you ended up not liking me?"

"Not a chance. I always go with my gut instinct and my gut tells me this is right."

If only.

Because she felt the same way. She'd waited all her life to meet someone like him. No, to meet *him*. She wasn't sure she could stand to see him with another woman. Or find herself with another man. *Bummer*.

"What about you?" he asked.

She drew in a breath and let it out. "I'd marry you in a minute, Cody. But we still have commitments," she reminded him, "and we need to honor those. I'm not even sure how we'd get out of them."

"I know, I know," he grumbled.

"Maybe they won't work out."

"Maybe." Then he smiled. "But at least we still have the rest of tonight."

Oh, yes.The rest of the night and with a man who thought her body was perfect. Thought she *was perfect.*

He rolled to his back and lifted her until she was astride him, his recovered cock bobbing against her pussy. He ran his hands over her thighs, down and up again, his eyes darkening as he did. "I love every one of your curves," he told her in a thick voice. "I wish I had some talent as an artist so I could paint you in the nude."

"You're very good for my ego, you know."

"It's just the damn truth. I can tell you I'd never get tired of looking at you. Ever. Your naked body really turns me on."

Her breath rasped as heat quickened within her. "Same goes."

He wrapped his fingers around his cock and rubbed it against her clit then down her slit. "You're wet." His voice was gravelly, thick with desire. "And ready."

"Yes." She could barely get her breath.

He grabbed another condom and rolled it on quickly. Then he lifted her just enough to center himself on her and slid her down on his swollen shaft until she'd taken all of him.

"Ride me, Libby," he said in a hoarse voice. "Take me on that wild adventure with you."

This was new to her. None of the men she'd been with had been interested in more than one time in the missionary position. But it excited her, and with Cody's hands on her hips to guide her, she caught the rhythm. Soon they were moving in sync, his cock hot and thick inside her. Slower than the first time, not as desperate but stretched out, ripples turning into tremors and tremors finally turning into spasms. Her muscles contracted around him, milking him, as the ride went on and on. And then, like a slow train picking up speed, the orgasm built and built until it rolled over them like wild thunder.

She fell forward on his chest, dragging air into her lungs, her head tucked under his chin. His heart jackhammered against her chest and it was such a nice, solid feeling. She turned her head toward the wall of windows that looked out on the surrounding snowcapped mountains. They had opened the drapes earlier to take advantage of the view.

"It's so clear out there," she murmured. "Almost like a scene from a painting."

At that moment they heard the peal of the church bells that rang twice daily, so loud they could hear them wherever they were. Even with doors and windows closed.

"Midnight," he commented.

"The start of a new day."

"Not until the morning." His hands idly caressed her back. "You're mine until the sun comes up. And I'm going to make love to you at least one more time."

He pulled her head to him and pressed his mouth to hers, his lips warm and firm, his tongue hot and demanding. And she melted into him.

Cody put his coffee cup down and looked across the table at

Libby. She'd been quiet during breakfast, and he hadn't felt like talking much himself. He had the nervous, edgy feeling he got when something was about to fall apart, and he was sure he knew what it was. Last night–*all* of last night–had been spectacular. They fit like two pieces of the same whole, but they had commitments and no idea how to get out of them. Or even if they could. After all, they *were* among those with special invitations to the Christmas week and fancy ball.

Tomorrow night?

Holy shit!

"Do you realize it's Christmas Eve?" he asked.

"It is?" Libby stared at him. "You're kidding. How could I forget something like that?"

"Didn't you have people to buy presents for?"

She shrugged, a delicate movement that tantalized him. "My parents are on a cruise and my sister and brother-in-law are in Jamaica. I sent them all cards."

"Nice holiday traditions," he said wryly.

"We've never been much on those."

He couldn't miss the sadness in her voice and he hated it. He'd spent every Christmas with his parents and Uncle Cesar and the ranch hands and their families. "Not even a Christmas tree?"

She did the little shrug thing again. "I usually get a small one for my apartment, but this year I just didn't see the need for it. By the time I get back Christmas will be over."

Me, too. And I hope to hell I'm engaged. I just hope my 1Night Stand is half the woman this one is.

"We're in a mess, aren't we?" He reached across the table and took her hand in his.

"Maybe our 'arrangements' will fall through," she laughed.

"Or we could try explaining what happened and beg out of them."

"There's a thought."

The waiter had just refilled their coffee cups when a lodge staff member wearing a Santa cap and carrying letter-sized envelopes approached their table.

"Miss Morris? Mr. Alvarez?"

They nodded.

"These are for you. Merry Christmas."

Libby frowned as she opened her envelope and pulled out the letter inside. She read it in shock, read it again and burst out laughing.

"Oh, my God." She had trouble catching her breath. "I can't believe it." She looked at Cody.

He sat in his chair with a stunned look on his face. "Me, either."

"What does yours say?"

"You first."

She cleared her throat.

Dear Libby,

I know you wanted an exciting one-night stand, something beyond your dreams. I wanted that for you, too. And sometimes Fate intervenes when we really need it to. When I read the application form Cody Alvarez, I got this strange feeling that something electric was about to happen. Then I opened your application right after his and I knew. Magic. If I could put the two of you together in the right circumstances, chemistry would take care of the rest. That's why I so carefully arranged for the two of you to be the only ones on the flight from Seattle to Castle.

My spies told me they saw the sparks in the beginning, but the two of you were a little slow off the mark. I was afraid I'd have to give you a nudge and I really wanted this to occur spontaneously. Then it happened, with all the magic I hoped for.

I wish you and Cody a long life together.

Affectionately,

Madame Evangeline

"Mine says almost the same thing," he told her.

She could barely contain her excitement. "Read it to me."

"Okay." He smoothed the paper out.

Dear Cody,

When I opened Libby's application right after yours, I had the strangest feeling that Fate was guiding my hand. I checked her thoroughly and discovered that she is exactly the woman you need. I had a sixth sense about it, something I've developed after all these years. Did you not wonder why you two were the only ones on the plane? I didn't want another couple to disrupt the magic. My spies tell me sparks flew at once but then things stalled much to my dismay, I must admit. I worried that I'd have to give the two of you another nudge, but thankfully you took care of it for me.

So now you have had your one-night stand with the woman I am certain will be the one to help you keep that ranch and build a rich full life. I hope to hear an announcement at the ball.

Affectionately,

Madame Evangeline

Cody stared at Libby. She stared back at him before they both burst into laughter again.

"Well," he said, catching his breath. "Let me ask you this." He leaned across the table, watching her intently. "Could you stand to live in Texas? With a couple of thousand head of cattle and a bunch of rowdy hands?"

Her lips turned up in a little smile. "Will you be there?"

"You bet."

"Then of course I could. Cody, I'm totally unattached. Free. I can go anywhere and do anything I want to."

He took both of her hands in his. "I know this is fast, but I also know in my heart what I want. Libby, will you marry me?"

She wet her lips and for a moment he was afraid she'd changed her mind. Then she grinned. "Yes. Yes, I will."

"Then what are we sitting here for?" He raised his hand to call the waiter.

"Aren't you going to call the attorney and share your news?"

"After."

"After what?"

"After I kiss you again to make sure you don't change your mind."

She grinned at him. "Never happen."

"And after I go to the front desk and get the ring I had them stash in the safe for me. Just in case." He stood up and winked at her then urged her from her chair, pulling her into his arms.

"The ring's just the icing on the cake, Cody. What I really want is that kiss."

And there in the restaurant, in full view of everyone eating there, he wrapped his arms around her and kissed her until they were both out of breath. The sound of applause startled them back into reality. When Cody looked, he saw everyone clapping for them.

"I assume congratulations are in order." A tall man with dark coloring, dark hair and a warm expression walked over to them and held out his hand. "Nick Castillo. I manage the property for the family."

Cody could tell Libby was as dazed as he was. He shook Nick's hand. "Nice to meet you."

"I had a heads up from Madame Eve. I hope you'll allow us to make the announcement at the ball."

Cody looked down into Libby's warm hazel eyes. "Yes, by all means. Tell everyone the future Mr. and Mrs. Cody Alvarez are looking forward to a long and happy future together."

~About the Author~

Desiree Holt's writing is flavored with the rich experiences of her life, including a long stretch in the music business representing every kind of artist from country singer to heavy metal rock bands. For several years she also ran her own public relations agency handling any client that interested her, many of whom might recognize themselves in the pages of her stories. She is twice a finalist for an EPIC E-Book Award, a nominee for a Romantic Times Reviewers Choice Award, winner of the first 5 Heart Sweetheart of the Year Award at The Romance Studio as well as twice a CAPA Award for best BDSM book of the year, winner of two Holt Medallion Awards of Merit, and is published by five different houses. *Romance Junkies* said of her work: "Desiree Holt is the most amazing erotica author of our time and each story is more fulfilling then the last."

Visit Desiree online at:
www.desireeholt.com

This Endris Night

by

D. L. Jackson

Chapter One

The cold kissed Shiya's cheeks as the sled raced through the night, gliding across the snow in the Alaskan wilderness. Yeah, she could have arrived like the other guests, by bush plane, but the siren's call of the icy world had been great, and she needed access to the wilds to put her plan in motion.

It had been too long since she'd last come home. Northern lights danced across the horizon, playing off icicles that gleamed on bent pine boughs—nature's Christmas trees. Overhead the stars glittered, something she'd rarely seen because of the city lights.

Something she'd missed.

The fur-lined hood of her red parka hid her long black hair and high cheekbones, her Inuit signature features. But not all of her appearance was Yupik. A fling her great-great grandmother had with a white man during the Yukon gold rush in the 1800s resulted in a freakish height of five foot eleven and green eyes that brought summer to the frozen tundra.

Though four generations had passed since her grandmother's affair, the genetics hadn't disappeared from her family line, making her a child of two worlds, not quite fitting into either.

Her mother had died giving birth, leaving her not only her name, an Inuit tradition, but her unusual attributes. Shiya was the only one in her tribe still alive who looked the way she did—a blessing and a curse.

Her family didn't want her here. Shiya had wanted to go to school—move to the city—live like a normal person, be someone other than she'd been raised to be. She'd rejected an arranged marriage, thrown tradition back in her family's face, and shamed them when she'd left for the city, found a modeling job, and made money off the heritage she'd walked away from.

The Eskimo Supermodel, a term that ostracized her from her people further. She cringed every time she heard it, but chose to ignore her internal reaction to the insult, knowing if she were to survive, she had to fit in.

Fitting in—that went well. Sought out for her appearance, Shiya no longer knew if it were possible to find someone who didn't want her because of her looks or money. Men hit on her everywhere she went. Overwhelmed by her sudden celebrity status, she'd stopped going out and secluded herself in her apartment, effectively cutting herself off from the real world. She spent her downtime online in chat rooms, flirting with people who couldn't see her, gaining some sense of security in her anonymity.

Until she'd picked up a stalker. She'd packed to run when she heard he was out on bail, not sure where she'd go or hide, as she wasn't welcome in her father's house. Her stalker owned a profitable corporation, with homes all over the world. He could follow her around the globe. And had. When running didn't work, Shiya changed tactics. She planned to make a stand—on soil she was familiar with, seizing the high ground in a risky maneuver.

She'd contacted an exclusive internet dating site, 1Night Stand, and arranged for an interlude, knowing she'd didn't plan to attend the party. The trip to Alaska had nothing to do with finding the perfect man, but luring a dangerous one to where she had a tactical advantage. Lucas wouldn't be able to resist the carrot she'd dangled.

The running would stop on her turf. She'd been careful to drop clues online, but also not be too obvious she'd set a trap. In the wilds of the Great North, safety came from the people who watched the sacred land. They took their calling seriously. When

Lucas arrived, which would be soon, the nightmare would end.

His flight into Anchorage would land at midnight, followed by a trip by bush plane. Shiya calculated she had at least three days to prepare for his arrival.

Ahead, the starlight caught a dark patch in the snow. "Whoa," she yelled. The dogs responded by slowing to a stop. A pool of what appeared to be fresh blood and splatters of crimson spots stained the pristine white surface. The metallic smell of copper clung to the chilled air, calling to memory the scent of a fresh kill, when her people butchered a seal or whale. Alongside, winding in and out of the blood were deep impressions, the familiar soles of boots. Overlaying and crossing the manmade treads were more chilling images, the wide, splayed tracks with a dish-sized, split, central pad and five toes. One animal in Alaska made that track. She pulled a high powered rifle from a sleeve and stepped onto the frozen snowpack. Her lead dog turned toward her and whined.

"Stay here." She pounded a stake into the frozen ground and secured their lead to it, tethering them to prevent the team from leaving her to die. Five miles could be like a hundred out in the hostile wilderness—people who forgot that lost their lives.

Shiya squatted down, removed a glove to dip her fingers into the puddle. Still warm—not good. She lifted her eyes from the mess and scanned the darkness. No movement, but it didn't mean the bear wasn't there. There was a minute chance that whatever man found his way into the beast's teeth might still be alive.

She glanced at the stained snow again. Gelled red filled the imprints left by the man's boot—a big man from the size of the boot, and the depth in which the track sank into the snow. Big or not, it was doubtful he'd survive a bear attack. But since there was a chance, she couldn't leave without investigating. Shiya began to follow the trail.

Master predators, the bears could smell the blood from miles away. If she found one—there would be more and not just that, it would draw other predators. Packs of wolves frequented this area and had been known to travel in massive groups.

What the hell was the guy doing by the glacier? The tracks appeared to stagger, leading off into a thick stand of trees.

So caught up in the reason a stranger might have traveled there, she failed to hear the monster behind her until he was on top of her. A rough chuff, followed by a hiss, and the impact spun Shiya around on the ice and sent her flying, where she slammed shoulders first into an icy bank. Her rifle flew from her hands, discharging when it hit the ground. She crab-crawled backward. The bear opened its mouth and roared, the sound shaking her to her soul.

Oh shit, oh shit, oh shit. Massive, twice the size of any bear she'd ever seen in the area, the herculean monster closed in, stalking forward on gigantic paws that looked like velvet-flocked snowshoes. Red stained his white coat, matting down the thick fur on his leg, and hot breath steamed from his mouth and nose like an iron train.

He grabbed her boot in his enormous jaws and dragged her back until he straddled her body, his face now inches from hers. Shiya threw her arms up, keeping them vertical. A Nanuk wouldn't turn his head to bite, or that's what her father had told her. *Make yourself bigger than the bear can bite, he'd said time and time again.* But there was no way to be bigger than this bear could bite.

Nanuk didn't have to turn his head to take her arms into his mouth. Her entire head could fit in those jaws lined with teeth at least four inches long and more like daggers than fangs.

Even stranger than his freakish size, his teeth hadn't punctured her boot or crushed her ankle when he'd grabbed her. Her mind let that thought slip as he leaned in and sniffed her. Another chuff ruffled her hair. Not gentle or friendly—a well honed killing machine.

A cloud of warm breath puffed from the carnivore's open jaws, washing across her face. The smell of minty toothpaste filled her nostrils. Shiya cringed. He'd already eaten the man, and from the smell of it, the toiletries the tourist had carried with him. *Ah, shit.*

The bear opened his jaws and roared again. His nose touched hers and he nudged her face with his muzzle, pushing her head back and exposing her throat. The sniffing, the huffing. Shiya couldn't move and didn't dare to breathe.

Here's the part where he'll tear my head off. Shiya closed her eyes, unable to look at death. She had many regrets, the biggest that she never had the chance to make amends with her family. It wouldn't matter. They'd never find her body—never know she'd come home. The monster wouldn't leave a scrap of her behind.

A coarse tongue licked her from chin to forehead. Her eyes opened and fixed on the beast before her. Shiya's chest tightened and her heart pounded, making it impossible to draw a breath. The bear roared again. Its great maw gaped open before her, displaying rows of lethal teeth. More steam rolled over her face and then darkness.

Gunnar stared at the unconscious woman. Her hood had dropped away and her long hair pooled around her shoulders like inky silk. A beauty. Her lips were slightly parted, and her breathing had slowed. She looked peaceful, much calmer than when she'd been awake.

He rummaged through her parka, looking for some form of identification to confirm his suspicions, but given her appearance, she might not have any on her. Mushers didn't exactly need driver's licenses for their dog sleds. His hands closed over a card and he pulled it free. Gunnar stared. She was who he thought.

His date.

He stroked his hand over her cheek and closed his eyes to inhale her scent. Nick, a local resort owner had paid him a visit earlier in the week at his work site, insisting he attend some fancy ball, and that his date was on her way. He'd agreed to get rid of him, and the next thing he knew, a Madame Eve from a company called 1NightStand, contacted him, attaching a folder to the email that disclosed anything he could possibly want to know about his date. He'd gotten as far as her name, didn't bother with the rest. Had been way too busy.

He'd planned to back out at the last minute, but now he had another idea. Perhaps he should attend this dance, claim he found her out here, unconscious? He could both play the hero and search the area near the lodge—which had been a challenge, as his bullet wound testified.

The wreckage needed to be excavated—all of it, before the people of this planet found any more. The ship had crashed hundreds of years before, and until the glacier began to melt, its discovery hadn't been an issue.

When a local Inuit boy came home with a relic, a chunk from the hull with glyphs across its surface and sold it to a local, who'd sent it to a professor at a university, it had triggered an article in a gossip rag. The only thing in their favor had been that the magazine the article was in wasn't taken seriously by the Terrans, but it didn't mean next time they'd be as lucky. Gunnar's people deployed a team to Earth to extract the evidence of their visit. The relic had been recovered, the professor, the boy and his tribe's minds wiped of the event. No small task, as the tribe tended to move around.

A lot.

His team had posed as members of an organization called *The Wildlife Federation*, stating they were on the glacier studying the declining population of polar bears. But hiding the ship and what they were doing had been tricky. They had to deal with both the locals who were but five miles from the site and the wildlife that wandered in unannounced and often hungry. With the lodge and tourists nearby it quickly turned into a nightmare scenario. But a solution presented itself when least expected. After an incident with one of the white bears, Gunnar's team quickly learned they could be used to keep the Terrans away.

Doppelgangers by birth, his people could take any form to blend with a planet's indigenous population. Sometimes they would assume the form of beasts. In this case, one of the most fearsome of Alaska's wildlife, one not just the city people and tourists kept their distance from, but one the local tribes revered, respected, and gave plenty of space.

When the woman wandered onto their site by following Gunnar's blood trail, he knew he needed to scare her away immediately. The electromagnetic shields on the ship had failed and she'd been footsteps away from seeing it. He'd only meant to drive her away—not scare her into unconsciousness.

The wound ached where the bullet had gone through his shoulder. Clean, which made it easier to repair, but if he hadn't gotten so close to the local village looking for bits of the wreckage that peppered the area, he wouldn't have been shot. He arrived back in time to see his shields overheat and his whole operation come into view. No time to treat the wound, he'd bled around the site as he worked to restore their invisibility. Gunnar had just slapped a nanite-infused patch on the injury when she appeared.

He scanned her body, memorizing every curve and dip. Tall for a female of this land, and her eyes had been green like soft grasses. So different from the indigenous peoples. When he'd caught her scent, he knew why. She wasn't Terran. The pheromones she gave off were unique. She was a descendant of someone who'd crashed here years before—making attending the ball an even more enticing situation.

He sat back and rubbed the bullet wound on his shoulder. He needed to keep a low profile until they'd recovered the wreckage and secured it in the hold of their ship. What better place than the lodge while he wined and dined the perfect woman.

The woman was also evidence. She hadn't come into the shift yet, but from the smell of the pheromones she kicked off, she would soon. And when she did, her inability to control changing her shape would draw attention—attention they didn't need. He'd have to question her about her family, make sure there were no others and unfortunately, they were coming with them when they left the planet. The alternative was death. The date would be the perfect means to inquire about her past and prevent unnecessary measures. Gods help her if his government called in a hunter to take care of her. Better he do it quietly and less violently.

He scooped her up and carried her to the dog sled, securing her with her bags and tucking her under several furs. Gunnar pulled a med-dart from his pack he'd left nearby, and gave her a shot in the neck, enough to keep her unconscious until they arrived at the lodge. He yanked up the stake and took his place at the back of the sled.

"Hike!"

The dogs took off, headed for the resort and what could be a most interesting date.

Chapter Two

Shiya groaned, pulled the covers up, and cracked an eye. *How did I get into a bed?* The last thing she recalled was that yawning mouth full of nasty teeth—a coarse stroke of Nanuk's tongue on her face—the smell of his minty-fresh breath. The memory seemed too real to be a product of her imagination, and her shoulder certainly wasn't subject to delusion. The pain couldn't be more real.

Unless I slept on it wrong.

"Good, you're awake."

Both eyes flew open to the sound of a masculine voice. She turned her head and spotted a tall drink of Viking, who stared at her from the corner of the room where he'd draped his body into a chair with predatory grace, making the otherwise substantial seat look like a piece of doll furniture.

"Who are you and where am I?" She didn't need to know his name to know a sexual encounter was imminent. It hung between them, vibrating in the air like a taut string ready to snap. Shiya shifted on the mattress as a ball of heat rolled through her.

"Not why am I alive?" He quirked a brow. The deep timbre of his voice moved through her, drawing the tension between them tighter.

"That too." He must be the reason she wasn't inside the guts of a beast.

"My name is Gunnar," he said. The clipped accent suggested Icelandic heritage.

Her gaze traveled up, taking in the mountain before her. Being almost six foot tall, she'd rarely met a man that made her feel petite. This one did—and good God, he was gorgeous. "Shiya," she mumbled, unable to take her eyes off him.

His gray thermal shirt stretched over a muscular chest, defined pecs, defined shoulders, defined everything. Her gaze traveled to hands big enough to circle her waist—working hands—a warrior's hands.

"A beautiful name." He sat forward and rested his elbows on his knees, studying her back. His eyes were a pale blue—mimicking the glacial ice, but not holding the chill. Warmth crept up the back of her neck at the intensity of his gaze.

"I'm named after my mother. She's dead," she stuttered.

His brow shot up again. *Okay—maybe that had been a little too much detail.* "Tradition," she stuttered, knowing outsiders just didn't understand and it wasn't worth trying to explain.

He nodded as though it were perfectly normal to tell a stranger your mother was dead, and something in that look told her he *would've* understood if she'd tried to explain. "I found you by the glacier—unconscious."

Shiya furrowed her brow. "No bear?"

"Didn't see one."

She sucked her lower lip between her teeth. The prints had been there. She'd dipped her fingers into the blood, felt the heat. Lifting her hand, she turned it and examined her fingertips. Nothing to prove it had been anything more than a hallucination. "There were tracks—blood."

"Didn't see those either."

She lifted her gaze back to his and furrowed her brow.

His expression said he hadn't, but the tone of his voice said otherwise. "I think you must have slipped and hit your head."

"You're sure?" She ran a hand through her hair looking for a lump on her scalp, or at least a tender spot that told her maybe she had a concussion. Nothing. As soon as the sun came up, she planned to go back to look—depending on how far away it was. The need to prove her sanity seemed at the forefront. "Where am I?"

"You're at Castle Lodge, the closest place from my camp where I could bring you for medical treatment."

"Did you say your camp?" She was almost at the glacier when she'd encountered the bear. There were a multitude of locations that would make a better camping spot. The guy was obviously a tourist with little knowledge about what kind of danger was out there. Knowing the land better than most, Shiya knew it was her responsibility to educate him and educate him she would—he'd saved her life. "Why would you want to camp by the glacier? The area is full of bears, has crevasses miles deep, and no shelter from the elements."

"I did say camp, and there are plenty of reasons a person would want to camp there. I'm a biologist with an organization studying the local bears in the area. There's been a sharp drop in the population. The glacier gives me the best vantage point to observe." He leaned back in his chair and crossed his arms over his chest.

Shiya's heart sped up. He knew her world and worked to protect it. Everything about Gunnar called to her baser desires. Too bad she didn't have time to explore the spark between them.

"And I'm also your date for the weekend."

Her eyes widened and her stomach did a crazy flip. Eve hadn't been kidding when she'd emailed she'd found the perfect man for her. Shiya had a packet with his full profile, but had never bothered to open it, since she hadn't planned on following through with the date.

Maybe she should have. Gunnar's sheer size made her feel safe and could he be any more perfect? Hero. Heartthrob. Gentleman? Shiya shifted on the bed and realized she'd been peeled down to her T-shirt and panties. "Who...?"

"A doctor. She works exclusively for the resort."

Shiya nodded and frowned. He had the uncanny ability to answer her questions before she asked them. How could any man be that tuned into a woman he'd just met? Too perfect—or perhaps he'd been doing his homework, and something about that screamed stalker, and thank you very much, she already had one too many of those.

"Do I know you?"

"Not intimately." He leaned in. "Not yet."

He said it with such confidence, not as though he were bragging, but stating a fact. Perhaps he was right in his assumption. Every second that passed, she wanted him all the more. It threw her off balance. And rarely did she feel clumsy, but this man had her emotionally stumbling all over herself.

"Oh." This is the part where she should tell him to get the fuck out of her room for making presumptions, but she couldn't. A part of her wished it hadn't been the doctor who'd stripped her. It wasn't a novelty for strangers to see her naked, but with him, it felt like it would be the first time someone truly saw her—all of her.

Behind the scenes of a fashion show, the models never had dressing rooms. She often stripped where she stood, sometimes still dressing as she headed for the catwalk. She was used to strangers seeing her naked. It didn't even bother her anymore.

Until now.

Gunnar had her shivering from the moment she'd opened her eyes. His Arctic blue eyes seemed to undress her soul and see between the layers she kept hidden from the public. The true Shiya. So intimate. So....

Bad.

He slid his chair closer, until she could smell the peppermint on his breath. "Do you wish I had removed your clothes?"

Yes. "I..." That scent—it seemed.... She pressed her fingers to her forehead and closed her eyes. The bear had eaten his toothpaste. Had been in his camp. So whose blood...? She scanned his body. Not so much as a Band-Aid. He should have some visible damage if he came face to face with the beast.

"There was no bear in my camp."

She screwed her eyes up. "Excuse me. Did you just answer a question I didn't ask?"

"It was the look on your face," he said. *I'm really good at reading people.*

"I guess you are." Shiya froze as she realized he hadn't said the last bit, at least he hadn't out loud, or did he? Maybe she had cracked her skull. She seemed to be imagining telepathy.

Are you imagining it? His mouth twitched and light danced in his eyes, as though he was amused.

Yes. No. Are you talking to me in my head? Shiya stared at him, waiting for him to do it again. *Ridiculous. Of course he isn't talking to you in your head. He said it out loud.* Nothing else would explain it. She rubbed her temples again, looking for the elusive injury that seemed to have knocked her silly.

"Does everything have to be explained?"

Shiya's eyes widened. *Yupik?* Had the entire conversation been in her native tongue?

His mouth curled into a full blown, very smug smile.

"You speak my language."

"I'm fluent in several. Inuit is just one of them." He switched to Russian or something that sounded Slavic, and then Chinese, and finally what sounded a lot like an African dialect. She hadn't a clue what he said, but he'd certainly made his point. "Take your pick. It's why I got the assignment, but you'd know this if you'd read my profile."

Busted. Shiya frowned. How could she explain?

"I don't care about why you didn't, but...." He reached out and touched her face, leaning in until his lips were only a breath away. "You didn't answer my question." His fingers brushed her skin with a tenderness that should be impossible for a man of his stature.

The world around her whirled. "What question was that?"

"Do you wish I'd removed your clothes?" He watched her, waiting for her answer with intensity in his eyes that made her squirm.

Shiya's stomach flipped and she pulled her face away from his hand, turning her chin until she looked at a painting of the Alaskan coast. He seemed way too perceptive to lie to, and who wouldn't want him to take their clothes off? She could think of a couple dozen women and men who'd die to have his hands on them. She flushed from head to toe. "Yes," she said and turned back to him.

"I thought so. I could smell your arousal the moment you first looked at me."

Her eyes widened in horror. *How?*

He slid his hand into her hair and twisted it around his fist, tugging her closer. Not gentle, not painful, but enough to let her know who was in control. "Then you won't mind if I kiss you," he said. Not can I—but I will—and he did.

Shiya's toes curled the moment their lips touched. Lightning rocketed through her body, exploding into a carnal storm inside her. She surrendered her mouth to him.

"You taste incredible." With his free hand he yanked the duvet off the bed and shoved it to the floor. "I want more." Again not a question.

He crawled onto the mattress. It dipped under his weight as he straddled her thighs. Gunner's lips traveled down her neck and his hands made short work of her panties, ripping the thin silk away.

"Please." Shiya bucked up, desperately needing him to touch her. Never had she done this, and she must have lost her mind—or left it on the glacier. She had no inclination to stop him—though she knew she should. Honorable women didn't behave this way. A whimper escaped her as he tore her thin T-shirt down the middle, exposing pebbled nipples. His hands moved up to cup her breasts, driving more jolts of energy straight to her center. His lips grazed the flesh on the top one of her breasts, while the pad of a thumb drew torturous circles around the nipple of the other.

"So beautiful." When he drew the tight bud into his mouth, she groaned and arched against him. Anything he wanted was his. She couldn't—wouldn't say no. She'd surrendered with one touch, unable to resist the compulsion. "Please," she gasped again, even more desperate. She ground her hips into him like a cat in heat, wanting to fuck so badly she shook.

He lifted his eyes and locked gazes. A crooked smile crept onto his face. "Please what?"

"Touch me—down there."

"Not yet." His lips went back to her breast; his tongue swirled around her nipple.

Shiya slipped a hand to his groin.

"You will not move unless I tell you to." Gunnar grabbed both her wrists and pressed them into the mattress over her head. "Not yet," he said a little more forcefully. Her chest rose and fell against his. God, she wanted him. The sheets grew soaked under her and her heart rate spiked. She opened her mouth.

"Don't." He let go of her wrists and cupped her face. "Let me savor you." He skimmed his fingers down her throat. "Let me show you what you've missed."

She left her hands over her head, even though the need to sink her nails into his flesh was almost more than she could bear. "What have I missed?"

"Did you think fate had nothing to do with this? Let me show you why we were matched. I think deep down inside you know what is going on."

Combustion. Why she didn't know, but one thing was clear—she needed him with every cell in her body. "Yes," she whispered. "I feel it." She lifted her hips from the bed and ground against his erection, causing him to groan. "I feel it very well."

"Willful." He smiled down at her.

"You have no idea."

No, he didn't but intended to find out. A primitive fuse inside him began to burn as she started the shift. The cells in her body were mutating, becoming pliable—doppelganger. He could smell it, taste it—hear the thoughts in her head. Feel the hunger that drove the males of his species into a frenzy when exposed to it. Every little whimper. Every little breath. This was not supposed to happen in the middle of nowhere with a half-breed. He'd waited his entire life to feel this.

The timing couldn't be shittier.

Gunner had already lied to her, betrayed her trust, and he'd continue to lie until he knew how many of the half-breeds were out there. Before this was over, the one woman in the galaxy meant for him would hate him and there wasn't anything he could do about it. But it wouldn't stop him from claiming her. He knew the moment he caught her scent on the glacier, he couldn't let her go. Shiya belonged to him and the sooner he made it clear, the better.

He slid down her body, tasting every inch of flesh. He nipped her belly and she bucked again, making him nearly spill cum inside his jeans. He grabbed her hips and slammed them to the mattress. "No." He tipped his head and bit her thigh, not hard enough to break the skin, but firm enough to warn her to be still. Control would be lost if she continued. "I said not to move."

Shiya quivered under him and moaned as she creamed again. Shit, the woman liked it. It shouldn't surprise him, even if she wasn't full-blooded. Doppelganger women liked aggressive foreplay. Pressure built in his balls and his body coiled like a steel spring. Not yet. He'd done enough to piss her off; the last thing he needed to do was add to it by hurting her.

Her first time during the shift would be explosive. He didn't want to damage her, but she made it difficult to be gentle, especially since he could smell just how hot the rough play made her. He used his forehead to nudge her thighs apart, unable to touch her with his hands and not lose the precious splinter of control he'd maintained.

When his tongue found her clit, she orgasmed. He licked down the pink slit and thrust his tongue inside her, savoring her flavor, as he'd told her he would. Now that he had a taste of her, she could never hide from him. They were linked. He could have kissed her to the same effect, but this method was much more pleasurable for both of them. The chemicals he secreted from glands in his mouth were absorbed by her flesh, not only marking her, but mutating her awakening cells, branding her with his DNA, a doppelganger aphrodisiac—one she could never resist.

Whenever she saw him, her first reaction would always be

lust. As the Terran aliens always said in their movies, "resistance was futile."

The corner of his mouth curled as his unique hormone surged through her body, infecting her with his essence. He slipped a finger inside her and she cried out, but didn't move, taking his warning seriously and a good thing she did. *A virgin? Dear gods.* He didn't think he could take much more, but this needed to be finished in a manner that pleased her.

"Gunnar," she whimpered unknowingly in his language, thrashing her head from side to side, deep into the cellular bonding, unaware of the changes in her body that would brand her forever as his. He speared his tongue inside again, giving her another dose of the hormone, winding her tighter. Her pussy clamped onto him and her juices ran into his mouth as she orgasmed again.

The link snapped into place, her future locked. He felt it the moment it happened. Now, she was ready. He pulled away and unfastened his pants. She stared at him through sex-hazed eyes. His personal addict and addiction from this point forward. Nothing would keep him from her.

Gunnar pulled a condom from his pocket and slipped it on. He slid up her body and placed his cock at her saturated entrance. "The first time always hurts and I regret that it will. I promise to make this up to you."

"I don't care. Please...." She tensed under him, but didn't do anything to stop what was coming. He thrust inside, breaking her virgin's barrier and stopped when he was buried inside her, waiting for her to adjust to his size and for the pain to subside. She didn't cry out. No tears. Nothing.

She reached up and touched his face. Her eyes sparkled. "More."

Gunnar began to move slowly, sliding in and out. Brave, brave woman. His woman. Perfect. Beautiful. His. He'd make sure she didn't regret the joining if it killed him.

Chapter Three

"I'll start us a shower," he said and kissed the tip of her nose before he slid off and went to the bathroom. After what seemed like her millionth orgasm, he'd finally seemed to tire. She watched his ass as he walked, muscular, strong, the finest she'd ever seen. Shiya fought the urge to follow him, grabbing on to the headboard as though it could possibly stop her traitorous body if it took a mind to go after him. Even after the lengthy lovemaking, she wanted more.

The door shut with a soft click and reality slammed home. The trance she'd seemed to have been in, dissolved. *Holy shit.* Shiya bolted up into a sitting position in the rumpled bed and let go of the rail. *What the hell was I thinking?* She'd not hesitated to give her cherry to him, even though they'd just met. With Lucas on his way, the last thing she should be doing was lying on her back while the enemy closed in.

What had come over her?

She snorted. Well, what had come over her was obvious, certainly more than one woman lost her wits to him, but falling in lust didn't make up for her serious lack of judgment. *Idiot.*

She gathered the sheet around her body and rose from the bed. Blood and juices trickled down her thigh. Her heart started to pound. *Fuck.* She wiped it away with the sheet and glanced around for her clothing, finding it folded in a dresser, next to the rest of her belongings—and his. *Oh, hell.* He'd moved her into his room.

"Are you hungry?" he called from the other side of the door.

"Not really." She grabbed her jeans and hopped into them, not bothering with digging in the dresser for her underwear. She wiggled them up her hips, snagged a camisole and pulled it on. Shiya followed it up with a bulky sweater, meant to swallow her figure and hide her curves. She glanced around, frantic to run before he came out. Her boots were nowhere to be seen.

Shiya eyed the blood-stained sheet on the floor, proof she hadn't imagined the encounter, and opted for barefoot, too panicked to stay. As the door to the bathroom opened, she slipped out of the room without looking back, not sure where she intended to go without her shoes. All she knew was she couldn't face the man.

Stupid. Stupid. Stupid. She trotted down the hall and began her descent of a grand staircase with twisted branch rails. A massive Tiffany chandelier with woodland scenes lit the space. Beautiful and any other time, she'd stop to study it, but she was on a mission and the faster she found the office, the sooner she could get her team harnessed and leave. From there she could catch a flight back to New York, where she should have stayed. *Tactical advantage indeed!*

Where to go? The lodge was enormous. The cathedral ceilings had to rise at least thirty feet with a massive windowed wall looking out over the water of the inlet where she could see storm clouds rolling in. No one could leave by bush plane today, or possibly for a few days with the look of the sky. Which meant no one could follow her out, unless they had an alternative means of transport, and then they wouldn't know the land like she did. She bit her lip and surveyed her surroundings, looking for the office.

Hopefully Gunnar had brought her sled team. She'd trained them from pups, had a special air-conditioned kennel built in New York to keep them happy. The lodge did have a kennel for adventurous souls who wanted to try their hand at sledding, but the bond between her and her dogs was too strong to leave them behind, especially when she might have to run for her life. When she'd decided to return, she'd brought her team, knowing there was no better way to get around. But somewhere in the moment, things had gone wrong—very wrong.

She'd never intended to come to the lodge and put any innocents in danger, which meant she needed to get out of this place as soon as possible. The guests' safety depended on her absence, and from the looks of it, the resort planned to have a huge party.

A tree at least twenty feet tall sat to one side of the circular room. It had been decked out with blown glass ornaments shaped like pinecones and petite birds, all for a holiday she'd never celebrated but found a beautiful sentiment. White lights twinkled from every bough, setting it alight like a starry night. The lodge had been trimmed with natural pine garland and the scent of the forest and cinnamon permeated the air, a heady smell of the Christian holiday season. She scanned along the entrance.

Shiya froze as her gaze landed on a man, the last person she expected to see here—this early. Had he flown in by Learjet? Her heart jumped into her throat, and she pressed her hand to the divot at the base of her throat. "Oh, God."

The man, not nearly as big as Gunnar, but tall by any standard, stood in the great room, unaware of her at the moment. The monster had almost killed her once. Shiya's pulse throbbed so hard in her neck it became difficult to breathe.

Not the average stalker, Lucas had both looks and power. Attractive with his dark hair and cocoa skin, he could have any woman he wanted, every woman but her. He'd followed her around the globe, determined they'd come to an understanding.

Any other woman would have fallen for him, but Shiya had lived her entire life around predators and knew one when she saw one. Dressed in Armani, wearing a twenty thousand dollar Rolex and custom-made Italian shoes, Lucas was smoking hot but deceptively dangerous.

She should flee before he spotted her. This was not the place to make her stand. A lump formed in her throat, and she swallowed, doing her best to summon the strength to run. The message failed to reach her feet. Instead, she stood in place, continuing to stare. Shiya balled her hands, damp from fear. *Run!*

Lucas looked up, locking gazes. Adrenaline punched through her midsection, making escape finally possible. She gasped and backed up, but a wall of muscle stopped her retreat. She yelped and jumped.

Lips pressed to her ear. "I thought I scared you away."

She spun around. "Let's go back to the room." She tried to smile, but couldn't summon the control and ended up giving him more of a nervous twitch, certainly looking more like a crazed woman than someone who wanted to flirt her way back into bed. Her hands shook. Her heart pounded. All she wanted to do was run and the damn man blocked her path. "Plea...please."

He leaned in and rubbed his nose to hers. "What's the matter?"

Her stomach fluttered. "I...." She glanced over her shoulder. Lucas hadn't moved. Not yet. "I'm just tired."

Gunnar reached up and ran his thumb along her jaw. Shivers moved through her. "You go back. I'll procure some food."

Looking in those eyes, she felt safe. So strange. "Okay," she said and gave him her nervous twitch again. Shiya glanced back one more time before running up the stairs and dashing into the room. She didn't stop until she'd slammed the door behind her and shoved the deadbolt into place.

What am I going to do? She leaned back against the door and slid down the solid surface to sit on her heels, rubbing her forehead. She couldn't drag Gunnar into this. Lucas would kill him—might even after he saw the contact on the stairs. He'd been ruthless in his pursuit and hadn't let anything get between him and what he wanted.

Lucas had stabbed her on an elevator back in New York, but before he could finish her off, the doors opened and security grabbed him. He would kill anyone who tried to keep her from him. The biologist was outgunned in this instance. He couldn't possibly have the funds or resources to stop Lucas.

"Brother," Gunnar inclined his head to the man in the lobby. Not a brother by blood but by planet and mission. Both served their world in a different manner on Earth. Lucas was charged with mind-wiping witnesses, and if they couldn't be mind-wiped, they disappeared. He carried the title of hunter, intergalactic assassin, and knew the job well. He could only be at the lodge for one reason.

"Don't get between me and my target, Gunnar. This isn't your concern."

Gunnar narrowed his eyes. He had bonded with her, and Lucas couldn't touch her without authorization from higher up. "Stay away from my wife."

Lucas shook his head. "You've been on Earth too long. You and I both know we don't take Terran wives."

"And you know she's no more Terran than you or I." The doppelganger mutation changed cells, overpowered other genetics. Though it might have been several generations since the cross-breeding, none of the Terran genes would have survived. Every mating created a child half-and-half, that within days of birth, mutated to full doppelganger, retaining only the physical appearance of its parents. Shiya, though a product of a mating several generations past, was full-blooded doppelganger and starting the shift.

Gunnar would also bet she'd never been to a hospital or physician who would have noticed the differences in her genetic makeup. From her heritage, he was certain that's why she'd slipped through the cracks and wasn't identified as a child. Her primitive life in Alaska had insured it, until she'd stepped out into the spotlight and caught Lucas's attention.

An adult doppelganger running around without knowledge of whom and what they were could be very dangerous to his people's secret. Lucas hunted her, and she'd be dead when he finished his task.

Not happening.

"I know what she is," Lucas said. "We can't leave her alive.

She's too big a risk to remain here, and she can't go back to our world. She could carry germs or viruses that could be harmful to our people who haven't been exposed to Terran diseases."

"We've developed immunity to the illnesses that plague this world. You know that's just an excuse to keep our people from taking alien mates. Her mother or grandmother may have been Terran, but she certainly isn't."

"It's the law and I'm ordering you to stand down."

"Which is only applicable to Terrans. You're going to have to go through me to get to her."

Lucas smiled and gave him a curt nod. He wouldn't do anything at the lodge, he'd draw too much attention, but the moment Shiya left its safety, Lucas would go after her. He didn't need to say anything further. Gunnar knew he'd have to kill him to protect her. Lucas turned and exited. The man wasn't going to make it easy—but then again, neither was Shiya.

What a nightmare. Shiya gathered her strength and grabbed her bag. She yanked all the drawers on the dresser open and began to cram her clothes into the duffle. She could run to her village. No one could find her there, but her people wouldn't exactly welcome her with open arms.

After seeing Lucas in the great room, Shiya knew she'd run out of options. Her sled, her dogs had to be at the lodge. Gunnar didn't seem like the kind of man who would neglect their care, and he was a biologist—an animal lover. The team would be the quietest method to run, but getting down to the kennel could be tricky.

Never had she been as thankful for the six weeks every year her father had trained her in the traditional Inuit skills of survival. For a period every year, her tribe would swap the roles of the male and female children. The boys were taken under the village women's wings and taught to cook and sew, while the girls were taken out and taught to hunt and track, even going out on the water in kayaks. Shiya knew the area better than most and wouldn't succumb to Alaska's vicious bite.

No, survival out in the elements wouldn't be an issue—survival here another matter altogether. She needed to get back to what she knew and that would be how she escaped. Her only regret would be to leave Gunnar behind. She wanted to know him better, explore the energy that seemed to sizzle between them. Unfortunately, dragging him into this wasn't an option. She still planned to kill Lucas and couldn't let Gunnar be an accessory to murder, even if in self-defense.

Here they would part company, so why did she want to throw herself on the bed and cry? It wasn't like she knew him all that well, intimately—yes, but she didn't know much more than that, and that he cared about her world.

She blew a breath out and found her boots in a closet. Blood covered the toes. Shiya flipped them over to see more had dried on the treads. Gunnar had lied to her.

Why?

Her guts twisted into a tight knot. Her feelings instantly went into conflict. Did he work for Lucas? Were they in it together?

The door opened and Gunnar stepped through. She looked up at him. He eyed the boots in her hands and then locked gazes. "I'm not working for him, but we are from the same place."

Shiya dropped the boots. "What?"

He nodded at the bed. "Sit."

She sank to the mattress.

"If you go anywhere without me, he'll kill you. I can protect you, but only if I'm by your side. Do you understand?"

She nodded. "Who exactly are you? Some kind of federal agent?"

"I'll explain later. Right now, I need to arrange our escape. You will go everywhere with me and not leave my side until I say we're safe. Do you understand?"

Shiya nodded. Even though he'd lied about the bear and the blood, the tone of his voice told her he didn't lie about what he said now.

"Good. We're here for a party, so we're going to carry on like nothing has happened and slip out to escape during the ball. I'll arrange for transport to a safe location with my people. Until then, we sit tight."

"Your people—as in people like Lucas?"

"No. They're with me, and they won't let anything happen to you. You can trust me."

"Even if you lied to me?" She eyed him, waiting for him to deny it.

"I had to—to protect you. Besides, I didn't believe you'd accept the truth."

"Try me."

"I really wanted to wait until later to talk to you about this." He sighed.

"I'm not going anywhere with you until you explain."

"Do you believe life exists outside of your world?" A serious expression covered his face. He continued to hold her gaze, watching for her reaction, waiting for her response, not saying anything further.

The air between them crackled and a shiver ran up her spine. What was he trying to say? He was an alien? Shiya nodded toward the ceiling. "You mean up there?"

"Yes."

"I suppose. There are many planets in the universe. It would be foolish to assume we have the only one with life on it."

"You're correct. Life exists on many worlds. Some of these planets are like your own, others not so much." He walked up to her and cupped her face in his hands so she couldn't turn away. "I'm from one of those worlds—a place like Earth, but very far away. So is Lucas."

Shiya screwed up her face. Did he understand how preposterous his claim sounded? She was willing to accept that other people existed out there, but he asked too much when he wanted her to believe she'd come face to face with an extraterrestrial—made love to an alien. *Really?* He couldn't be serious. Shiya pulled her face away.

"I'm serious."

"Uh, huh." She bit her lip. Why did she always manage to find the crazy ones? "It appears I've stumbled onto a lodge full of escaped mental patients. From the frying pan into the fire. I guess I got the one night I'd never forget—as promised."

"You're not making sense."

Shiya spun around. "Okay, let's review this conversation. You know my stalker—actually you're both from another world and just happened to end up in Alaska at the same time I did, and this somehow has something to do with me being attacked by a giant bear. How does that not sound like a really bad acid trip?"

"The bear didn't attack you."

"Yes it did." Shiya pointed to her boots. "It knocked me to the ground..."

"...and licked you."

Shiya jumped to her feet. "You were there. I knew it. I didn't imagine it, and the blood on the bottom of my boots more than proves it." She poked him in the chest, furious. "And you're asking me to trust you—to stick to you so you can protect me from the other crazy in the lodge. You're as insane as Lucas. I'm leaving and taking my chances with Nanuk."

Shiya twisted and Gunnar grabbed her arms stopping her. His lips sealed over hers and her world froze in time, hanging suspended in the moment. All her anger, all her intentions vaporized and her traitorous arms reached up and pulled him deeper into the kiss.

Gunnar took her pack with a change of clothes, her boots, and parka, and set up the dog sled as she changed for the ball. Shiya smoothed the white velvet over her curves and fastened a diamond necklace around her throat.

Her gown was sleeveless, with a deep plunge in the front and a slit on the side up to her hip. A sexy number for Alaska, but it also suited the location. The creamy fabric reminded her of the bear that had almost taken her life. Strange that she'd chosen to bring the dress, especially when she'd never intended to come to the party, but something about the gown called to her, demanded she bring it. So she had, and as she looked at herself in the mirror, she truly wondered how much fate governed her future.

Shiya couldn't help but feel the gown was exactly Gunnar's taste—for him alone. She turned side to side and then bent over to slip her heels on, unafraid of the height they'd add, knowing she could never be as tall as her Viking who claimed to be from another world.

The door opened as she buckled a strap on her silver stiletto.

"It's all...."

Shiya lifted her head and smiled. Gunnar froze where he stood. His jaw dropped open, and his hand clamped onto the doorframe so hard his knuckles turned white.

"It's all what?" she asked.

"Done," he said so low the vibration rolled through her and centered in her torso, sending zings racing through her blood. "My gods, woman. You look like sex in the snow."

Shiya took her time buckling the other strap and then stood enjoying the way he visually feasted on her. "You like then?"

He nodded.

Her stomach flipped at the hungry expression on his face. She didn't bother to tell him underwear couldn't be worn with the gown because every line showed. A trickle of anticipation of him discovering that fact shivered through her.

Crazy really, she didn't intend to sleep with him again, or at least that's what she'd told herself over and over after he'd left the room. And it had been settled—until he opened that door. Now, she wanted him again. Crazy or not, the man did things to her with one glance she'd never thought possible, but she needed to push those urges aside and focus. Her life and his depended on it.

After she escaped the lodge, Shiya planned to ditch Gunnar at the first village or town and head deep into the wild country, her territory.

Out there, she had control. Leaving him behind felt wrong, even though it wasn't. She didn't have time to develop feelings for

Gunnar, nor had she had the chance to grow attached, but here she was, full of regret. The sooner they left, the sooner she could take care of unfinished business. "Shall we go down?"

Gunnar stepped forward and kicked the door shut behind him. Shiya gasped as he stalked forward.

"Gunnar?"

He backed her against a wall, pressing both his palms on the surface, caging her in. He leaned in and sniffed her neck. "Go down. Yes." He dropped to his knees and slid both hands under her skirt, shoving the fabric up on her hips. "No panties?" He tipped his head back and gave her a smoldering look. "How wicked." His fingers found her clit and drew a circle around the throbbing bud. "You're just looking for trouble, aren't you?"

And from the expression on his face, trouble meant that tongue thrust inside her. Cream flooded her pussy. "No," Shiya gasped and fell back against the wall. "I'm avoiding panty lines."

"Um hmm." Around and around his finger went, circling her clit, drawing her tighter, setting her core on fire. He cocked his head, never taking his gaze from hers. "Is that so?"

"Yes," she mumbled and moaned as his finger slipped inside and he began to fuck her. In and out, slow and tortuous, until she was ready to climb backward up the door, or fire off like a rocket. A second finger joined the first. Both twisted and curled up, nailing her in her G-spot.

Launch. Her igniters blew as the orgasm overtook her with such force she couldn't breathe. She cried and threw her head back. Her hands clamped on his shoulders, the only thing keeping her upright.

In and out—faster and faster. Wave after wave rolled through her. No end—no beginning. Throbbing spasms rocked her with seismic force, and yet he continued stroking, drawing out the pleasure, taking her deeper into his own brand of possession. There was no denying what he did. He'd claimed her and made it clear she wasn't going anywhere without him and she'd be out of her mind to try.

"You were planning to run from me?" He spoke as though he'd

read her thoughts from moments before.

"No," she lied, shaking her head back and forth, denying her intentions.

"Let me show you what you'd be running from." He licked her thigh and a second orgasm tore through her, stronger, more intense than the first. It pulsed around his fingers. He hooked one of her legs and rested it on his shoulder. His lips traveled up and she gasped. The man was sexy—crazy as shit, but oh, my God, sexy.

Chapter Four

Her escape hadn't gone as planned. Gunnar swore backup would arrive soon and they could make their departure, but that had been hours ago and still no backup. She hadn't seen Lucas since the encounter on the stairs, but her instincts told her not to let her guard down. He didn't back down from a challenge.

Gunnar must have sensed it too. He hadn't let her break physical contact. Always touching her arm or hip, so close she could hear him breathe in the crowded and very noisy room. She'd had to pee for the last hour, but couldn't seem to summon the control to break contact. His touch settled her nerves.

Finally, she couldn't hold it anymore. She excused herself to go to the ladies' room. As she washed her hands and leaned over the counter to reapply her lipstick, a gorgeous redhead walked in and stood beside her at the sink.

She turned and smiled at Shiya. "Isn't this just the most romantic place you've ever been?"

"I used to live in Alaska." Shiya shrugged, even though she had to agree with her.

The woman turned back to the mirror, tugged at her neckline, lowering the cleavage a fraction of an inch. She eyed Shiya out of the corner of her eye. "Lucas wanted me to give you a message."

Shiya dropped her lipstick in the sink and her hand shot to her breast. "You're here with Lucas?"

The corner of the woman's mouth curled into the most unfriendly smile she'd ever seen. Shiya stepped away, putting distance between them. The woman moved closer and leaned in. "You can't run."

Shiya stepped back and bumped into the wall. Her mouth opened but nothing came out. He had minions. Everywhere. Lucas had sent a message all right. Wherever she went—she'd never be safe. Even in the land she knew better than most.

The redhead did a head-to-toe appraisal and looked back up into Shiya's eyes. "Lovely dress." She gave Shiya a friendly smile, grabbed her clutch from the counter, and turned to exit the ladies' room, pausing at the door. "You either go to him, or he's coming for you. Choose." The door clicked shut behind her.

Shiya threw her hands on the counter, dropped her head, and sucked in a deep breath. Her heart pounded so hard she could barely breathe and her head spun. The encounter brought questions to the surface. If the pretty redhead worked for Lucas, who else did? Was this whole party a setup? Had she been lured to this lodge to die?

One thing was for certain. She needed to run. She couldn't wait for backup to arrive, and she couldn't go anywhere with Gunnar. His life would be in danger if he remained in her company.

If someone wanted to commit murder, Alaska was a great place to lose a body—or two. She should have thought of that before coming home. It had always felt so safe, a place she could run to for security. At the moment it felt like the most dangerous place on Earth.

Shiya closed her eyes, took another deep breath. No more waiting around for a knight to come to her rescue. It had been foolish to think she could find security in the arms of another. If she wanted to get out of this alive, she'd have to do it on her own.

She lifted her chin, opened her eyes, and froze. The woman in the mirror staring back at her in her snowy velvet dress was the redhead.

Shiya screamed.

&

Gunnar looked up when he heard the scream. Lucas lifted his chin at the same time. The room was loud and chaotic. Nobody else seemed to notice. Which was a good thing.

A redhead in white burst from the ladies room and ran for the kitchen and back doors. It took Gunnar seconds to register the woman was Shiya, and she'd gone into the shift, triggered by endorphins from fear or their earlier sexual encounter. The way she ran, he'd say it was fear. Not good—especially with Lucas witness to it.

She threw the swinging doors to the kitchen open and darted through, disappearing behind them as they shut. Lucas shot Gunnar a quick look and headed for the front exit. *Game on.* Gunnar took Shiya's route, and as he ran by the chef and his staff, a snowmobile screamed past the backdoor with Shiya on it.

Gunnar rushed outside. "Shiya!"

She didn't look back—she hadn't heard him. The sound of a second engine rent the night. The bright red Polaris roared past, hot on her tracks with Lucas on the back.

As Gunnar went to acquire a snowmobile of his own, someone grabbed his arm. He didn't have to turn to see who. His teammate who was supposed to be distracting Lucas by shifting her appearance to Shiya's. He shrugged her off. "You were supposed to distract him."

"I was in the ladies' room." She grabbed his arm again. "Let her go. You know the law."

He glanced over his shoulder to see the attractive redhead behind him. This time she'd pulled a laser and set the sights on him. He should have known better than to trust her. She'd tried several times to have sex with him and form a bond since she'd arrived on Terran soil. Jealousy clearly reflected in her eyes and contempt filled the sneer on her face.

"The law doesn't apply to mates." He'd rushed the bond to

protect Shiya, knowing eventually he planned to take her as a mate anyway. His only regret was that he couldn't take the time to court her in a proper manner, and Regan saw it as an indication he wasn't serious about Shiya. "If she dies, I'll have you brought up on charges of murder."

"Clearly, she's going to die."

Gunnar struck so fast Regan didn't have time to blink. She slumped into a heap at his feet. Pulling her up onto his shoulder, he picked up her laser and ran for a shed where the snowmobiles were stored and he could dump Regan until he could deal with her later. Hopefully, the delay wouldn't cost Shiya her life. If it did, Regan and Lucas would both pay.

Chapter Five

Shiya heard the snowmobile seconds before it struck the back of her sled, spinning the Arctic Cat around like a top on the frozen inlet. The sled hit a rut and stopped. She didn't. The centrifugal force sent her flying from her seat where she hit the ice and slid toward the water's edge.

Shiya clawed at the wind-slicked surface, breaking her nails, frantic to stop before she went in. A rough chunk of ice caught the strap on her shoe, stopping her slide, but breaking the buckle and gouging her ankle. The stiletto continued across the ice for several feet, until it dropped into an open area of the inlet with a plunk.

Lucas fired several times, hitting the area around her. With each impact she yelped, expecting the bolt to hit her. Instead, the frozen surface began to glow with an eerie green light, seeming to take on the energy from the blast. The glow faded as quickly as it had started, followed by a popping and crackling sound. Several fractures moved through the ice and underneath her.

Blood dripped from her forehead, freezing on impact. Pressing her hands flat, she pushed to rise, but the surface began to crack around her palms and knees, spider-webbing across the glassy surface in every direction. Shiya went still. The next move could be her last.

"Shiya, Shiya, Shiya. You've given me quite the challenge." Lucas stopped fifty feet from her location, safe on the thicker ice near the bank. He swung his leg off the snowmobile, dismounting in a casual manner, as though he murdered people every day. "You've been a hard woman to kill." He waved the strange gun around casually. "I regret what I have to do," he said, "but you understand. I can't allow you to go around shifting your appearance in public. This planet isn't ready to accept our existence."

"You sent that woman into the ladies' room."

He gave her a nod. "You aren't who you think—you're a loose end—a doppelganger—one of us."

"So that's what this is about?" Shiya swallowed. Yeah, she got that Gunnar hadn't been lying, but why did that mean she had to die? "I won't tell anyone your secret."

"Our secret." He tsked. "That's the problem. You can't control it. You haven't been taught how. That shift you did earlier proves it, and it was all the evidence I needed to terminate a rogue mate. Regrettable. There are few females with your talent and beauty."

"I can learn." Shiya lifted her head and gave him a pleading look. The ice cracked some more. Her heart jumped. "Please, don't shoot me."

Lucas tipped his head back and laughed. "I'm not going to shoot you. The water will swallow you. This is for Gunnar. He should have backed off when I told him to."

"Don't hurt him. He only protected me."

"Sorry, he gave me no choice. I don't like looking over my shoulder, which I'll have to do for killing you. We mate once in a lifetime." Lucas shrugged.

In the distance a motor hummed, growing closer by the second. Lucas smiled and turned his head toward the sound. Shiya's heart began to thump painfully against her ribs. "Don't do this, Lucas."

"Sit back and enjoy the show." Lucas spun around and lifted the laser, firing as Gunnar came around a bend in the inlet. He dove off the sled as it exploded into ash, tucking and rolling across the snow. Lucas raised the laser again.

Gunnar had gone from rolling to rushing forward on his feet

like a linebacker. His clothes dropped behind him as his body stretched. Fur rippled across his skin, covering his bare flesh in velvet white. Gunnar leapt into the air, his hands stretched forward. As they came down, they landed as giant paws. His face extended into the all too familiar Roman nose of Nanuk.

Lucas fired. Gunnar dodged to the side. Snow and ice exploded into the air where he'd been, not slowing his charge in the least. Gunnar roared, launching across the shore at Lucas.

Lucas took the time to aim. His arm came up steady, as though danger didn't approach.

Calm, collected, ready to make a kill.

"Watch out," Shiya screamed and scrambled to her feet. The ice caved around her. It took only a second, but in that second Lucas glanced back to see her go in. The distraction gave Gunnar all he needed to reach and tackle him—the last thing Shiya saw as she went under and blocks of ice slammed shut over her head.

Gunnar's jaws closed on Lucas's forearm as he threw it up to protect his face. Grizzly fur quickly filled his mouth. A giant paw came around, swatting Gunnar in the head and sending him flying back into a bank. Lucas circled as Gunnar rolled to his feet and shook off the impact.

He pulled his lips back, eying the spot Shiya had gone under. If he could get around Lucas, he could dive in and pull her out. The cold would keep her alive a little longer—the only benefit of going into the arctic water.

Lucas wasn't having any part of it. He posted himself between Gunnar and where Shiya had gone in, letting him know if he wanted to get to her, he'd have to go through him. Lucas raised a paw and batted at the air in raw challenge.

Come and get her.

Gunnar put his head down and charged. He didn't have to beat him. He only needed to get into the water to retrieve Shiya. At the last second he dodged to the side, toward the gap in the ice she'd gone through.

Lucas anticipated his move. Claws at least six inches long

ripped across his side, laying open his hide as cleanly as a filet knife. Ribs snapped like twigs along the gash. The raw power of the strike had been more than Gunnar expected. He staggered and went down halfway to his goal, too far from the water, and too hurt to get closer. Blood pumped from the wound onto the ice, painting it red. Lucas swung around. Triumph filled his eyes.

I've won. You die.

Gunnar groaned and lifted his head. That had not been the way to go. He stared, waiting for the fatal blow, a million regrets flashing through his mind. He'd failed her when he'd promised he'd save her.

Lucas raised a paw, a smile on his maw.

Death.

The ice cracked and exploded around them. A killer whale broke through the frozen inlet and took Lucas under the ice with it. Waves splashed up, soaking Gunnar. Shiya could still be alive if he acted quickly, but he couldn't move.

Frothing water splashed everywhere. If the Orca gave Lucas enough time to focus on shifting, it would be over for the whale. Fins, slashing paws—a roar as Lucas's head broke the surface—silence as it sank back under. A violent struggle of life and death ensued beneath him and he could do nothing to retrieve the woman who desperately needed his help.

The grizzly came up again, claws sinking into the edge, frantically seeking purchase. A pleading look filled his face. Lucas began to shift back into his true humanoid form, unable to hold his focus in the frigid water. Fur retreated, bones popped back into place, cracking and crunching. Soon, human hands fought to keep hold of the slick surface.

Save me, brother.

But to shift his shape with his injuries would be a death sentence. He wouldn't have the strength to shift back and without immediate medical attention, the wounds in his human form would kill him. The whale would end it quick.

Lucas's hands slipped and he dropped into the water. Seconds later his head submerged into the icy depths. He'd only been doing the job he'd been assigned, but that job had threatened the woman Gunnar protected. He regretted his death. This matter could have been solved in their courts.

Now, fate had decided and all would die. Even if he located her, Gunnar wasn't sure he could bring her to the surface. The better solution would be to drown with her. He kicked a back leg, pushing his bulk toward the edge.

Lucas resurfaced, thrust up onto to the ice by a massive black and white head. The whale backed away and locked gazes with Gunnar. Human eyes—Shiya's eyes.

She lived. He tried to crawl forward but couldn't move. His body had gone numb from the blood loss, and his heart struggled to beat with the dropping pressure.

She sank below the surface and came back up again. This time her dark hair swirled around her head in the water. "Gunnar," she said.

Lucas rolled over and looked in her direction. Seconds later, his hand extended out toward her. She eyed it for a moment before she reached out and let him pull her naked body from the water. Shiya immediately crawled over to Gunnar and stroked his face. He licked her hand. "He's dying," she said.

Lucas nodded.

"Please help me save him."

Gunnar's vision grew fuzzy. He blinked, but couldn't reopen his eyes.

"Will he be okay?"

"Okay? Never. He's always been a strange one, but he'll recover if that's what you mean."

Gunnar opened his eyes and glared at Lucas. The surroundings were familiar. His ship—his quarters—his bed. "Look who's calling me strange."

Lucas smiled. "Your woman and I came to an understanding."

Gunnar raised a brow.

"I won't kill her and she'll learn how to control her abilities."

"And who's going to teach her?"

Lucas crossed his arms. "I'd volunteer, but I think you've already staked your claim."

"You think right."

Lucas nodded. "Treat her well. She's a remarkable woman. I'm glad I didn't succeed in killing her. Keep her out of trouble and you won't see me again." Lucas turned and walked out.

"So where do we go from here?"

Everywhere.

"You're doing that talk in the head thing again."

"Yes." The universe belonged to them. There was so much he wanted to show her—teach her about her ancestors and the people of their world. Once the mission was over, and the ship recovered, he intended to show her wonders, take her places that would leave her breathless. But until that time, he'd like to make her breathless. He eyed her. *Naked and breathless.*

"Let's start over." Gunnar reached his hand out and took hers, pulling her onto the bed and face to face. "Hi. My name is Gunnar. Where have you been all my life?"

"Waiting for you to rescue me." Shiya leaned in and kissed him. "And is that what you're doing—rescuing me?"

"Whatever you want to call it." He grinned and went for her top.

~About the Author~

D. L. Jackson is a writer of urban fantasy, science fiction, military romance and erotic romance. She loves to incorporate crazy plot twists, comedy and the unexpected into her worlds. As a U.S. Army veteran, she naturally adores men in uniform and feels the world could always use more. She does her part by incorporating as many sexy soldiers in her novels as she can. When she isn't writing or running the roads, you can often find her online chatting with her peers and readers. Grab a cup of iced coffee, pull up your virtual chair and say hi. She loves emails and blog visits from her readers.

Visit D.L. online at:
www.authordljackson.com

All She Wants for Christmas is Her Dom

by

Stacey Kennedy

Chapter One

The suite in the Castillo Lodge far exceeded Blake's expectations. Rustic in appearance with log walls, hardwood panel floors, and the rich scent of evergreens filling the air, it was exactly what he requested and fit the mood for a Christmas getaway. The room delighted him, but the woman who stood before him enchanted him more.

He led the blindfolded Taryn over to the four-poster wooden bed with a quilt on top and placed her hands on the railing over the footboard. "I suggest you present yourself." She bent over, spread her long, sexy legs, and angled her hips to expose her ass decorated by a thong. Her straight brown locks hung loosely down her back, covering the crimson lace bra that looked lovely against her pale skin. "Nicely done."

Her chest rose and fell quickly. *Nervous?* The thought only lingered on his mind a moment—no one paired with him would hold anxieties. As a Dom, he demanded much of his submissives. He needed them to be strong and obedient. And Madame Eve, a matchmaker out of Las Vegas who had arranged the encounter, had been well aware of that fact. As he examined her more closely, he equated her reaction to being aroused, and relished the thought that his mere presence caused her reaction.

"I'm here to please you, Sir."

The fire in the large stone fireplace on the far side of the large room cast a lovely glow over her skin. "Your desire to entice me is working." He pressed his hard cock against the seam of her ass to declare she hadn't been the only one affected. "I appreciate you addressing me with such respect, but for now, we can do without it. I'd advise, though, to use the term when you believe I want to hear it." He rubbed himself against her and held back his groan. "Is my cock what you want?"

"My pussy aches for you."

He chuckled before he moved away and saw her stance falter. "That kind of pleasure you'll have to earn."

She proved she was a skilled submissive as she recovered her position without pause. "I want to earn it, Sir."

He strode toward his bag on the floor by the stone fireplace and took out his flogger. She tensed as he flicked his hand to allow her to hear the sound of the tails whooshing through the air. "Do you have a safe word, my pet?"

"Marshal."

He positioned himself behind her and trailed the flogger over her backside. "Explain why that word holds significance?" He smacked her ass with a hard hit to test her limits.

"I'm a U.S. Marshal in Texas." She groaned. "Supervisory Deputy to be exact."

He ran the flogger over her bottom again to tease her. "Is that why the submissive role appeals to you, because of the job you hold?"

"It feels wonderful to give up the control I carry in my day-to-day life." She moaned as he issued another hit. "And I enjoy being punished."

He'd already known she enjoyed pain play. Madame Eve had sent him an extensive list of her limits, but he preferred learning for himself where those limits were drawn. "How long have you lived the BDSM lifestyle?"

"Five years." She squeaked as he delivered a hard hit on her back then let the tails of the flogger tickle down the sweet cheeks of her ass.

"But you haven't had a lifestyle Dom?"

"I—" She paused. "I'd prefer not to discuss it."

Unacceptable. He hit hard twice. She bowed her head and cringed. "I didn't ask what you preferred. Answer the question."

She breathed deep as he hit lightly along her thighs. "I did have someone, but not anymore."

"Would he be jealous that I'm your Dom tonight?"

"I'd imagine he would be." She gasped when he flogged her on the shoulders and continued down her back.

"I suppose then, I'll need to leave my mark on you for all to see, so they're well aware who you belong to now." He hit harder.

Her flesh turned a lovely shade of red, but he knew she could take more. He needed to up the intensity and push her further. "Reach into your panties and rub your clit. But if you orgasm without permission you will displease me. Am I understood?"

"Yes, Sir." She lowered her hand into her thong and moaned as she played with her clit.

He raised the flogger and slapped her again, repeatedly moving his arm in a figure-eight pattern. Her skin burned red as he whipped her without mercy. She cringed, complained with yelps, but he suspected she enjoyed every damn minute of it.

She impressed him. Her control, ability to handle pain, and desire to please him had been honorable. That is, until he caught sight of something that tightened his jaw. Her body trembled but not in a way that informed him the pain had been too intense. No, she had defied him.

He hit her twice and meant the strokes to hurt. "Did you orgasm?"

"I'm sorry, Sir." She panted.

He gripped her hair and pulled back to expose her face. The blindfold had not moved. Her parted lips trembled as she sucked in deep breaths and her cheeks were as red as her ass. "You did not answer my question."

"It's been so long since I've been flogged. It felt incredible. I couldn't help myself, Sir."

He *tsked.* "If you had asked permission, I would have granted you the right. Now, though, you will need to earn back such luxuries and be punished for your mistake." He approached his bag again where he grabbed out two five-pound weights and his whip. "Raise your arms to shoulder height and do *not* lower them."

She complied and he placed the weights in her hands. "Turn slowly in a circle and keep those weights high."

He took a step back then sent the whip to connect with her torso, flicking his wrist in time with her spin so with each turn she made, the whip connected with a new area on her body. She sucked in a breath and flinched away.

Red marks decorated her skin. Her moans, mixed with pleasure and pain, drifted over to caress him like a warm hand stroking his cock. He continued until her arms shook from exhaustion and he'd marked her body beautifully. "You will not orgasm again without permission. Do I make myself clear?"

"Yes, Sir." Her legs trembled and her voice shook. "My arms are hurting, Sir. May I lower them?"

She'd been punished, which was his intention—to make sure she never disobeyed him again—but he'd not let her off that easy. She had asked for his punishment to end instead of him granting it. She had defied him again. "You're inability to do as I ask is disappointing."

"I don't mean to fail you, Sir."

"I'm finding that hard to believe since you continually do so." He took the weights from her, tossed them aside, and massaged her arms. "If such were the case I would find myself rewarding you more than I am punishing."

Taryn's Dom rubbed her arms and relieved the soreness. His procedure of punishment seemed so familiar. Her ex-boyfriend punished that hard and always made her work for her reward. She shook the thought from her mind. Past lovers should have no place in her mind now.

She wanted to look at him, but he hadn't allowed her to remove the blindfold. When she agreed in her questionnaire to

Madame Eve that she'd been comfortable with the idea of shielding her eyes, she had assumed it had been the way he wanted her to be presented to him. She had not expected she'd be blindfolded the entire time—never to see him at all.

He released her arms, and she listened as he strode to the other side of the room. Her heart raced for what was to come next. She held no doubt he would make an example of her failures. Part of her welcomed the pain she expected would be soon upon her. The other part was fearful of his harsh punishments.

His presence returned a moment later. Even though she couldn't see him, his energy simmered around her and her mind played with images of what he looked like. Tall, dark, and handsome with a body that made her damp between her thighs—or so she hoped.

"Lower to your hands and knees."

She obeyed and positioned herself on all fours, and did her best to make the pose as sexy as possible to entice him.

He tapped her back and she recognized the feel of a cane. The burn that followed the hit was undisputable. "Do you want to earn back how much you've disappointed me?"

"With all that I am, Sir." It had been years since she'd been in the submissive role, and anger at herself for not having more control set in. She wanted him to acknowledge her as submissive, be proud of what she accomplished, and even more so, wanted the reward of a job well done.

"Well then, my pet, you'll take what I'm going to give you with little argument. Am I understood?"

"Yes, Sir."

He struck her lightly between the shoulder blades, but even a gentle tap with a cane was painful. She dipped her head and breathed deeply. She'd learned the skill long ago to bottle the pain and convert it into something brilliant—use it to bring herself to a higher level of arousal.

The hits continued to travel along her torso, to her bottom, and travelled down to the back of her thighs until the cane met the arch of her foot. She hissed but didn't dare voice her pain with words. No, she needed to please him, for him to stop punishing her, and be in awe of her submissiveness.

"Reach your hand out." She did and he placed a bullet vibrator in her palm. "Find a way to turn it on, then lower your head down to the floor and place it against your clit."

She fumbled as she attempted to find the on button—she eventually did—then placed her cheek against the hard floor and arched her back. She positioned the vibrator into her panties and the buzz along her clit made her eyes roll back into her head.

"I will not have to remind you of what you must ask for, will I?"

She forced herself to draw away from her pleasure and find her voice to answer him. "No, Sir. I will not come without permission."

She heard the sound of the cane swoosh through the air before the hard wood hit her bottom. She nearly cried out, but swallowed it back. He walloped her with such force she suspected welts would be a reminder of tonight.

Not that she minded. She deserved the punishment—enjoyed the treatment he gave her—and she sucked in the pain with each breath. She pushed the vibrator harder against her clit in a demand that her body ignore the sharp sting.

He placed his foot between her shoulder blades to pin her and continued with hard smacks against her sore flesh. She worked the vibe feverishly against her clit to offset the agony. Yet, as he spanked her ass in between the torment of the cane, she couldn't hold back.

She screamed as heat burned through her body. The increase of pain introduced the rise of her climax. The sensation stole all of her reason and overloaded her nerve endings with pleasure. "May I come, Sir?"

He removed his foot, placed his hand on her nape, and caged her in his grip. "You may. But you damn well better make it impressive." He slapped along her body—from her neck all the way to her sore ass—and never missed a piece of her tender flesh.

His hits stung, but they held no comparison to the

overwhelming surge of pleasure erupting in her body. Her clit pulsed, pussy contracted, and she vocalized her pleasure to allow him to hear the intensity of her orgasm. She had not come so hard in years and she lost herself completely with the force of it.

It hadn't been until his finger trailed down her arm did she return from the blissful place she'd been sent to. "Stand, but take it slow." He helped her up, steadied her, and even supported her for a while. "Are you feeling light-headed at all?"

She groaned as the world spun around her. Her heartbeat raced and a cold sweat washed over her body. She exhaled slow and steady, and waited for her body to recover from his harsh treatment.

Many minutes later, her feet felt more stable on the floor and her body no longer tingled. "I'm feeling better now." He pushed on her slightly and her bottom connected with a cold, smooth surface—the log wall she assumed—and the coolness against her sore rump came as a relief.

"Don't move." He released his hold on her arm, and she heard shuffling before he closed back in on her. She worried for a moment that he might issue more pain, but when he pulled her from the wall and applied cool cream along her bottom, she sighed. The smooth lotion eased the sting on her skin and soothed her. Still, she doubted she'd sit right for a week.

He used a gentle touch as he tended to her. She flinched a few times at the marks that had clearly been the worst, but felt more relaxed than she had in a long time. There, she found her peace. It wasn't spa days, or therapy sessions—this was where she could release all of her strain. Euphoria filled her soul.

He covered her whole body with the cream, finished up at her ankles and stood. She heard him move in front of her while he rubbed the remaining lotion into his hands. Each breath she took only seemed to draw out the moment of complete silence.

"You've done well tonight."

He trailed a finger down her cheek, and being already sensitive, she shivered. More so, the pride sounding in his voice brought forth emotions long hidden. She'd withstood all his punishment and she'd done right by him. Her self-confidence rose to a level it hadn't been at in years.

"Thank you, Sir."

"You're quite welcome."

His voice wavered in such a way that made her hesitate, and the sound drained all of her pride and happiness. "Sir, why does it sound as if our night is over?"

"Because, my pet, it is."

"But I've taken your punishment." She paused. Yes, he'd rewarded her with a climax, but she had yet to have him. She wanted his cock and the ache in her pussy declared she needed him. "What have I done to displease you, Sir?"

"No more formalities, please."

"What have I done then? Tell me what I did to upset you that you will not offer yourself to me?" Tears rimmed her eyes behind the mask. She'd been taken on a high, soared along the fantastic ride, only to be dropped with no net.

He took her hand and squeezed. "You've done nothing wrong. In fact, you did everything right." His voice sounded so different than it had this whole time—almost unsure.

It unsettled her. Before she had a chance to ask him more, he released a low deep breath. "Remove the blindfold, Taryn."

She blinked beneath it and tried to process what she'd heard. Up to that point, her Dom had not said her name and the sound of it hit her with a memory.

It can't be.

She yanked the blindfold down, so she could laugh at herself for thinking that this man just then sounded so much like her ex-boyfriend. But as her vision adjusted from being held in the dark for so long, warm hazel eyes greeted her, along with a charming smile.

"Blake?"

He grinned. "Surprised to see me?"

Chapter Two

Blake had no preconceived notion about how Taryn would react, and had been surprised she hadn't recognized his voice, even though he tried his best to disguise it. He didn't want her to know who mastered her because he wanted to remind her of what he had to offer. Now, he merely let the seconds tick by until she had resolved her thoughts.

She finally blinked, but still stared blank-faced at him. "How can this be?"

"Madame Eve contacted me three weeks ago—as I'm sure she did you—and invited me to the Christmas celebration here at the lodge to meet my match, and also extended an invitation to attend the gala on Christmas Day. It's my hope that you'll join me."

She shook her head as if she were unable to process what he told her. "Are you telling me we met again by chance?"

"No." The Christmas Eve encounter had taken not only planning by Madame Eve, but he'd had to make life changes in order to be the man he needed to be when he saw Taryn again.

"Then, what?" Her confused expression shifted to a scowl. "You set this up? You knew you were meeting me tonight and said nothing?"

"You agreed to keep our identities a secret until tonight," he gently reminded her. "Madame Eve must have thought it was appropriate that I knew we were being matched, but she didn't disapprove of my wanting to surprise you."

"That means nothing—who cares what Madame Eve thinks? *You* should have told me." She glared. "I cannot believe you did this." She strode over to her suitcase, grabbed a pair of pants, plus a shirt, and set about getting dressed. "You should have warned me. Told me it was you. You had no right to assume I even wanted to be with you again." She never looked back, but he could tell by her curt tone that she loathed him.

She dressed and he saw her wince as the clothing settled over her sore body. He wanted to help, but knew better than to approach her right then. He leaned against the wall, crossed his arms, and waited for her to calm down. The Taryn in front of him was one he knew well. If he said a word, she'd trap him in an impossible situation he'd never recover from—nothing he did would ease her. He waited for her to stop being so angry, to allow herself time to think.

"And there you go—like you always did—saying nothing while I'm the only one letting my feelings be known." She scowled at him. "You have nothing to say?"

He shook his head. *Not right now. Not when you've cornered me.*

Her eyes narrowed, her face turned a dark shade of red, and rage wafted off her. "I'm so fucking angry with you." She spun on her heels, heading for the patio door, only dressed in the T-shirt and a pair of jeans. "Go home."

He sighed, annoyed, infuriated, and frustrated. He hoped she'd be more receptive to him—that she missed and wanted him as much as he did her—but her demand had been firm. She wanted nothing to do with him.

It only confirmed he had made the right choice in how he approached her. If he had knocked on her door or even called her, she would have run—just like she did now. He wanted to show her the spark that existed between them, and he held no doubt she'd witnessed it tonight. He suspected her hesitation came from the night he broke her heart and she broke his—too swamped with old pain to see straight.

He had lived that life for the past five years, and he wouldn't walk in the shadow of despair any longer. He hadn't gone through all he had to ensure this night happened to let her walk out of his life again.

Fuck this. She's mine.

He snatched the quilt off the bed and strode out after her. The snowy mountains of Alaska stood picturesque against the moonlight sky. The ski hill was lit up and he could hear laughter as guests enjoyed the cold winter's night. His focus remained on finding Taryn. Each step he took into the deep snow froze his feet as the icy air made him shiver.

He passed a large snowdrift, and she appeared standing beside an evergreen tree. Her head was in her hands and she sobbed. He sighed in relief. Her first reaction might have been anger, but as always, she'd break down and let him in.

He stepped in behind her, placed the quilt over her shoulders, and turned her to face him. It tugged at his heart seeing the pain in the depths of her eyes—pain he'd put there. "Are you ready to talk now?"

"I wasn't expecting this," she said so softly he barely heard her. "Why wouldn't you tell me it was you?"

"Because I wanted to remind you of how good we are together before you knew that I was with you. I didn't want you to react exactly like you did."

Her eyes narrowed but there was no heat in her gaze. "How else was I supposed to act? You blindsided me and violated the trust."

"I did nothing you didn't agree to. Madame Eve told you exactly what would take place here. You knew you'd be blindfolded, brought into a BDSM scene, and you agreed to know nothing about me before tonight. You, not me, set the limits. I merely followed them." He cocked his head. "Did you not question why I never engaged you sexually?"

"You...." He saw the argument rise on her expression before she stopped herself. "You're right. You made me pleasure myself and never touched me in that way."

"Nor did I kiss you. I acted as your Dom and nothing more, which had all been things you agreed to. In fact, you wanted sex if I remember and didn't I refuse you? I might have gone about this in a way you disprove of, but I would not have taken you without you knowing the truth."

She studied him—the sadness, dismay, and even the anger dissipated from her face—she looked exhausted. "How did Madame Eve know about us? How did she arrange this?"

"I hired Madame Eve four months ago, filled out the questionnaire in search of a lifestyle submissive, and as you know she asked about previous relationships."

"So you told her about me?"

He brushed his knuckles across her cheek and it pleased him when she leaned into his touch. "Of course I would."

"But...." Her chin quivered. "But I don't understand. You let me go."

He deserved to see how much his actions hurt her, and she hid none of it in her expression. "What was I to do? You came to me and spoke of big dreams in Houston."

"You could have come with me."

A tear fell down her cheek and he caught it with his thumb. "I couldn't and you know that. I had the contract to build the new library in Sackville. I would have lost the deal and that project made the company what it is today."

"You lost me."

His heart clenched. The truth hurt. "A bad decision on my part, but not one I'll make again." It took a good part of the last two weeks to organize his life and get his priorities straight. But he'd not live another day in a life he didn't want and be away from the woman who fulfilled him. "I sold the business a week ago and moved to Houston last weekend."

Her eyes went huge. "You sold the business...for me?"

"It's always been you, Taryn, and *will* always be you. It hadn't been until Madame Eve contacted me and told me you had signed up with her services, did I realize I couldn't live another day without you. I saw that I had submerged myself in my work to try to forget you but that I failed miserably—all that remained was an empty man."

"Blake," she whispered.

He needed to explain himself and pressed on to share his soul with her. "Madame Eve felt regardless of what happened between us, that we were a perfect match and I happened to agree with her." He leaned in and her warm breath tickled his lips as the crisp air nipped at his skin. "I've made enough money. Yes, I could make more, but without you I have nothing."

She exhaled so deep the air fogged around them. "I have waited five years for you to say what you just said to me. There has not been a day where I haven't thought of you, missed being in your arms, and craved to be your submissive. If I wasn't as cold as I am now, I'd think I was dreaming, but I doubt I'd feel frostbitten in a dream."

He chuckled. "Best we warm you up then." He gathered her in his arms, trudging through the snow with one intent—spend the rest of the night reminding himself and her how right it was for them to be together.

&

Taryn welcomed the warm air from the suite as Blake shut the sliding door. He turned back to her, his eyes intent and her insides melted. She dropped the blanket to the floor as he latched onto her arms and yanked her toward him. He placed his lips over hers and set to make her forget her own name.

She swiped her tongue across his as he kissed her deeply. It'd been so long since she had his lips on hers, she'd forgotten how good the man could kiss. No one kissed her with the fevered pitch that he did, and no one but him could make her legs wobble.

He backed away, only a moment, and removed his shirt. She ran her hands over his chest, down his toned abs, and was delighted when they clenched beneath her touch. He'd always been muscular, but not like this. Her pussy ached for him at the feel of each groove beneath her fingers.

He left her mouth, to kiss along her jaw, to her shoulder where he bit. She gasped, but the throb along her clit only pulsed deeper. He touched her just how she liked it—rough and never hesitated. It made her burn. She raised her arms when he grabbed her shirt and lifted it over her head. He wasted no time removing her bra, pants, and panties then stepped back to examine her.

"I want you to know that it had been a torment not to see you naked—not to be able to touch your splendid pussy." He cupped her moist heat and squeezed tight. She ground herself against his hand. "Fuck, Taryn, you're a sexy woman."

The crackling fire lit his face in a warm glimmer. *My Blake. My Dom.* She'd missed him terribly, and seeing him like this, so powerful in front of her—she wondered how she'd gone so long without him. She had mourned their break-up for the past five years and her heart welcomed the healing.

He must have seen the happiness in her expression because he smiled. "We could exchange sentiments, but I'd much prefer to let your body speak to how happy you are that I'm here with you now." He gestured to his pants. "Remind me of what I've been missing these past five years."

She sank to her knees, kept her gaze focused on his, and undid his belt. His eyes burned with a wicked light and butterflies danced in her stomach. His black slacks pooled at his feet as his heavy cock rested at eye-level. She ran her hands up his thighs, licked the tip of his dick, and savored the salty liquid on her tongue.

He threaded his fingers through her hair and stared hungrily at her. She kissed his thighs, ran her tongue along his muscular legs, and trailed her hands along his abs. He tensed as she blew lightly on his cock and then slid her tongue up his shaft in a firm stroke. She brought him into her mouth and took him deep into her throat.

She backed away not a moment later and moistened him with her saliva before wrapping her hand around his erection to spread the warm liquid along his cock. She flicked the tip with her tongue to tease him, drew in a long breath, then went wild on him.

His hand tightened in her hair as she bobbed her head while she stroked his cock without mercy. His moans washed along her skin, raising goose bumps, as his cock hardened even more against her tongue. Each sound he made urged her to suck harder, stroke faster, and within only minutes, he jumped away from her.

"That...." He sounded breathless. "That was one hell of a good reminder." He leaned down to cage her face in his hands and took her mouth with a hard kiss that dampened her pussy.

He broke off the kiss, and she gasped at the loss of contact. "Nothing pleases me more than having the scent of my cock on your mouth."

Her clit pulsed at the low growl of possession in his tone.

"You are to remain kneeling there." He approached a bag on the floor and took a large square black velvet box. He turned back to her and smiled. "I got you something."

She took the box from him and ran her hand over the rich fabric. "What did you do?"

"Go on." He gestured toward the box. "Open it."

She glanced back to the gift, opened the lid, and gasped when sparking diamonds greeted her. "Oh, Blake...."

"Stand and let me decorate you."

He took the jewelry out of the box and it appeared to be a long necklace. She stood, turned her back to him, and he flicked her hair across her shoulder. "This, my pet, will be what I expect you to wear when we are in a scene together—a statement that my diamonds are along your skin and the knowledge that you are worthy of wearing such treasures."

Her breath hitched as he tightened the choker around her throat. The statement he made brought tears to her eyes. She ran her fingers along the choker, down the two rows of diamonds between her breasts and continued until she hit the belly chain as he fastened it. Nothing had ever felt so right.

He turned her to face him and his eyes shone with adoration. "You look perfect, exactly as you should, and now you understand what this symbolizes."

A marriage proposal meant something to some people, but in

her world, this meant so much more. "You've collared me and claimed me as yours."

His powerful gaze burned scorching heat through her body reaching down to her center. "Yes, my pet, I've collared you, but I haven't claimed you—not completely, anyway."

Chapter Three

The diamonds enhanced Taryn's beauty, and Blake would never grow tired of looking at her. She'd been marked as his and had accepted him as her lifestyle Dom. But his needy cock reminded him to stop admiring her and claim her.

He approached his bag and took out the last of the items he'd brought—four pieces of long black rope. Her breath hitched as he returned to her, confirming she still enjoyed the feel of restraints. He took her hand, led her in front of the footboard then turned her around so her ass rested against the wood, and she faced him. If he could have placed her on the bed, tied her down and done the wicked things he wanted to, he would have. But her body would be sore from the punishment earlier and her well-being stayed on his mind.

He sank to his knees, took one of her ankles, and tied the rope tight against her skin. He attached the remaining rope to the post on the bed before he repeated the move on the other ankle, and then did the same to her wrists to leave her caged between the posts on the bed.

His cock ached to slam into her slick pussy, but he'd not stray from what he'd craved for years. "Every day since you were gone, I thought of how you taste and your sweet honey tormented me." He licked out to savor her and groaned as her cream delighted his tongue. "Exactly as I remembered."

He smacked her pussy and hit her clit hard. “I grant you the right to not address me as Sir as long as you tell me nothing but the truth. Tell me how much you want my cock?”

“I’ve thought of your cock every time I masturbated. I’ve dreamed of how it used to fill me up, and I want you to make me come like you always could.”

He took her clit between his fingers and pinched. “While you fucked yourself, what did you think of?”

“I-I....” She moaned. “I thought of how you used to make me feel. The way your power would wash over me, just like it did tonight, and how I’d do anything I could to please you.”

He inserted a finger inside of her, then another, and her pussy tightened around him. “Did you do this while you thought of me?”

“Yes, always.”

He grasped her hip and he thrust his fingers inside of her with a steady rhythm. His muscles burned as he fingered her, and she bucked under his touch. He flicked her clit with his tongue and she shook, indicating a rising climax, but he wanted his mouth to offer her orgasm, not his fingers. He withdrew them, slid his tongue into her moist heat, and she hissed as she stared at him. Her hooded eyes made his cock stiffen further. He grabbed it and stroked himself.

The sight clearly pleased her since her eyes darkened as she watched him jerk off. He used his free hand to pinch her clit again and her moans encouraged him. He increased his speed with his tongue until her breath froze, her eyes widened, and her body quivered—all followed by a whoosh of air from her, indicating she was in the throes of her orgasm.

He swirled his tongue and her body trembled against his lips. He gave her a final, deep lick all the way up until he reached her clit then kissed it. He sat back on his legs and ran his fingers lightly over his shaft, while he waited for her to acknowledge his presence again.

❧

The haze cleared from Taryn’s vision and she watched Blake

as he touched himself in a way to make her spent body awaken. "I'm not the only one who is incredible with their mouth."

He winked as he stood, and then approached his pants on the floor. He took out a condom from his wallet, applied the latex over his rock hard cock, and then looked back to her. His gaze looked nothing less than a man who planned to fuck her savagely and, she eagerly awaited him.

He returned to her, gripped her hip, and placed his cock against her slick entrance. "Are you ready for me, my pet?" She nodded and he pushed in. She groaned—a sound he mirrored. "You're fucking tight."

"I should be." She gasped. "I haven't had sex with anyone since you."

"Nor have I."

The acknowledgment he'd not been with another made her blissfully happy, but she was too lost in the pressure along her pussy. She watched as he rubbed his cock along her heat and tweaked her clit. She shifted her pelvis forward and circled her hips in time with his touch. Her moves inched him into her tight pussy, but slowly. He allowed her to take him in and his only help had been when he stepped forward so she could wiggle her way onto him.

By the time he was fully seated inside her, her pussy released to accept him, and his thick cock stretched her in a beautiful way. He grabbed her hips with both hands, placed his forehead against hers, and closed his eyes.

"I've craved to be right here for so long." He dipped lower and fucked her in the exact way she liked it—hard and ruthless. Each thrust made her moan, squirm, and made her pussy so wet.

He withdrew his cock, dragged his arousal over her anus, and then rejoined her. He grabbed onto her bottom, gave it a tight squeeze before he dipped his hand between her cheeks and inserted a finger into her tight bud.

She gasped at the initial intrusion, but pleasure immediately followed, flooding her with sensations. He continued to thrust in her pussy with primal strokes that had her struggling against the bonds.

He lowered his head to bite the sweet spot along her neck and she cried out. The burn along her skin, paired with the pressure in her pussy awakened her climax. But just as her body hinted at a release, he withdrew his cock.

"Don't stop."

He grinned haughtily. "You don't think I'd let you come that easily, do you?"

She should have known better. His finger in her bottom moved and it awakened a new sense of pleasure for her. Her clit and her pussy ached for him to return but as he denied it, only to offer it somewhere else, it stole her breath.

"I know your pussy hasn't been fucked, but has your ass?" He continued to stroke the tight knot. "Has anyone used your ass like I used to?"

"No," she barely managed.

"This shall be a real treat for me then." He removed his finger and strode back over to his bag. He took out a bottle of lube, and her body scorched in need of him. He applied a new condom before he spread the clear liquid to his cock and coated it. He dipped some onto his fingers and threw the bottle to the ground.

He returned to her and ran his fingers over her ass, and inserted his finger to ready her. She moaned, but he drank in her sounds as he took her mouth so rough she could barely keep up. He loosened the binds on her ankles, then grabbed her hips to angle them forward, which tightened the ropes around her wrists but she welcomed the burn.

Whenever he got rough in his kisses, it meant his end was near and that meant he'd fuck her senseless. He smacked his cock against her clit, and already being aroused, she gasped against the intense sensation. He ran the tip of his dick down her pussy and pulled her hips out further to gain access to her. The rope dug into her wrists, but as he reached her anus, she forgot the pain and he gave a steady push.

She hissed at the pressure, but did her best to relax. Gripping her hips, he angled her more toward him and pushed in deeper.

He leaned in to kiss her again as his cock passed through the tight rim. Running his hand along her stomach to her clit, where he circled the little nub, he started to thrust in and out of her with ease.

Her eyes widened as a rush of erotic fulfillment titillated her senses. Her wrists burned from the hold, the pressure built along her ass, and her pussy ached for his cock but all the opposing sensations spiked her climax.

"Fuck, woman, I love every damn thing about you." He all but growled. His skin smacked against her as her pleasure skyrocketed.

"I love you, too," she shouted. "Make me come with you."

"Yes, sweetheart, come for me." He backed his chest away, dipped even lower, and pushed his fingers into her pussy.

She lost her breath—immediately consumed with a rich source of energy. Everything else disappeared as he finger-fucked her while his cock pounded her ass. Her head fell back, eyes shut tight, and she screamed against the pressure building inside of her. Her body had been overwhelmed with some pain and some pleasure—all of it extraordinarily fantastic.

Every muscle tightened as though a bomb went off in her center. A rush of pure and unadulterated pleasure awakened every nerve. He thrust in an unforgiving way until he buried himself deep and roared out his satisfaction.

She returned to the present when he withdrew. Her body felt used—sore in all the right places, and in other places that might have been wrong to some. He made quick work to rid her of the ropes and her muscles held no strength, but before she could slump to the floor, he had her in his arms.

She glanced at him and his warm, powerful gaze stared back at her. She hadn't expected any of this to happen but Madame Eve had been right—they were a perfect match. She might have told herself she'd gotten over him and that her career stood above all else, but it had all been a lie.

Blake adored her in a way no one else dared to and treated her exactly how she wanted to be treated. He knew all her deepest, darkest desires, and he didn't run from her fantasies, but fulfilled them. "I'll never leave you again."

He smiled and kissed her lips in a gentle way that showed how complex a man he really was. "And I'll never let you go."

~About the Author~

Stacey Kennedy's urban fantasy/paranormal and erotic romance series have hit Amazon Kindle and All Romance Ebooks Bestseller lists. If she isn't plugging away at her next novel, tending to her two little ones, she's got her nose deep in a good book. She lives in Ontario, Canada with her husband. Be sure to drop her a line at www.staceykennedy.com, she loves to hear from her readers.

I'll Be Mated for Christmas

by

Rebecca Royce

Chapter One

Bethany Johnson rubbed her nose. The movement constituted a nervous habit left over from childhood. When she wasn't standing in her stepfather's living room staring at a past she wished to forget, she didn't do it anymore. Her psychiatrist would have a field day with all the small, troubling behaviors that showed up in the ten minutes she'd been home. Truthfully, she knew in about thirty seconds, if given the chance, she'd desperately seek out an eating binge.

It must have been the Christmas tree. Every year, her stepfather got the same size Christmas tree and the whole family decorated it with ornaments people in his family had collected for hundreds of years. *Well, maybe not hundreds of years—maybe it only seemed that way.*

The fire in the fireplace crackled and sputtered, desperate for someone to throw another log on it before it died completely. She rubbed her nose again. Should she bother to let the flames grow?

"You look so fantastic." Bethany whirled around at the sound of her brother Jack's voice. He leaned against the doorframe of the front door. "I know you said one hundred pounds, but I had no idea how you would look. You don't even resemble the same person, Bethy."

She knew that. Weight-loss surgery and hard work had finally, for the first time since her fifth birthday, let her live in a non-morbidly obese body.

"Well, one hundred pounds off will do that." She shrugged, hoping to make it seem like less of a big deal. "Where's Cara?"

Her sister had promised to be there, too. Bethany made very specific plans before coming into town. Her psychiatrist helped her map out the whole scenario and she didn't want to screw it up. Even if her therapist didn't know all the details of the complications that defined her family....

"She's on her way. Maybe two minutes behind me. And Dad says to give you his regards."

She nodded and smiled. Devron Davis had tried to raise her the best he could. To Cara and Jack, he'd been an ideal father. But he hadn't had the first clue how to raise a purely human child. Things between them were rough before her mother died. Werewolves had a hard time accepting that their mates could have a child not their own—even if it had happened two years before they'd ever met. But he hadn't dropped her off at an orphanage when his mate died, and for that she supposed she should feel grateful.

Maybe she'd understand it better if she were a wolf. She shook her head. She needed to concentrate on the purpose of this visit: to say goodbye. She'd lost one hundred pounds, dealt with the death of her mother—finally—and taken a new job she'd start at the first of the year. The time had come to let the things that didn't work for her go. Unfortunately, that included her half-brother and half-sister. Trying to fit into their world—even for quick holiday visits—forced her to live in a toxic environment that didn't make anybody happy.

"Tell your father I said hello back."

She'd let Devron know weeks ago she never intended to return. He'd done her the favor of allowing her to come and tell Jack and Cara herself. She did love them, even if she could never see them again. They didn't understand her and never would.

"Wow, Bethy, look at you."

Cara entered in a whirlwind of energy. Jack laughed and crossed to throw another log on the fire. The blaze burned brighter, grateful someone had paid attention to it. She reached out to embrace Cara.

"Oh, stop." She gave her a sister a pat on the back before she let go. "It's not that big of a deal."

Except that it mattered more than anything else ever had before and the fact that she couldn't talk to them about it, that they would never understand what it meant to be overweight because werewolves physically were unable to be, illustrated her reasons for saying goodbye better than anything else.

Jack sat down on the couch. "And you were able to lose all that weight from some band they stuck around your stomach?"

"Uh-huh." *And diet. And exercise. And tears. And psychotherapy.*

"Weird." Jack picked up a candy cane from a bowl on the table. "You know us wolves—we have to eat like thousands of calories a day or we don't make it."

She knew. Because once upon a time she'd eaten just like them. "So the reason for my visit...."

Jack cut her off. "Did Dad tell you any of the craziness going on here? We finished a war this year, Bethy. You should have been here to see it. Three different families, everyone having an Alpha competing to take over after Paul faced defeat. The whole thing defined insanity." His eyes glowed to show how exciting he found the *whole thing*.

Her stepfather's family didn't want to be Alphas. No, they'd always been the right hand of the Alpha. It looked like they'd once again backed the right horse, or in this case, wolf.

"He mentioned something about it." Right after he'd stopped listening to her talk about surgery. Bethany steeled herself. She'd lived thirty years, not thirteen. She didn't need the attention of any of them. She had friends and a career.

Cara sat down next to Jack. "Luke won. He's dreamy, Bethy. In fact, he should be here soon. He said something about picking up some of the financial paperwork Dad keeps in the study. He wants to go over it this weekend."

She straightened up at the news. That meant she needed to get out a lot faster. The last thing she wanted was to be sneered at by another Alpha while her brother and sister made excuses for the fact that their mother had been married before she'd mated with their father. And went on about how weird it was that humans did that.

"Okay, so the reason I'm here is to say goodbye."

Cara moved in her seat and Jack scratched his head. Finally, he spoke. "You arrived minutes ago."

He seemed generally forlorn by her announcement, which made her feel badly, but it didn't alter her path. "Yes, and I'm not coming back." She cleared her throat as she rubbed her nose. "Maybe ever."

Cara jumped to her feet. "What?"

"I'm leaving Alaska altogether. I've given up my apartment in Anchorage. I've quit my teaching job. As of the first of the year, I am going to be teaching English in Italy. Doesn't that sound amazing?" It probably didn't to them. Wolves liked territory. They never left it, if they could avoid it.

"When will you be back?"

"I won't." She held out her hands to stop their questions. "I don't belong here. This is your life. It was Mom's. She loved being mated to your dad even if she happened to be one of only three non-wolves here. But I'm a human. I don't belong here. I love you, but it's time for me to be me. I can't continue to be the human sister of two of the strongest wolves in the Delta pack. Do you understand?"

"You're leaving?" Jack got up and paced to the window. "You're our sister. It's bad enough you live an hour away. How are we supposed to protect you in Italy?"

Jack had always been the sweetest boy. She wiped away a tear that spilled down her cheek. She need not have bothered; they could smell her emotions even if most of the time they ignored human feelings that seemed too out of control. Her brother and sister might be half-human, but they were all wolf when it came to sensing emotions.

"You're not. I'm going to protect myself. It's what humans do. We don't have packs."

"You're going to leave?" Cara hadn't moved. She stared at her like she had two heads.

"Pretty much. First, I'm giving myself a bit of a Christmas gift. But then I'm leaving, yes."

"What gift?" Cara took her hand and squeezed it. "I can't believe you won't be here for the holidays anymore."

"Let's face it, holidays don't go so well when I'm here." Bethany let go of her hand and walked a few paces away. "I've signed up for a dating service called 1Night Stand. It's promised me a night I'll never forget."

Jack growled. "You're going to have sex with a stranger and you're doing that on purpose? Why? What could you possibly be thinking?"

"It's run by a woman named Madame Eve. I think it'll be good for me. You can read all about it on the Internet if you want. I filled out a form. Anyway, it's a long story. But, I need this. Humans don't mate like you guys. You know this."

Cara shook her head. "Mom did."

"I'm not the mate to anyone in this pack. I refuse to go wandering around the world searching for wolf packs to see if I happen to have a mate. I'm a human. I'm going to live like one. And humans are lucky if they marry for life. All of this is beside the point. I need to feel better about myself. I need to look in someone's eyes and know that they don't see the weight loss or the plastic surgery that made my skin look less stretched out."

Jack stepped forward. "That happened?"

She rolled her eyes. "Yes. Now come and give me hugs. I'm leaving."

Her brother and sister moved slowly to her side. They usually bubbled with energy, but this constituted the most subdued she'd ever seen them. She squeezed them both tightly. Cara finally spoke. "Maybe in a few years we can see each other again."

"Maybe."

Luke ran toward the Davis house. He needed those papers and he didn't feel like listening to Devron prattle on. If luck took his side today, he still had a couple of hours before the man returned home from the errand he'd sent him on. Devron could do accounting better than anyone, but he drove Luke crazy with his total lack of social graces.

His ears perked up. He was still blocks from the house, but he could hear Cara, one of his newly acquired pack members, sobbing. She made wild, keening noises. Luke knew grief when he heard it. Sniffing the air as he moved, he didn't sense any danger.

He pushed open the door without knocking. This house sat on pack land. *My pack's land.* And he didn't have to knock. Ever.

"What's going on?" Cara and Jack jumped apart and hit the ground into their required kneel. "Get up."

They both stood, their eyes diverted. Cara sniffed, wiping away her tears and Jack looked like he was struggling with strong emotions.

"What's going on?" He hated repeating himself, but it didn't seem either would answer unless he did. A scent drifted in the air, catching his attention. He'd never smelled anything akin to it before. What made that scent? Floral and clean....

"Our sister left moments ago. She's not coming back. Ever." Cara choked on the last word.

"You have a sister?" She hadn't appeared on any pack reports. He'd not met her. She didn't come to his ceremonies. He didn't appreciate surprises that left him unprepared.

"She's human." Jack sighed. "Our mother was human, as you know. She had a husband who died. Bethy came from that marriage. Humans do that, they can mate more than once."

Luke waved his hand in the air to shut Jack up. "I grew up with humans, hidden amongst them to keep Paul from killing me at birth. I don't need to have human behaviors explained to me. I get them perfectly, and in some ways I prefer them. We could use some of their compassion in this pack."

He walked around the room quickly, taking in the furniture and decorations. He'd not spent a lot of time there due to his personal dislike of Devron. But Jack and Cara seemed like good pack mates. They were strong wolves and loyal to a fault. He would have to amend his decision to avoid their father.

"Why did she leave?"

"It's complicated. Sometimes it's hard to understand Bethy." Jack took a step toward him. "We love her so much, but sometimes it seems that everything we do only makes her hate herself."

"She's going to *Italy*." Cara sobbed on the last word as she dissolved into a mess of hysterical tears. Jack took her over to the couch. This, Luke could understand. Nothing mattered more than family. Where had Devron gone? Why had he not convinced his stepdaughter that she needed to remain with her siblings? If she was family, she was pack.

End of story.

He moved over to the bookshelf and his senses went on high alert. His claws descended from his fingertips and a growl formed in his throat. He didn't feel angry, no. But the scent where he stood wafted so much stronger. She must have stood there and not too long ago. And yet, too much time had passed.

Luke had never met the person whose scent he memorized, but he *knew* it. The aroma belonged to *her*. His destiny. His one and only. His mate.

Realization dawned on him as Jack and Cara jumped to their feet. Jack fell to his knees on the floor.

"What is it, my Alpha?"

"Your sister. She just left?"

Cara followed suit and dove to her knees. "Yes, my Alpha."

"And where is she now?" Cara's words suddenly rang in his ears. *Italy*. "Did she leave for the airport?"

If would be faster if he ran as a wolf, he could cut her off at the pass....

"No, she's going on the first of January." Cara looked up. "Why?"

"She's my mate." Saying it aloud brought pleasure to his soul. He'd not seen her, but it didn't matter if she had three arms. She was his. Forever. To love and cherish. Emotions he'd long suppressed threatened to spill over. He needed this woman. *Now.*

"Are you sure?" Jack sounded concerned, but obviously not afraid any longer as he staggered to his feet.

"Are you questioning my nose, wolf?"

"No, my Alpha." Jack's face broke out in a grin. "But this is great news. Because now she can't leave."

Luke took a look at the bookshelves. No, she wouldn't be leaving. Not ever. He stared at the picture frames that decorated the room. Where did her picture sit? "Where is she? What is her name? Bethy?"

"Bethany. We don't have too many pictures of her. Dad and Bethy have issues and she never liked seeing herself in pictures. But I think we have one from Christmas two years ago. She didn't come last year."

Cara scampered around him and pulled out an album. She handed the photo to Luke. It showed the whole family. Cara and Jack sat on each side of their father and to Cara's right sat his beautiful mate. She had brown hair and blue eyes—the saddest blue eyes he'd ever seen. His heart lurched. This would not be allowed to continue. One way or another she would find happiness. There would be no other way.

"That was when she was fat."

The violence of his anger startled him and it wasn't until he had Jack by the throat did he realize he might kill the young pup. Taking a deep breath, he dropped him to the floor.

"You don't ever talk about my mate like that. Am I clear?" His voice sounded half-human, half-animal. It had been twenty years since Luke lost that much control. At forty years old, he should be better at handling his temper. Usually, he did.

"I love her. I don't care if she's fat," Jack said.

Luke hadn't seen "fat" when he looked at Bethy. By contrast, all he noticed was how gloriously beautiful she looked, how she belonged to him.

Cara spoke in a squeaky voice. "She's lost one hundred pounds. The human doctors put something in her—a band around her stomach—and it made her not so hungry all the time. Then she had some kind of plastic surgery."

Luke's heart clenched. *She put herself in danger by going under the knife more than once?* "That must have been horribly painful."

"I guess." Cara averted her eyes.

"Did you not take care of her afterward?"

Jack rose from his knees. "She didn't even tell us she did it until after. Maybe Dad knew but he didn't tell us."

Things for Bethy were going to change. A horrid thought struck him. "Is she married?" The rational side of him tried to stay calm while his wolf called for the death of any potential competition.

"No." Cara smiled. "No boyfriend either. But she just signed up for some kind of dating service. She's going to have a one-night stand before she leaves for Italy."

"Like hell she is." Luke growled. "Where is her apartment? I will go and get her now."

"Luke." Cara touched his arm gently. "I don't know if that's how you should approach Bethy."

"What do you mean?" He wanted out of the man's house where his mate had not been happy. His whole focus turned from looking over financial papers to finding and holding his mate until he never saw that sad gaze again. *Ever*.

"I don't understand humans as well as you do. I've only ever known the few that lived here, and Bethy spent so much time trying to fit in until she left, and then she didn't try...."

Jack nudged her. "You're rambling."

"Right, well, if you go to Bethy and you tell her you're her mate right away, she might run. She really, really seemed to want to be out of here. I'm afraid she might not even give you the chance."

It had never occurred to him that his mate could reject him. But Cara spoke correctly. Her sister was human. Once they mated, she would be as bound to him as a wolf would be, but until then she could deny her feelings as wolf instincts did not factor into her decisions.

Cara's eyes gleamed. He tried to take a deep breath. "I assume your intense gaze means you have an idea."

"I do."

"Well?"

"You should contact that Madame Eve who runs that 1Night Stand thing. You can be Bethy's one-night stand. Let her get to know you. Then she'll want to come home with you and be with all of us forever."

It seemed like a good idea. Luke tapped his foot. It wasn't as speedy as hunting Bethy down and keeping her locked up in his house until he made her his own. But it would be a more human approach and his mate might appreciate a gentler touch.

He held the picture in his hand. Once again, all he could see were Bethy's sad blue eyes. Could she wait a little while longer? Could she survive with sadness like that?

"Pull up the website, Cara. One way or another, this is starting now."

Chapter Two

Bethany didn't want to imagine what she looked like right at that second. She didn't like flying and she particularly didn't like doing it in a bush plane, even a private one with a very nice pilot. She smoothed down her hair and tried to smile at the receptionist who signed her in. To her left, she saw a man sporting a beard talking on the phone in a private office. She wondered if that was Nick Castillo, who ran the Castillo Lodge in Castle, Alaska.

Madame Eve had been downright mysterious when she'd e-mailed, telling her to get some warm clothes together and something nice to wear to a gala because she had to leave immediately for the Castillo Lodge. She didn't have any other plans, having quit her job, so it wasn't a problem. But still. It had been a little odd. Did Madame Eve handle all of her client's dates that abruptly?

"You're all set, Ms. Johnson." The receptionist smiled at her and held out a key. "Down the hall is the elevator. Take it to the second floor. Mr. Denarius is already here."

"He is?" She tried to swallow away the nervous lump in her throat.

"Yes, ma'am. He arrived quite early this morning."

"I see." She hoped the receptionist didn't notice her sweaty hands as she took the key. She had been counting on being there first. It would have given her some time to relax, take a bath, and make herself look somewhat presentable before she had to face her date.

As if in a daze, she walked toward the elevator. What had her so spooked? This was exactly what she wanted. One night with a stranger who could fulfill all of her yearnings. She'd get it out of her system and then she'd go on to Italy the confident, capable woman she knew she could be.

Lucian Denarius constituted a means to an end. Maybe he'd be a nice guy who she could see again someday if the situation presented itself. She shivered at the name. Madame Eve hadn't sent his picture in the e-mail, but the name alone inspired all sorts of ridiculous fantasies for her. He sounded mysterious.

She entered the elevator and took it to the second floor. The elevator traveled swiftly. In the morning, after she'd had her night of wild sex, she'd explore the lodge. It looked beautiful, like something out of a fantasy. She'd never been on vacation. Wolves didn't take trips away from home and when she'd ventured out on her own, there hadn't been the money to do those kinds of things.

With determination in her stride, she walked up to the door. Should she knock? Would he be found inside or had he gone skiing?

She leaned her head up against the door and forced the panic attack threatening her to go away. Just because she'd never had sex before didn't mean she had to go her whole life without it. This was her Christmas present to herself. Madame Eve knew about her virginity. She'd put it on the form. He must be fine with having an inexperienced partner or he wouldn't be in there.

Lucian Denarius would be fine. Better than fine. He'd be what she needed.

She put the key in the lock, turned it, and entered the room swiftly. Hopefully she looked better than she imagined she did.

Immediately, she saw him. He leaned up against the window. His gaze met hers instantly and she caught her breath. *Heavens, the man defines the word gorgeous.*

He was at least a foot taller than she, which would make him about six-foot, five-inches. She'd grown up with wolves. They were all tall and intimidating, but outside of a pack she didn't see men this big and strapping—even in Alaska. He had dark brown hair, almost black, and at least a day's worth of unshaved stubble on his face. She loved that look on a guy. His cheekbones were high and well defined.

Without a word, he moved quickly toward her, giving her a good view of his broad shoulders and strong gait. He stood before her, hand extended, and took her bag from her hand. She stared for a second at his fingers on top of hers. He had working hands. They were scarred on his knuckles. The hands of a strong, capable man.

He seemed to be every fantasy she had ever created in her mind of the perfect man. She almost turned and ran.

Finally, he spoke. "I'll put your bag down on the luggage holder, Bethy."

His voice showed no discernable accent. He stared her right in the eyes when he talked and the heat there as he did made her core wet. That was the expression—that was what she'd always hoped to see when a man looked at her.

His words finally penetrated her haze and she nodded, watching him take the bag.

"Hi." She hoped she didn't sound dumb. "Thank you."

"You're welcome." He lifted it like it weighed nothing and placed it down on the luggage rack. "How did your flight go, Bethy?"

She blinked. She needed to start as she intended to continue. "Some people do call me Bethy, but I really prefer Bethany, if that's okay." There, she'd said it. She hoped it didn't make her seem like a bitch.

"Bethany suits you." He smiled at her, a strange emotion she couldn't identify in his gaze.

She stepped further into the room. He smelled like the woods, like fresh-cut trees, and the breezy wind she'd grown accustomed to her in youth. The thought stopped her short. No way should she be thinking about that now.

"And you're Lucian, right?" She hoped she didn't sound as

nervous as she suspected she did.

"That's right, but no one calls me that." He put his hands in his pockets. "I think maybe I'd like you to, though. I like the way it sounds coming from your lips."

Her cheeks heated up until she knew they must be red. "Lucian is kind of an old-fashioned name, isn't it?"

"My parents are old-fashioned and I'm older than you by ten years. I just turned forty."

She grinned. "Oh wow, you're ancient." Not everyone liked her sarcasm and usually she tried not to be, but the response popped out of her mouth.

He laughed, a joyous sound and she wished she could keep him laughing all the time. "Sometimes I feel like I am." He extended his hand to show her the sitting area. "Do you want to sit down?"

"Um." She resisted the urge to rub her nose. "Sure, that would be great."

She moved further into the beautifully decorated room. Clearly, the designer had been going for a rustic look to match the rest of the lodge. Warm colors complemented the breathtaking view of Alaska that the windows provided. The chair she sat down in had been designed for comfort as well as utility.

"Did you have to travel far to get here?" She loved the sound of his voice and hoped to get him speaking again.

"Not far. I live in Alaska. I was born in this area but then we moved away before I was a year old. I guess Montana would be where I think of as my childhood home even though we moved a lot."

"Were your parents in the military?"

"No." He shook his head. "My uncle wasn't a nice man. My parents were determined I would grow up without his influence in my life." She wanted to question him more about that, but he continued to speak. "Can I get you something to eat?"

"No. It's not time for me to eat yet. I mean, I did actually eat earlier. Oh, drat." She hadn't wanted to discuss the topic but now, for some reason she couldn't grasp, she was compelled to keep talking. "I actually had weight-loss surgery. I eat when I'm hungry, but small amounts. I just ate so...."

"You're the most beautiful woman I've ever seen. Don't look down, ever, when you talk to someone. Nothing about what you just told me warrants any kind of shame or uncomfortable feelings."

His comment stunned her silent. "I hadn't realized I'd done that." He was right. She always avoided eye contact when she talked about her weight problem. "Thank you for saying I'm attractive, but if you had seen me before you would have understood why I had the surgery."

He stood up and crossed to her. Then, he sat down on the arm of her chair. That close to him left no question as to his sexual appeal. Power radiated from his every pore, sending her libido into overdrive. "I didn't say you were attractive. You're much more than that. You're beautiful." He tilted her chin up until she looked him straight in the eyes. Their dark depths called to her soul. She hadn't expected to be that moved by her one-night date. "And I would have thought you were beautiful if I'd met you then, too."

He brought his mouth down on top of hers before she could argue. The clock said three o'clock in the afternoon, but his one kiss made her lose all track of time. She pressed herself into his embrace. He broke it only long enough to lift her out of the chair and reposition her on top of him in the chair she'd been sitting in. She straddled him, dying for another kiss.

His tongue sought out hers and she heard herself moan. Her nipples got hard and she ached to take her bra off. Pulling back, she regarded him for a second. "I don't usually behave like this."

He pushed her hair out of her eyes. "I don't mind. Isn't this what you wanted?"

"Yes. No. I don't know." She bit her lip. "I thought this would be the first step in getting to know myself better. I'm carving out a new life for myself."

"How can you not know yourself? I knew you the second I first saw you."

He looked so sincere she actually believed him. "I've changed a lot and not just with the weight loss. I've had to figure out why I ate the way I did. I think I've been pretty lonely."

"I know that feeling. I've been so lonely, too."

She ran her hands down the stubble on his cheeks. "How could you be lonely?"

"It's possible to be all alone in a crowd. I've had so much pressure over the last few years, it has completely isolated me from everyone."

She kissed his cheek. He looked gorgeous, but like she had always been hidden by her outside appearance, he had clearly had the same experience. Gorgeous and built didn't necessarily lend itself to internal happiness.

"I can't lie to you." He took her off his lap and placed her on the floor.

"You don't find me attractive, do you? You were being nice...."

"Hush." He pulled her up against him. "Does that feel like I don't find you attractive?"

She could feel the hard push of his cock on her leg. He really was turned on. What could he possibly have lied about?

"I know who you are because I am actually the Alpha of your family's pack."

The ground dropped out from underneath her. Or at least it seemed like it did. This whole thing—her family had done this to her. Why? Why would they have interfered?

"I don't understand. Why are you here? Why this elaborate guise? Why did my family make you get involved in this? Did they not think I could even handle a one-night stand without their interference?"

She wanted to throw something. The whole experience had signaled the beginning of a new life for her, and now it had been tainted.

"I insisted. I couldn't let you have a one-night stand. You're my mate. I'd have to kill whomever you slept with."

"What?" She shook her head. "This is the first time we're meeting. Even I know how mating works. The ones involved have to at least see each other. You couldn't have arranged this knowing I was your mate."

What was wrong with her that she kind of liked the idea even as it infuriated her? The old version of herself had wanted to be part of the pack, to be accepted, to mate. Not the new Bethany.

"I smelled your scent in your family's home the last time you were there. I knew instantly and then when I saw your picture it confirmed it for me."

"When you saw my...." She sank into the chair. "I can't imagine it made me look very good." She closed her eyes.

"What's the matter? I told you I think you're beautiful. I thought it then, too. I would think that whether you weighed nothing or a million pounds."

She opened her eyes, suddenly more tired than she'd ever been. "I wanted to lose my virginity to someone who had never seen me fat."

"This is your issue. Not mine. I will always find you incredibly attractive. I will tell you as many times as you need to hear it."

"It doesn't matter." She stood up, looking for her bag. *I have to get out of here. Now.* That's right, he'd put it on the luggage rack. "I can't be your mate. I'm going to Italy. And even if I were not, I can't go back to all those full moons alone."

He scratched the stubble on his cheeks. "Full moons alone?"

"The whole pack goes off, they do their wolf stuff and I wander the house by myself, always alone for not only one day, but three every month during the cycle. It's hard enough being alone without knowing you will never be able to do what everyone else does."

"I never thought about what that must be like. To simply be abandoned by your entire family for three days." He stroked her cheek and she wanted to close her eyes and return to the feelings she had for him when she'd first arrived.

"Go find another mate. I can't be her."

"Sorry, not how it works." He smiled. "Which you know."

"I would be the worst Alpha mate in the whole world and if you think I am going to sit at home and not have the adventures I planned for myself because you happened to come along and decide I was yours, you've got another think coming."

He raised an eyebrow. "Then I suppose it is beholden to me to convince you to change your mind." He pulled her up against him. "You're mine. Your body knew it instantly. You've waited your entire life for me, as I have for you."

This time when his mouth took hers it wasn't gentle or calming. No, he laid claim to her. She didn't even attempt to deny him. Not when her body buzzed as though alive for the very first time.

"Oh," she whispered between kisses. "This was how I imagined it could be, but I didn't think it could be real."

"It's real between us. We were made for each other."

He picked her up like she weighed nothing at all. She knew how strong werewolves were and Alphas were supposed to be even more so. She shuddered at the power the man possessed.

"Why did you suddenly get scared?"

He set her down gently on the bed, coming over her. A small gold pendant hung down from a small chain he wore under his shirt. She hadn't noticed it before. Most weres that she knew didn't own jewelry. The fact that he did looked strangely beautiful.

"Are you going to make me a werewolf, too?" She'd always wanted to be, but now that the possibility could be real, it made her stomach flip-flop.

"No. That is illegal. Not all humans can survive the transition. You will be human—my human—until we are both old, grey, and decide to depart this world together."

His words relaxed her even as she recognized them for the "line" that they were. No one got to decide when they died.

"I haven't agreed to be your mate."

He raised an eyebrow. "Haven't you? You know what it will mean if we consummate this relationship. You will be mine. You will belong to me."

"I'm human, not wolf. I could still choose to leave." She didn't even know if she believed what she said or if she would follow through on her threat. She wanted him. Her body begged for his attention.

"You won't." He exuded confidence.

Can I do this? Could she change all of her plans and go back to that world for one night with him?

His hands reached down as he began to slowly unbutton her shirt. She knew she could stop him. So why didn't she?

"I'm a powerful man. I trained from the moment I came into this world to lead the Delta Pack. I fought for the right. I'm dangerous." He bent over to nuzzle her neck, sending shivers of pleasure down her spine. "The only person in the universe who has no reason to fear me is you. From now until I die, I will be yours to command. You own me, Bethany."

His swift fingers undid the last button, leaving her bare to his inspection. His finger trailed up her stomach to her bra clasp, which he quickly undid. No matter how hard she worked at it, she'd never be as physically perfect as she would like and yet he looked at her with so much desire, it made her heart stutter. In the room with her, making love to her was a man who could have any woman on the planet, but wanted her instead.

"I'm scared of doing the wrong thing," she whispered. "I'm terrified of regrets."

"Then I guess you have to ask yourself what you would regret more: not going to Italy to teach English, or not loving me?"

When he put it like that, it seemed silly she even questioned not becoming his mate. What existed in the universe more important than love? So what that her mate came in a package she'd never thought to have?

She wrapped her arms around his neck, pulling him down on top of her for another kiss.

"Your mouth is so fantastic. But I want to see and touch all of you and if you keep distracting me with your sweet lips, I'll never get to love the rest of you."

She wanted to touch the rest of him, too. She had years to make up for and she got to do it all with a man who possessed the body of a god.

He bent over to suck on one of her nipples. Pleasure

threatened to overwhelm her and her back arched off the bed.

"So responsive. What a joy you are to make love to."

She hoped he meant what he said because she'd never done this before, so she had nothing to go by other than what he told her. His hand massaged her other breast. She tugged on his shirt, desperate to get it off him. He smiled as he pulled it over his head.

She fingered his gold chain with a questioning glance. He shook his head. "I'll explain later. Right now, beautiful, I have to get your pants off."

Chapter Three

Luke thought if he didn't get inside of his beautiful little mate soon, he might literally explode from the heat inside his body. His wolf ached to howl his frustration, and Luke struggled to keep his beast under control. She might have been raised with siblings and a stepfather who bathed in the moonlight, but he doubted she was ready to deal with his beast in bed.

Not while she still remained a virgin—something he hadn't expected and it humbled him to have been given the gift. She belonged to him and would know the touch of no other man.

He pulled at her pants until they came down her shapely legs. "Do you run?"

She giggled. "Badly. No one would ever call me an athlete."

"You have the legs of a runner." He pulled her leg up until he could kiss the top of her toes.

He wanted to taste all of her. He lived with the soul of a wolf and his wolf liked to taste things. She had become his new favorite toy.

"I couldn't run anywhere nearly as fast as my siblings, even when they're in human form."

"Even in their human form, they are genetically predisposed to be faster than you are." He kissed down her legs and she shuddered. God, she was so hot. "Some night I am going to spend hours making love to your legs."

There could be no doubt about it—he was a lucky man.

He pulled his own pants off. When the time came, he didn't want anything between them. A thought dawned on him and he was glad he'd prepared for the one-night stand requirement of wearing a condom.

"Sweetheart, I brought a condom. You're my mate. We'll be a very good fit for baby making. If we're not careful, you could get pregnant every year. Do you want a baby or shall I cover it up as Madame Eve said I was required to do?"

Her eyes got huge as he spoke. She visibly swallowed, her neck muscles straining. "I recently lost all this weight. I don't know if it's the healthiest time for me to have a baby right now. I'm not a wolf, I'm more fragile."

"I know that." He said a silent prayer that he'd always be able to keep her safe. "I'll cover up until you tell me not to."

He was a little bit relieved. It might be nice to have some time alone with his mate without children.

She raised an eyebrow. "I'm new to this, but don't you have to take off your briefs before that becomes necessary?"

"You're sassy, aren't you?" He loved it. "Yes, I will remove both your panties and mine."

She grinned, showing off her bright smile. He loved the happiness in her eyes. If he had to keep her in bed all day and night to keep her smiling, he would gladly do so. Why should they ever leave the bedroom? Except to, say, occasionally do it in the kitchen. Or the living room....

She pulled down his briefs with a shriek. "I beat you to it. I took off yours."

"You did." He laughed. She kept surprising him. When he'd come here, he'd expected to have to coax her slowly to this point and now she directed him. "I guess I'll return the favor."

He yanked her panties off. A growl of possession formed in his throat. Her pussy lay before him crying for his attention.

"I'm going to feast on you now."

She sucked in her breath. "What do you mean?"

He bent over until he could reach her warm core. "Your pussy calls to me. I need you so much. I need to see you come, pretty lady."

His fingers stroked her, starting at her inner thigh and moving slowly to the place where he wanted to be most in the world. She trembled beneath his touch. No one had ever stroked her like that and he needed to remember it, despite all her bravado. He smelled her nervousness.

He caressed her beautiful curls before slipping a finger inside of her. God, she was tight. His cock jumped with anticipation. He would not hurt her; he would not allow it. He had to make her ready to take him.

Taking a moment to explore his mate, he finally found the small bundle of nerves inside of her and began to play with it. She responded to every pat, every movement he made. Then she began to pant when he found the right rhythm.

Damn. His mate appeared so beautiful and he got to look at her extraordinary face for the rest of his life.

"Lucian." Her voice had gotten husky. "I feel like I might explode."

"Let yourself, baby. That's a good thing." And oh yes, he wanted to explode inside of her.

Her neck arched back on the bed. Her eyes closed and she cried out with her first orgasm. Watching her discover her pleasure looked so beautiful; he knew the image would be imprinted on his brain for all time. It would be his joy to play with her clit anytime she wanted or to find other ways to pleasure her like that with his fingers.

But damn, he couldn't wait any more. He needed to be inside of her. Right that second. While she still panted, he slipped on the condom as fast as he could. It fit him tightly, which was good, because it would keep him from coming too fast. Using his fingers to loosen her slightly, he gently eased himself into her inch-by-inch.

She gasped, gripping his arms in her embrace. "Wow."

"Easy. I promise, we fit."

"You're inside of me. I'm so happy to have you there."

He leaned down to kiss her nose. "There's nowhere else I would rather be."

As gently as he could, he began to move. Her muscles clenched around him and he nearly came. He was forty years old; he had to keep it together and keep this from ending in two minutes flat.

"You feel so damn good." He wasn't even sure he sounded coherent.

"I didn't know it could be like this. Ever. I couldn't imagine."

Neither could he. But then there was no holding back. In and out he moved; she met him thrust for thrust. She gasped, moaned, and writhed beneath him, making him feel like the luckiest guy in the world. He got to do that for the rest of his life.

She cried out his name, her fingers digging into his skin. Her pleasure triggered his and he couldn't hold back any longer. His body exploded. Yes, that was the moment he'd been waiting for, to lose himself inside of her. His teeth elongated as he gave into the urge and bit down on her neck right up against her shoulder blade, marking her as his for the rest of his life.

His mark would never go away completely. It would fade, but all wolves would know she belonged to him. Luke closed his eyes, losing himself to the pleasure surrounding him in her arms.

He woke up to a strange sensation. It took him a moment to realize what was going on. She rubbed her thumb over his knuckles. He inhaled deeply to take more of her floral—he'd decided lilies—scent into his soul.

"How long have you been awake?"

She smiled, picking up his hand to kiss his knuckles. "A couple of hours actually. You were out cold. I didn't want to wake you. I guess I couldn't keep my hands to myself. Sorry."

She didn't look sorry and he was glad she didn't seem that way. She should always feel comfortable waking him up whenever she wanted to.

He stretched. "I guess I must have been exhausted. It was a bit of a long year."

"I didn't listen too much when Devron talked about the Alpha challenges, but from what little I gathered, you came back to the pack to take it from Paul? And you had to fight off three other challengers?"

Luke ran his finger up her thigh. He knew that any second he'd be hard for her again. But his mate wanted to talk, so they would do that. *First.*

"When I was born, Paul smelled me as he does all the new pups and he could tell that I would someday be strong enough to challenge him. My father got wind that he'd ordered my death, so my parents took me and ran. Paul was my uncle, my mother's brother. I wasn't the only child Paul ordered killed, but I was only one of four who got away." He sat up all the way to pull her into his arms. These were not happy memories for him, not at all. It helped to have her presence; she helped to separate the past from the present. "When it became clear that Paul's leadership would irrevocably destroy the pack, I came back to oust him. I did it and then I fought to keep my position."

"I guess you didn't talk Paul into stepping down and then negotiate peace treaties with the others?"

"I've told you, my mate." He kissed her neck and she sighed. "I'm dangerous but not to you." He'd love the challenge of finally taking what had been his to take since birth. "I'd kill for you."

Her face fell and wariness flitted across her gaze. "Don't kill for me."

"If the situation were to arise where that level of violence became necessary, I'm not going to exactly stop to discuss it with you first."

She closed her eyes and pressed her face against his chest. "Do you think I'll be a danger to you?"

His little mate didn't know him well yet. Very little, short of apocalyptic conditions, could cause him any real danger. "Why would you think that?"

"Because you're going to spend half your time fighting off challenges from the wolves who will try to kill me for being human."

"Bethany." He pushed her head back gently so he could look her in the eyes and so she could see his resolve. "Why would wolves try to kill you for being human?"

"When the pack shifts on Full Moon nights, they're so completely in their animal forms that they try to kill the humans who are around. It's why I had to hide in the basement behind locked doors with the television for company every month."

Luke tried to digest what his mate had told him. She had grown up thinking that her family might actually kill her while they were in wolf form. Did every human member of his pack think that? Was that why they never showed up for anything?

He took a deep breath and forced back the anger that made him want to kill Paul again.

"A good Alpha is always in control of his pack. When I won the challenge, the Delta pack took a blood oath to me. That means they are always in the back of my mind, even when I am not with them." He wasn't, at the moment, going to explain to her how daunting it had initially been to have that many minds connected to his own. It had taken some getting used to. "Even when they are in their wolf forms, I can stop them from doing bad things. Having said that, I've never encountered a werewolf who would choose to kill a human member of the pack, even in wolf form."

"But that's what happened. To my mother." Her voice rose barely above a whisper, but he would have heard it across the room.

"What?"

"A rogue wolf attacked and killed her."

He touched her face, wiping away the one tear that slipped from her eye. That single drop of liquid made his soul ache. There were so many things he couldn't ever fix for her, no matter how much he wanted to. He leaned down to lick the side of cheek where the tear had been. If he couldn't make those hurts go away, he would share them with her.

Her skin tasted salty and sweet at the same time but, moreover, she tasted like his.

"A rogue wolf is not pack. But the fact that he could get

anywhere near your mother shows how weak the pack was. No one gets that close to my territory."

"Even now while you're away?"

He didn't like not being there but he could feel all the wolves in his pack. They were fine, doing mundane things, cooking, cleaning, and getting ready for bed. Nothing to get worked up over.

"Your brother and his friends have taken it upon themselves to patrol while I am away with you."

"Jack?" She laughed. "Really?"

"He's more capable than you might think."

Her smile fell. "If you hadn't told me you were a werewolf, I never would have known."

"Why?" If he could reach inside of her and pull out her unhappiness, he would do it right now.

"Because you seem to feel things, really feel them, and every werewolf I've ever known shies away from human emotions like they're a disease."

"When I came upon your family, the day I found your scent, your sister wept uncontrollably because you were leaving forever. Werewolves feel emotions just fine. We don't like to feel other people's pain. I can smell, taste, and hear your pain. Everything in me cries out to make you happy. Perhaps what you've interpreted as shying away is actually an attempt to make you feel better, to not make you feel worse by bringing them up."

She looked down. "No one ever explained it to me that way, Luke."

"I liked how you called me Lucian. Could you keep doing that?"

She smiled as she looked back up. "Yes."

"Good." He kissed her nose. The feel of the gold necklace he wore scratched his chest and he jumped. He'd almost forgotten about it. In one tug, he got it off his neck. "This is for you. It's your first, of many, Christmas presents."

She took it from his hands and he smiled at the way she seemed to hold it like it might break. "It's beautiful. Is it an angel?"

"It's a Guardian Angel. My mother gave it to me before she died. She told me to give it to my mate someday, and if she wore it then she would have all the love and protection my mother could send from the great beyond."

"Oh, my God." Tears flowed in earnest down her face, but Luke couldn't smell any sadness. Simply—happiness? "Are you crying because you're happy?" Maybe she was right; maybe even with his understanding of humans, he would never really get them because this made no sense to him. None at all.

She threw her arms around his neck. "I don't have anything to give to you."

"Did you bring a pretty dress to wear to the gala?"

She sniffed. "I did."

"Then seeing you in it will be my gift."

He'd gotten a mate for Christmas. It was more than he could ever have asked for. "Were you happy with your one-night stand?"

"What do you think?" She whacked him on the arm and he laughed. "I'm wondering if I can get my money back for all of those Italian language classes I took."

"I'll take you there. Soon. We'll go this year. You can't stay and teach, but we'll go. Would that be something you'd like?"

In his whole life, Luke had never, ever wanted to travel. They had to move all the time to avoid his uncle finding them. He liked territory and pack—they both represented safety to him. But mated to his woman, all he wanted was to do whatever she wanted.

"I'd like that."

He would, too.

January 15th

Bethany woke up with a start. *What was that?* She flipped on the light, anxious to see what had awakened her. Lucian wouldn't be back yet. It was four in the morning and only the first day of the full moon cycle. She'd be lucky if she saw him before noon.

Five wolves stood at the foot of her bed and one to her right. She gasped and pulled the covers up to her neck. Her mate had promised her she was in no danger, but what if he was somehow wrong. Her heart beat wildly.

The wolf to her right nudged her hand. That must have been what woke her in the first place. She blinked. Did she know that wolf? She had no idea. Lucian had white fur on the top of his head, but other than that she'd never been able to tell one werewolf from another since she'd never been allowed to be with them when they shifted. She knew she'd have to work on that.

The wolf whimpered and tugged at her sleeve. "What's the matter? Is Lucian hurt?"

The same whimpering sound answered her. She jumped up and threw on her boots under her flannel nightgown. It was Alaska in January. Without her mate in the bed with her, she'd gone for warmth instead of sex appeal. She grabbed her coat as she followed the wolves out of the room. Her fear for her own safety had rapidly been replaced with utter terror for her mate. She couldn't have lost him after she'd finally found him. No, fate couldn't be that cruel. Tears threatened to spill and she pushed them away as she followed the wolves out through the night.

They didn't have to walk very far. A few blocks from her house she spotted the storage warehouse where the pack kept extra supplies in the event a snowstorm stopped them from going out for more. Several wolves hung around outside. The wolf behind her nudged her through the door.

Wolves gathered everywhere inside.

"Bethany."

Lucian's voice had her turning to look to her left. He leaned against the wall.

"What are you doing?" She rushed over to him. "You're not supposed to be turned back yet for hours. The moon is still up in the sky."

"I'm the Alpha. I'm stronger than the others. I can turn whenever I want."

She wrapped her arms around his waist. "You look exhausted. What is going on?"

"I am exhausted. This is my surprise for you."

"What?" She really had no idea what he meant.

"Usually, we run until we pass out and we all gather into a big hoard of bodies like puppies do to sleep. Then we wake up and all sort of slump home."

She knew all about this. She'd heard about it for years. It was supposed to be very relaxing and pack affirming.

"Right."

"I can't be comfortable if you're not with me and I'm the Alpha, so what I want is law. Even with me warming you up, you can't sleep on the ground in Alaska in the middle of winter."

No, she couldn't. Not unless she did it in a thermal tent and even then....

"So, I decided this would be our stopping point. Every full moon, we will run until we're exhausted and then come here to sleep as a pack. You and the other human members will be here waiting for us and then we'll all sleep together."

"Um." Tears clogged her throat, which seemed to be a constant occurrence for her when she was around him. He was so considerate and thoughtful. "You did this for me?"

"We all did. Everyone wanted to."

She snuggled into his embrace. "I don't have words. It's too much."

"It's a little thing." He shrugged as he kissed her hair. "Come on, everyone is starting to pass out now."

She took his hand and let him lead her to the center of the Delta pack sleeping group. Her mate's movements were sluggish. He desperately needed to go to bed. She wasn't sure she could sleep; she experienced too much excitement. But she knew one thing for sure: Lucian was the best Christmas gift she'd ever gotten and if she was ever to meet Madame Eve, she'd give her the biggest hug in the world. The woman had helped her make all of her dreams come true.

~About the Author~

As a teenager, Rebecca would hide in her room to read her favorite romance novels when she was supposed to be doing her homework. She hopes, these days, that her parents think it was worth it.

She is the mother of three adorable boys and she is fortunate to be married to her best friend. They live in northern New Jersey and try not to freeze too badly during the winter months.

She is in love with science fiction, fantasy, and the paranormal and tries to use all of these elements in her writing. She's been told she's a little bloodthirsty so she hopes that when you read her work you'll enjoy the action packed ride that always ends in romance. She loves to write series because she loves to see characters develop over time and it always makes her happy to see her favorite characters make guest appearances in other books.

In her world anything is possible, anything can happen, and you should suspect that it will.

www.rebeccaroyce.com

Her First White Christmas

by

Liia Ann White

Prologue

Remy Sommers leaned back in his seat and smiled at the perky airhostess who brought him the drink he ordered. Taking a sip, he looked around the cabin and noticed a woman sitting across the aisle. She caught his eye and offered him a wink. Usually, he would have made a move, fed her some suave line, and joined her in the bathroom for a quick, mid-air fuck. But he'd grown tired of his playboy ways.

For years, he'd lived alone, spending night after night with different women—sowing his wild oats. Until recently, the lifestyle had suited him perfectly. He could travel, work, and enjoy a social life without worrying about a woman waiting for him at home. However, attending his younger sister, Zalia's wedding over the past weekend had triggered something inside him.

She'd met her soul mate, Xavier, through an online dating service. Remy had always been suspicious of the whole scene. As Zalia informed him, a lot of successful adults turned to the services because they either didn't have the time to date or had been out of the game for so long they had no idea how to meet new people.

That was Remy. He'd played the bachelor for so long, he'd forgotten how to go about finding a serious girlfriend. Reaching into his jacket pocket, he pulled out the business card Zalia had given him. Madame Evangeline had a knack for bringing people together, apparently. Turning it between his fingers, he eyed the woman across the aisle again, surprised to feel no need to hit on the stunning brunette. Yeah, he'd contact 1Night Stand when he landed in Orlando.

Bella Donna threw her handbag across the room, watching its contents spill out on the living room floor. She flopped on the couch, held a pillow over her face, and screamed as loud as she could. Removing the cushion, she found her best friend looking at her with raised brows.

"Tough day at the office?" Sebastian sat next to her.

"Why do I attract assholes, Seb?" she asked. "Am I a sleazebag magnet?"

He pursed his lips and frowned. For years, Sebastian had sat by her side and listened to her bitch and moan about bad dates. If she weren't so angry, she'd have felt guilty for complaining to him yet again.

"I'm never going on another blind date."

Sebastian placed a small card in her lap and smiled. "One more. If this fails, we'll have to hook up."

She managed a light chuckle at his words. "Just what I need, a pity fuck from my bi best friend. No thanks."

"It wouldn't be a pity fuck. It'd be a pity relationship." He nudged her. "Seriously, go to this site. They're brilliant. They hooked Gabe up with his new boyfriend."

"Really?"

She wasn't exactly skeptical, but Bella Donna had used dating services before and ended up bitterly disappointed. At thirty-five, she was running out of time to receive her happily ever after. *Why is it so hard to find a decent man?* Even in a big city like Melbourne, they all hid from her.

"What's so special about this 1Night Stand place?" Flipping the card over, she noted the web address.

"There are no profiles as such. You fill out an online form. Madame Evangeline takes all your information and finds your perfect match. It took three months for her to find Gabe a match, but when she did, he was perfect."

She thought it over quickly. What did she have to lose? She'd exhausted all other avenues. Random guys in bars were sleazes, mutual friends fell flat, and other online dating services hadn't helped one bit.

Bouncing off the couch, she grabbed her laptop and visited the website. Sebastian leaned over and watched as she entered the intimate details of her life on the online form.

"Oh, don't forget to mention that you've never orgasmed from sex."

Bella Donna scowled at him. "I wish I'd never told you that." She'd never orgasmed from a man's touch. No matter how aroused a lover got her, they never managed to tip her over the edge—so to speak. In fact, she barely managed to climax through masturbation.

"Hey, that's what you get for playing truth or dare with a bunch of dudes." A grin spread over his handsome face. "Now, hurry up and finish. I can't wait to see who she finds for you."

Chapter One

Bella Donna leaned forward in her seat and rubbed her neck. Sleeping on a plane was never comfortable, but on a seventeen-hour flight, she'd had no choice but to nap for a while. The ride on the bush plane had been even more uncomfortable. Until she saw the snow-capped mountains that signaled her arrival in Castle, Alaska and all her discomfort disappeared, replaced with awe at the raw beauty.

She couldn't stop the excitement that built inside her. She'd never seen snow before. And now she'd been flown to Alaska for a white Christmas—her first. Grinning from ear to ear on the way to the Castillo Resort, she probably looked like a tourist, but didn't care. The surroundings were stunning. Stepping inside the beautiful—and warm—lodge, she pushed her sweater sleeves up. The cheery check-in clerk greeted her.

"I'm Bella Donna Thereaux—"

"Yes, Miss Thereaux." The receptionist cut her off with a chirpy voice. "Everything is ready for you. You have the day to yourself; Mr. Sommers isn't arriving until tonight. Here is your key, Paul will show you to your room, and enjoy your stay."

The woman spoke in the rushed yet professional way of hotel staff everywhere. Bella Donna smiled to herself, amused. She followed the bellhop down several hallways to her room. He carried her suitcase in and left her to her own devices. Closing the door behind her, she stared out the window on the opposite side of the room.

"Holy shit."

The scene before her was like a postcard. A body of frozen, blue water surrounded by snowy white mountains with a few rocks and trees scattered about. She'd always dreamt of having a white Christmas. Now she would, in the most picturesque setting she could have imagined.

Her phone buzzed, jolting her from her musings. Sebastian. Of course, he rang her.

"You're like a mother hen," she answered with a teasing tone.

"You were supposed to call me as soon as you got there, young lady."

"I just got to my room and am taking a moment to enjoy the view."

"What's it like?" He seemed as excited about her adventure as she was.

"Exactly like the website. Gorgeous. No, that's an understatement." Her gaze ran over the scenery again. "It's like the gods' own private paradise. It's perfect."

Sebastian laughed on the line. "You're more excited about seeing snow than you are about your date, aren't you?"

"Well, I haven't seen him yet. He could be a total douche for all I know."

"Madame Evangeline took six months to find you the right man, Bell. I bet you he's perfect."

"I hope so." While she didn't place all her hopes on his being "the one" for her, she wanted him to at least be a nice guy. "He's not arriving until tonight, so I've got the day to myself."

"Anyway, you're probably exhausted." He was right. Drained from the long flight, she wanted nothing more than to lie in a steaming hot bath and relax for a while. "Go and rest up for your date. You'll be getting no sleep tonight."

She snickered at his insinuation. "I'll see you in a few days."

"See ya, babe."

She hung up the phone and opened her suitcase to retrieve

some clothing. Her ball gown lay on top of her other items. She'd bought the beautiful blue, purple, and black patterned dress for a friend's wedding a few months before and been delighted to have the opportunity to wear it again at the ball Madame Evangeline had mentioned in her invitation.

Bella Donna hung the dress in the closet by the bathroom and grabbed her toiletry bag, ready for a bath. *Wow.* Her jaw dropped when she entered. A bathroom as big as her bedroom at home. Floor-to-ceiling marble tiles decorated the room, a huge mirror sat above the basins and granite counter top on the opposite side of the room. She beamed when her eyes lit upon the enormous spa bath that could seat at least five. *Yep, I'll soak in it right now.*

Remy couldn't believe he had butterflies. *When was the last time I got nervous about meeting a woman?* He couldn't remember. Yet he stood in front of a closed hotel room door with sweaty palms and a racing heartbeat.

Come on, man. Grow some balls.

He sucked in a breath and ignored the nerves as he slipped his key card into the lock. His date had already arrived. Bella Donna. When he first read the unusual name, the image of a busty blonde goddess came to mind. Which amused him, because he'd always preferred brunettes.

Strolling through the living area, he stopped and placed his bag on the floor next to an open suitcase and assessed the room quickly. It didn't surprise him to find the epitome of luxury. The Castillo chain was well known for not sparing a cent when it came to the comfort of their guests. They used only the best of everything.

A small squeak from behind distracted him. He turned to find a tall, leggy blonde standing outside the bathroom door wearing nothing but a towel. Now, he was *very* happy he'd caught an earlier flight to Alaska.

A flush spread across the woman's cheeks, travelling to her

chest. He smiled, loving the way her pale skin blushed a light pink. *Oh yeah, I have a fun night ahead of me.*

"I'm sorry," he said to the beauty before him, "I didn't mean to interrupt."

His gaze fell on her legs. He couldn't help it; he'd always been a leg man. And this woman had a great pair, long and toned with creamy, white skin that he wanted to lick from hip to toe.

"I'm Remy." He closed the distance between them and held out his hand.

She cleared her throat and smiled. "Bella Donna."

Shaking his hand, she held onto the top of her towel.

"I didn't expect you until tonight."

"I managed to catch an earlier flight. And I'm glad I did."

His gaze traveled up her body again until he caught her gaze. She had deep, chocolate brown eyes he could drown in. He shook his head at his rudeness. Staring at a woman he'd just met no doubt made her feel uncomfortable.

"Sorry, I'll wait in the living room until you're ready."

"It's okay," she said with a smirk. "I just need a change of clothes." Bella Donna squatted in front of her suitcase and rummaged around. "Those long flights are horrible—I had to have a bath to feel human again. If you'd shown up twenty minutes ago, you probably would have run away. I looked like a zombie."

Remy laughed. Just what he'd been looking for, a woman who shared his typical, dry Aussie sense of humor. "Now, that would have been terrifying."

She flashed him a quick grin as she stood and disappeared into the bathroom.

"Holy hell," he mumbled to himself, running his fingers through his cropped hair.

Beautiful. The image he'd had in mind was spot on. Remy crossed the room and eyed the room service tray that sat next to the big fireplace. Along with a bottle of expensive bourbon, a plate of meringue desserts with cream and assorted pastries had been laid out. A bottle of chocolate syrup stood to the side with a note propped against it.

Everything here is vegan, including the body chocolate. Have a fun night.

Madame Evangeline.

Wow. The woman thought of everything. Apparently, Bella Donna was also vegan and.... *Wait. Body chocolate?* Curious, Remy picked up the squeeze bottle of chocolate syrup and flicked the cap open, tasting the treat quickly. Delicious. He couldn't wait to pour it all over Bella Donna's body and lick it off.

"You're starting without me?" She stood a few inches from him with a sexy pout. "Just don't finish without me, okay?"

The sultry smile that spread across her full lips had Remy's cock twitching. "You've got quite a naughty mouth, don't you?"

"Only a naughty mind would interpret the things I say as dirty."

Yeah, he could expect a fun night. The saucy minx only wore a small skirt and top that had her full breasts almost spilling out of the neckline. Remy held out the bottle of syrup. "Care to try some?"

"Gladly." Grabbing the bottle, she held Remy's hand and squirted a little dollop of chocolate onto the tip of his index finger.

His stomach flipped and his heart did a happy little jump. He'd truly met his match in Bella Donna. Every move she made turned him on. When she put his finger in her mouth and sucked, arousal flooded him. His heart rate jumped as she licked the syrup off thoroughly, swirling her tongue around the tip of his digit before removing it from her mouth.

Licking her lips, she moaned quietly and caught his gaze with lust-filled eyes. "Tasty."

"Oh, I know I'm going to have fun with you," he said in a voice so husky it sounded alien to his ears.

"That's what we're here for, isn't it?"

Chapter Two

Bella Donna's heart raced, pumping endorphins through her veins so fast she couldn't believe it. Everything about Remy aroused her. Short brown hair, soulful green eyes, and the chiseled features of an Adonis. He stood tall and broad, his presence exuding confidence. Her body cried out for his, her fingers tingling to run through his hair.

The moment she'd slipped his finger into her mouth, wetness had pooled in her core. She imagined doing that with his cock. He'd grip her hair and guide her as she drove him to madness with her lips and tongue.

She felt guilty for complaining to Sebastian that Madame Evangeline took so long to find her a suitable date. Remy was well worth the wait.

"So, where should we start the fun?" His Australian accent held a slight twang of American. That intrigued her. He'd obviously been in the United States for a while. "We can drink and talk or head to the bedroom."

Her cheeks flushed at his words. Bella Donna wanted nothing more at that moment than to be pinned beneath his body as he pounded into her. But her stomach had other ideas. It growled loudly. She blushed even more when Remy chuckled.

"Food it is."

How embarrassing.

"I haven't eaten in about eight hours."

He stared at her, the skin on his forehead wrinkling slightly when he raised his brows. She had no idea why, but she'd always found that particular expression sexy. "Eight hours? We definitely have to get some food into you."

I'd like something else in me right now. Bella Donna snickered at her thought. She'd always been forward when it came to sex, but Remy had her mind on a filth overload.

"Come on, let's get you a proper meal."

Shaking her head, she smiled. "I'd rather skip the meal and go straight to dessert." Remy's eyes danced with amusement and she realized what she'd said. "I didn't actually mean for that to be dirty. I've always had a sweet tooth—I prefer desserts."

He laughed lightly and stepped forward until his body almost pressed up against hers. The small of her back tingled in anticipation and her mouth went dry.

"I plan on taking you over and over tonight. You're going to need all the sustenance you can get."

The husky tone of his voice had her panties soaked. Remy's head lowered and his lips came crashing down on hers. Gripping either side of her face, he tilted her head back farther to deepen the kiss. His tongue invaded her mouth, and Bella Donna couldn't stop the low moan that escaped from her throat.

His lips and tongue worked on devouring every inch of her mouth while his hands moved from her face to grip her waist. Needing to touch him, she ran her hands up his chest, feeling the contours of defined muscle beneath the thin fabric of his shirt. His shoulders were broad and toned, his neck sinewy. She cupped his face, enjoying the feel of slight stubble under her fingertips. She loved a few days' growth on a man.

Remy broke away and let out a gentle sigh. "Well, that was nice."

"Nice is an understatement." Bella Donna licked her lips and took a step back from him.

"Now let's get you some food."

He gripped her hand in his and led her from the room.

Remy subtly shifted the crotch of his pants as he walked hand in hand with Bella Donna toward the restaurant. His cock had hardened to such an extent that it felt incredibly uncomfortable as he moved; each step had it rubbing against the zipper of his jeans. It took a lot of self-control on his part not to throw her on the bed and fuck her until she screamed his name.

But he wanted to drag out her pleasure. She would need all the energy she could get for tonight. Her ass swayed as she followed the restaurant hostess to the back of the establishment. A natural wiggle, rather than the exaggerated movement so many women used when trying to appear sexy.

Her hair fell in golden waves over her shoulders when she turned to face him.

"Is this table okay with you?"

She gestured to a cozy booth, almost completely secluded. Going by her sultry smirk, Bella Donna planned on using the private table to their advantage. Saucy woman.

"It's perfect." He looked to the hostess. "Thank you."

Seated next to each other, they ordered drinks and entrees quickly. Remy waited until the hostess was out of earshot. "Planning on enjoying the privacy, are you?"

She grinned, her eyes showing amusement and arousal. "I have no idea what you're talking about." She ran her hand up his thigh, coming incredibly close to his crotch before she stopped.

Oh hell, this woman's going to have me begging to see her again after tonight.

With a wink, she squeezed his leg lightly before removing her hand. *Two can play at that game.* He saw a waitress approaching with their drinks and quickly moved to touch Bella Donna's thigh, stroking her soft and silky smooth skin.

Remy moved his hand up until he reached the juncture he sought. Running a finger along the band of her panties, he grinned, enjoying the way her skin flushed. She sucked in a breath and shot him a look of slight embarrassment, along with enjoyment and the lust he'd sought.

Remy moved his fingers over her mound, his cock jumping when he found the material of her panties completely soaked. Quickly, he slipped his digits beneath the cotton and parted her slick folds. Bella Donna squealed and clamped her legs together the moment he touched her clit.

The waitress stood before the table and smiled at them, clearly oblivious to what went on under the table. "Two bourbons and a water?"

"Thank you," he replied casually.

Bella Donna let out a breath and regarded him with wide eyes. "I can't believe you did that while she stood right here."

"Really?" He found her entrance and he paused for a moment. "What about this?"

He thrust a finger inside her, enjoying the way she gasped and gripped his wrist. He moved his finger in and out, wriggling it around until he located her G-spot. Enjoying the way her cheeks flushed, he stilled his motion and reached for a drink with his free hand.

Raising his glass to her, Remy waited until she grabbed hers. "To us."

Bella Donna clinked her glass with Remy's and toasted before swallowing half of the bourbon. For someone who had trouble climaxing, she was awfully close. And he'd only touched her clit and fingered her a bit.

Fuck me.

She squeezed her thighs together and tried not to concentrate on the throbbing in her core. It wasn't exactly an easy task. Especially since Remy added a second finger and thrust them in and out as though they were in complete privacy rather than a restaurant.

"I do enjoy the way you blush." He leaned in and spoke into her ear, his breath hot on her skin.

Shivers trailed down her spine and she bit her lip to stop

herself moaning. Remy removed his digits from her and raised his hand.

No, he wouldn't.

A shudder spread throughout Bella Donna's entire being when he put his fingers in his mouth and sucked them. Usually, she'd be repulsed by the act, but when Remy did it, she found it incredibly erotic.

"You taste even better than I imagined."

Completely lost for words, she pulled his face down to hers. She kissed him deeply and thoroughly; both of them moaned when she pulled back.

"You're going to pay for what you did, later." She barely recognized her own voice. Husky and lust-filled, she sounded like a sexy siren.

"I can't wait." He winked.

The waitress arrived with their meal and Remy behaved in her presence this time.

Bella Donna eyed off his delicious looking stuffed field mushrooms and baby spinach salad. The cannelloni and Greek salad she ordered appeared far less appetizing. He must have noticed, because he put a piece of the mushroom on his fork and held it up for her.

"Have a taste." When she hesitated, he grinned. "I promise I'm not going to smear it in your face."

That wasn't what she'd been hesitant about. Slightly taken back by the romantic gesture, she'd paused for a moment. Nobody had fed her before. Ever. Without another thought, she took the food into her mouth, licking her lips. *Did Remy just shudder?* Apparently she wasn't the only one having trouble controlling herself.

"So," she started, "where are you from? Your accent's a bit muddled."

Remy's eyes crinkled as he smiled. "Originally, I'm from Melbourne. I've been living in Orlando for the past ten years, though. I travel around the US a lot for work."

"What do you do?"

"I'm the CFO for BA International."

She stared at him blankly, feeling like an idiot for not knowing what either set of mysterious initials—CFO or BA International—represented.

"It's a charity organization."

"Oh?" She looked at him, puzzled. "Pardon my ignorance, but what's a CFO?"

"Chief Financial Officer."

"Right, so you're a smarty, then."

He lifted a shoulder in a casual shrug. Even that small movement had her libido raging. Everything he did was sexy. "No, I'm just good with money. What do you do for a living, Bella Donna?"

She loved the way he said her name. "I run an animal shelter, specializing in abused animals and power breed dogs. Pit-bulls, Rottweilers, German Shepherds—those types."

He raised his eyebrows. "Very nice. Intelligent, beautiful, vegan, and you love animals. You're the perfect woman for me."

She blushed, feeling incredibly flattered. "Remind me to thank Madame Evangeline for finding you for me."

"Ditto."

Chapter Three

After dinner, Remy led Bella Donna back to the hotel room, barely managing to keep his hands off her. They tingled, needing to be all over her body, and his cock strained painfully against his zipper. He'd been rock hard all evening. He hadn't ever been with a woman so responsive.

When she shut the door behind her, he pushed her against it and kissed her. His excitement obviously took her by surprise, because she hesitated for a moment before kissing him back. Her tongue thrust in and out of his mouth, massaging his own.

Pinning her in place with his body, Remy used his hands to explore her. Gliding up her thighs, he skipped over her skirt and caressed the skin under her top. With her hands tugging at his hair, Bella Donna ground her pelvis against his, eliciting a groan of arousal from him.

Remy pulled away and looked at her. Cheeks flushed, breath coming in small pants through her kiss swollen lips—she was perfection.

"Do you mind if I skip the romantic gestures and take you now?"

Her pupils dilated and her body shuddered. Oh no, she didn't mind one bit.

"Are you going to do it or talk about it?"

"Naughty girl," he growled and picked her up, bridal style.

He grinned when Bella Donna let out a quiet squeal of surprise but threw her arms around his neck, using her lips to tease the sensitive skin beneath his ear. Reaching the bed in a few strides, he gently set her down and went about removing her clothing. Her shoes slipped off easily. As did her skirt. She'd removed her shirt while he worked on the rest and now sat on the bed in her underwear.

Remy's insides did a flip, his heart hammering as he sucked in a sharp breath.

Flawless.

He couldn't just fuck her their first time. He had to take his time, taunting and teasing her until she begged for release.

Bella Donna raised an eyebrow at him. "What are you waiting for?" A grin spread across her luscious lips. "Are you a tease?"

Remy let out a hearty laugh. The woman was too much. "I'm merely admiring the view."

Crawling onto the bed, he leaned over her. Capturing her lips in a sweet kiss, he gently pushed her back, holding his weight up on his arms. With surprisingly quick fingers, she undid his shirt and pulled it over his shoulders.

He broke the kiss to shrug off the garment and bent once more to nuzzle her neck. She smelled of vanilla and cherries, a scent so alluring he could have spent hours memorizing it. He traced his tongue from behind her earlobe to the hollow of her neck. Her body shuddered beneath his and she raised her hips to grind her mound against his painfully hard erection.

Fuck. If she did that any more, he'd come in his underwear. A small moan escaped her lips as his hand brushed against her breast. *Someone has sensitive breasts.* With a smile, he pulled back and looked at the black, lacy bra. Damn, no front clasp.

Bella Donna sat up, reached around her back, and undid her bra. She removed it and threw it on the floor. Remy's mouth went dry when the milky mounds of flesh bounced free. They were two handfuls easily. And all his to play with.

Her rosy pink nipples already began to bunch. Catching her gaze, he gave her a mischievous smile and lowered his mouth, taking one peak into his mouth. The moan she rewarded him with pleased him. So responsive—he loved it. After a few minutes on one breast, he moved his mouth to the other, ravaging the nipple and flesh.

Bella Donna's shallow breaths were music to his ears. He placed small kisses down her chest, across her stomach, and made his way to her center. The place he'd been waiting to bury himself in since he first laid eyes on her.

Hooking his fingers beneath the waistband, Remy pulled the panties down her legs and eagerly returned to the juncture. Completely shaved apart from a patch of curls at the top, he had never seen a more mouth-watering sight.

"Fuck, babe," he rasped. "You have no idea what you do to me."

Her response was a light snicker. He used his thumbs to part her glistening folds. Her musky scent was like a drug, turning his mind into nothing but a pile of aroused mush. All he could think of was fucking her brains out.

He took her clit into his mouth and groaned when he tasted her. Her tang was even better than he'd expected. Bella Donna arched her back and gasped as he suckled and flicked her bud with his tongue.

"Oh fuck, Remy."

He slowly inserted two fingers into her slick passage, thrusting them in and out until he found a spot and rhythm she responded to. Her breath came in pants and she trembled around him. When her thighs clamped around his shoulders, he added a third finger.

Her inner muscles clenched around him and her hips bucked. Using his other hand, he held her pelvis down, and continued to work her into a frenzy. Blood rushed in his ears, excitement building at the thought of her coming. Of making her come. He couldn't wait to hear her moan his name in a moment of pure bliss. He flicked his tongue over her engorged clit and filled with pride at her loud cry.

Not a second later, her whole body trembled. Her muscles

tightened, hips bucking again as she cried out in ecstasy. He looked up to see her flustered face: eyelids shut tight, mouth open, breasts bouncing with her panting breaths. He'd never witnessed anything more astounding.

Bella Donna slowly floated back down to Earth. Every inch of her tingled. She'd never experienced an orgasm so intense in her life. And she'd never—*ever*—climaxed at the hands of a man, no matter what sexual act they partook in. This man who appeared made for her had brought her to climax with his hands and tongue. It took a moment for her to realize she was crying.

Remy hovered over her with a concerned expression on his face. His fingers gently wiped at her cheeks then he placed a kiss on each.

"You okay?" His voice conveyed the same concern his face did.

Embarrassed, she bit down on her lip and nodded as she sat up. "Sorry." Feeling like an idiot, she wanted to get away from him. Who cried from climaxing? When she tried to shuffle off the bed, Remy moved to sit between her legs.

"Don't run from me, honey."

Her heart swelled at his softly spoken words. *Does this man have any faults?*

"Talk to me." He caressed the side of her face. "Please."

She pulled her legs up to her chest and sniffed. "I feel like such an idiot. I don't know why I cried."

He eyed her and pursed his lips. "Yes, you do."

She ran her fingers through her hair and swallowed nervously. "I've never had an orgasm from sex."

"Never?"

She shook her head, slightly irritated by his apparent amusement. "I've only ever climaxed from masturbation. And you made me come without even fucking me. I guess I got a little emotional. I didn't expect to have this connection with someone."

"So, I'm kind of like your first." He grinned. "Honey, you're so responsive, I've never had a woman who aroused me more. Seeing your cheeks flushed makes me rock hard."

She couldn't stop the blush that rose to her cheeks.

"Yeah like that." He kissed her softly on the lips. "I'm glad you enjoyed yourself."

"Enjoyed myself." She laughed. "You're an idiot."

"Yep." He moved so his body towered over hers again. "Now I'm going to fuck you until you scream my name and come harder than you ever could have imagined."

His words had her arousal peaking again. Her clit throbbed, core moistened, and her nipples hardened. She looked at the Adonis who hovered over her, running her fingers down his sculpted chest to the waistband of his jeans.

"So you get to play with me, but I don't get to play with you?" She pouted, happy when his eyes darkened at the gesture. "That's not very fair."

"Babe, if you play with me too much, I'm afraid I'm not going to last more than a minute."

A wicked smile spread across her face. "I have an idea."

Slipping out from underneath him, she dashed out of the room and grabbed the bottle of chocolate syrup. The label said body chocolate and she planned on lathering his body in the syrup and making herself a sexy man sundae.

Chapter Four

When she returned to the bedroom, Bella Donna found Remy stretched out on the bed, completely naked. His erection rested against his stomach, long and thick. She stopped and took in the sight before her.

Oh yeah, this man's perfection.

The look on his face told her he was very happy with her reaction.

"Body chocolate, huh?"

She shook the bottle quickly and wet her lips with her tongue. "I'm going to have my dessert now."

The small of her back tingled and arousal caused her heart to flutter. Crawling across the bed, she settled herself between his spread thighs and flicked the cap of the bottle open.

"Where to start?" She squeezed a drop of syrup on his cock, giggling when it twitched. "Here?"

Quickly licking the chocolate, she rested back on her knees and drizzled a long line from his navel to his neck. She smiled and bent forward. "No, I think I'll start here."

Remy's stomach muscles spasmed as she lapped the chocolate off his skin. She enjoyed the combination of salt and sweet as she ate the dessert treat she'd made for herself.

"Mmm, tasty," she mused and grasped the base of his cock.

The moment her fingers touched him there, Remy let out a

low groan. Smiling to herself, she squeezed the bottle and let chocolate syrup cover the head and run slowly down to the spot where her hand covered his wide length.

"Now, this is my favorite kind of treat."

A combination of an aroused growl and laugh rumbled from Remy's chest. "You're going to be the end of me, woman."

She grinned at him before bending her neck. Running her tongue around the tip, she took her time sipping the chocolate off his cock. She worked her way down, licking and sucking every inch of him until she'd lapped up all the syrup.

When his muscles clenched and his breathy moans became grunts, she'd achieved her goal. She'd wanted to drive him into an excited state, just like he had with her before she climaxed. Moving up his body, she offered him her chocolate-covered finger.

He sucked it into his mouth, using his tongue and lips to clean the digit. Pleasure shot straight to her core and her clit throbbed, suddenly more alive than it had been earlier. Bella Donna straddled him and pressed her breasts against his hard, smooth chest, before claiming his mouth with her own.

She kissed him deeply and thoroughly, her pussy moistening with every stroke of his tongue. Remy's arms wrapped around her waist and rolled her over to switch their positions, without breaking the kiss. She couldn't wait any longer. She needed him deep inside of her right now. When she wrapped her legs around his waist, he stiffened and pulled away.

"What's wrong?"

"Can't forget the condom."

She nodded, glad he remembered. "Right. I don't want a baby daddy right now."

He smiled and leaned across the bed, rummaging through a drawer on the nightstand.

Bella Donna took the opportunity to run her hands over his muscular thighs. How could a body so sculpted and toned be so comfortable to be pressed up against? Once he'd opened the packet and sheathed himself, she rested her hands on his shoulders and pulled him down to graze her lips against his.

Poised, at her entrance, he held his position rather than thrusting in. Too turned on to take things slowly, she wrapped her legs around his waist and propped her hips up so his head pushed inside her.

"Naughty girl," he growled in her ear before surging forward.

In one slick movement, he buried his cock to the hilt. She'd never felt so full. Closing her eyes, she concentrated on the movements Remy made that drove her to near madness.

When he found that sweet spot that had her every muscle crying for release, he circled her clit with his fingers and she was a goner. Everything inside her exploded. White light burst behind her closed eyelids. Her muscles clenched and spasmed as she cried out her release, digging her nails into his back.

Remy soon followed, his cock twitching and pulsing inside her as he held her close. She opened her eyes to find a satisfied smile on his lips.

Bella Donna kept her legs secured around his waist, wanting him inside and around her for as long as possible. Wiping a bead of sweat from his forehead, she leaned up and kissed him gently. *Wow. What a man.*

"I can officially say that's the best sex I've ever had, combined with the best orgasm I've ever had."

He chuckled, the sound ringing in her ears. "In case my trembling muscles didn't give it away, it was the same for me."

The overwhelming feeling of home filled her. Never before had she been so comfortable with someone. When he moved to dispose of the condom, she felt empty and cold. He returned with the satisfied expression still on his face and lay on the bed, scooping her into his arms.

She snuggled into his chest, resting her head where she could hear his heartbeat, and linked her legs with his. She'd officially fallen for a man she'd known mere hours.

Remy woke to an empty bed. Stretching his weary muscles, he

noticed some food on the nightstand. And a note:

I wasn't sure what you wanted for breakfast, so I got a bit of everything.

Love, BD

P.S. I'm outside enjoying snow for the first time. Come join me when you wake up.

With a grin, he sat properly and looked at the food. She really had gotten a bit of everything. There was tofu scramble, imitation bacon, cereal, toast, a bagel, coffee, tea, and hot chocolate. All still hot. She hadn't left long ago.

He quickly showered and dressed, grabbing bites of food while he prepared to brave the Alaskan December. He was probably far too eager to see Bella Donna, but he didn't care. The woman had stolen his heart last night and he ached to be with her.

Making his way through the lobby, he passed a few other seemingly happy couples and smiled to himself. Assuming Bella Donna felt the same way, he'd be one of them now. When he found her outside near the ice skating rink, caught her eye, and saw her light up, he knew she did.

With her wavy blonde hair pulled back into a high ponytail and cheeks pink from the cold, he saw her as a true picture of natural beauty. He vowed never to forget this week.

"What do you think?" she asked, bouncing toward him, a beaming smile on her face.

He followed her gaze and saw a small, lopsided snowman standing at the end of a row of others. "You made a snowman?"

She nodded eagerly and brushed her snow-covered gloves against her pants. "This is the first time I've ever seen snow. I had to be a cliché and make one. I also made a snow angel." Her musical giggle echoed in his ears.

"You're too beautiful." He scooped her into his arms and gave her a quick kiss. "Are there any other clichés you'd like to partake in today?"

She pursed her lips thoughtfully and looked past him. "Actually, I would like to make love by the fireplace." Clasping her hands over her heart, she forced a sigh and batted her lashes.

He chuckled and kissed her again. “We can do that whenever you want.”

“I want to do it now.”

That caught him by surprise. Although he was standing to attention as soon as he saw her, he’d been sure she’d want to do some skiing or ice skating before they retired to the room for another round of lovemaking. “Really? Now?”

She pressed her body against his and grasped his crotch with a gloved hand. “I’ve made a snowman and a snow angel. I’ve had my fill of snow. Now I want to have my fill of you.”

“Far be it from me to deny a beautiful woman.”

She grinned and nipped his lower lip. “Let’s go.”

Chapter Five

Bella Donna lay on the floor cushioned with a thick quilt and propped herself up on her elbows facing Remy. Still slightly puffed from their last round of lovemaking, she enjoyed the pinkish hue exertion brought to his tanned skin. He lay on his back with his arms crossed behind his head, his half-lidded eyes filled with adoration.

"So, why did a guy like you have to contact a dating agency?" She traced small circles around his stomach with a fingertip.

"A guy like me?" He raised a brow.

"You know, suave, sophisticated, successful, and hot."

"Stop it, you're going to make me blush." She hit him lightly and scoffed at his words. "Honestly, I went to my sister's wedding a few months ago and something changed for me. I used to play the field, doing what every guy does while they're single, and I guess I got sick of it. But I had no idea how to go about meeting a nice woman to settle down with, especially an Aussie. My sister found her husband through 1Night Stand and told me to give it a go." He rolled onto his side and propped himself up on an elbow. "And I'm glad I did. Because now I have you."

A blush heated her cheeks and butterflies flitted in her stomach. She was very happy she'd contacted the agency as well. If she hadn't, she never would have met a man who came even close to being as special as Remy.

"What about you?" He ran his fingers through her hair slowly. "How come some guy hasn't snapped you up?"

"I think I'm a douche magnet." She smiled when he laughed at her honesty. "Seriously, I dated so many jerks. The last blind date I had took me to a movie and expected me to have sex with him. In the theater."

She rolled her eyes at the memory of the moron her friend set her up with. But when she looked at Remy, all her frustration melted away.

"But I'm happy I dated all those duds. If it wasn't for them, I'd have never contacted Madame Eve."

"Remind me to thank them for driving you to such lengths," he murmured and pulled her on top of him.

While working another condom onto his rigid cock, Bella Donna giggled and then squirmed until the head of his hard erection poised at her entrance. Leaning over, she licked his bottom lip and gazed into his eyes. "You ready for round two, stud?"

Remy pushed his hips up, holding hers still and thrust inside her. At the intrusion, a shudder tore throughout her body.

"Oh, fuck me," she panted.

With a devilish grin, Remy sat up, leaning back on one arm, keeping the other firmly around her hips. "Okay."

He pulled out and thrust inside her again. It only took a few movements of his thick cock pushing its way in and out of her slick pussy for Bella Donna to become overwhelmed with pleasure.

Resting her forehead on his, she let out a sob and begged him to take her over the edge. When he pressed his thumb against her clit, she lost control.

Her muscles spasmed out of control as her orgasm took her onto a plane of bliss she never thought she'd experience. Holding him close, she clung to Remy like a lifeline that anchored her to the conscious world. Every muscle tingled, her core ached, and her head spun. She'd never been so happy in her life.

"Oh. My. God." She managed through her labored breaths. "I never thought I'd experience anything like that."

Remy placed a few soft kisses around Bella Donna's face before placing one on her lips. "You just needed the right man to take you there, honey."

Resuming his movements inside her, Remy's muscles tightened. Seeing Bella Donna orgasm was enough to get him off. He'd never imagined he'd find such a beautiful creature to fall for. With half-lidded eyes, she rode him, keeping perfect time with his ministrations. Her inner walls clenched around him, holding him like a tight fist.

With a groan, he shifted his position slightly, completely buried inside her when he thrust up. Bella Donna's lids closed and her breaths became whimpers.

Oh fuck—he was gone. Holding her still, he pounded into her, waiting until he couldn't hold off his climax any longer to rub her clit.

Remy followed Bella Donna on the ride to bliss, spilling his seed as every muscle in his body lit with completion. His breaths came out shaky and he dropped back, a sated, boneless pile of flesh.

Collapsing on the floor, he pulled her with him, holding her against his chest. He could stay like this forever.

"I love you, honey," he whispered into her hair.

She looked up at him, a brilliant smile on her face as she whispered in reply, "I love you, too."

Sealing his admission with a kiss, Remy beamed, happy to know he'd be spending the rest of his days with this beautiful woman.

Epilogue

Bella Donna paced her living room, unable to sit still because of the excitement building inside her. Remy had called her when he landed. He'd be at her house any moment now. She still couldn't believe he was moving back to Melbourne.

It had been a month since their stay in Alaska. She had managed to get time away from the animal shelter to spend a week with him in Orlando, but she hadn't seen him since. Two weeks. Two whole weeks of phone calls and web chats. She wanted to touch him, wrap her arms around his broad shoulders, and hold him tight.

Sebastian watched her with amusement as she continued to walk back and forth. "You need to sit down—you're making me tired watching you."

She shot him a frown but stopped pacing. "I can't help it. I've never been this excited about anything before."

"I still can't believe he's moving here for you. You've only spent two weeks together."

"It's true what they say. When you meet the one, you know." She crossed her arms and bounced on the balls of her feet, unable to keep completely still. "When you meet him, you'll understand. We were made for each other."

The doorbell rang and her breath caught in her throat.

She wanted to jump around like a lovesick teenager. She'd never been in love before. Not truly. Remy had told her the house he owned and had been renting to his sister had been vacant in the months since her wedding. He'd transferred to the Australian base of the company he worked for, broken the lease on his Orlando home, and did it all as though his extraordinary actions were an everyday occurrence.

She flashed a happy grin at Sebastian, who waved at her. "Go get your boyfriend. Bring him in when the love fest is over." He added a wink before she left.

With a spring in her step, Bella Donna opened her front door. Remy wore a big smile on his face and carried a bouquet of Gerberas.

"You're here." She threw her arms around his shoulders.

Pulling away, she looked down at the flowers she'd nearly crushed and felt a blush creep up her chest and cheeks. Nobody had ever given her flowers.

"Bella Donna." He said her name like it was the most beautiful thing in the world, as he held the flowers out to her. "I've missed you, honey."

Tears burned her eyes as she embraced him again, burying her face in his neck. "I missed you, too." She stepped back and wiped her cheeks quickly. "You're really sure about moving back?"

He gestured to the car sitting in her driveway—there were at least three suitcases. "Nothing could keep me away." He kissed her softly. "I'd move heaven and earth to be with you."

"I don't know what I did to deserve you," Bella Donna said.

"There's one condition on me moving back to Melbourne, though."

Her grin disappeared and she could have sworn her heart stopped beating.

Remy pulled something from his pocket and dangled it in front of her face. A set of keys. "Move in with me."

"Really?" she choked out, as another wave of emotion hit her.

"I don't want to live another day without you by my side. I want to wake up to see your face each morning and go to sleep with you in my arms each night."

New tears spilled from her eyes and she launched herself into his arms, almost knocking him over. “I love you so much,” she whispered into his ear.

“Should I take that as a yes?”

She leaned back in his embrace, looking at him. “Of course that’s a yes, you idiot.”

Remy’s eyes crinkled as he laughed and kissed her quickly. “I love you, honey.”

Giddy and blissfully happy, Bella Donna embraced him once more. She couldn’t believe how lucky she’d been to find him. And she couldn’t wait to spend the rest of their lives together.

❧

~About the Author~

I’m an Aussie writer, born and bred in Perth, WA – the best city in the world.

I love all things paranormal. I spent my childhood daydreaming about far-off lands and living in my own little fantasy world. I watched shows like ’Unsolved Mysteries’ and read books on witchcraft, fairies, demons, ghosts and all other sorts of supernatural creatures, including mutants (I love X-Men). I’m a complete geek and collect Disney and Star Wars memorabilia.

When not writing, I can be found reading, playing video games or spending times with my adorable doggies. I’m a big animal lover and vegan. I live in Perth with my family, which includes two adorable dogs, two birds and a handful of feisty fish.

I’m always interested in meeting new people, so drop me a line at my Facebook or Twitter. I am also a member of Romance Writers of America, Romance Writers of Australia, Passionate Ink, Futuristic, Fantasy & Paranormal Chapter of RWA and Young Adult Chapter of Romance Writers of America.

Hope to chat with you all!

www.liia-ann.com

Silent Night's Seduction

by

Clarissa Yip

Chapter One

Lily McCormick fumed as she stared out the window. White met her eyes. Snow-capped mountains and trees covered the landscape as the plane lowered its elevation, the engine rumbling loudly. The luxury surrounding her didn't faze her. She hated flying.

She gripped the seatbelt strapped across her chest and prayed for her life, all the while cursing out her older brother who'd dragged and forced her onto the aircraft. His parting words: *Payback is sweet. You'll thank me.*

More like kill him. All because she'd set him up with 1NightStand not so long ago, and now he'd done the same for her. Shane had gone to Las Vegas and met their town's librarian, Mia, whom he'd been dating since he'd returned home to Rover. Their happiness was sickening.

Her ears popped as a lodge came into view below. Lily drew in a deep breath, leaned against the seat, and closed her eyes.

Shane had refused to tell her where she was going. Only that Madame Eve had everything planned. He'd obtained a special invitation after signing Lily up with the service behind her back.

She could do this—meet her date, turn him down, and have a mini-vacation by herself. Lily McCormick did not do one-night stands even though her friends insisted she needed to get out and get laid, but coming from her brother? That was just wrong. So what if she hadn't dated in years? What if she hadn't slept with anyone since her ex-husband?

It didn't mean she was still mooning over Rafe.

She frowned at the thought of her ex-husband. It'd been three years since she'd left him in New York City. As the newly appointed district attorney, he hadn't had time for the naïve cowgirl who didn't fit into his lifestyle anymore.

Stop it, Lily. Don't think about him. It's over.

Memories flashed before her. The happy times, the arguments, and then leaving her husband of two years. It'd been for the best. She was a cowgirl at heart, needing open landscapes and space to sprint free.

The vibrations of the plane forced her eyes open. They were landing. She held onto the armrests as the aircraft propelled downward. She hated plane rides. Put her on a horse or in a sports car, and she'd run wild with the wind, but being in the air made her sick. Nor did it help that she was meeting a stranger for sex.

The sputter and jerking motion of the aircraft had her stomach lurching forward. She bounced in the seat when they touched ground. Looking out the window, the bright glare of the sun on the snow made her shield her gaze with her hands. They came to a stop and Lily glanced toward the cabin door.

She waited patiently as she undid her seatbelt and relaxed. She would definitely give Shane a piece of her mind once she returned.

"We're here, Ms. McCormick." The pilot appeared in the cabin and lifted the lock before pushing the door open.

Getting up from her seat, Lily gave the pilot a flimsy smile as she clutched her purse to her chest. Her knees wobbled. A strong brush of cold air met her face and she sneezed. "Where are we?"

The pilot grinned. "Why, Alaska. It's beautiful, isn't it?"

Lily descended the stairs and looked around, nothing to see but white. Tall trees covered in snow lined the area they'd landed on. She was in winter-wonderland-hell.

A breeze brushed her buttocks under her denim skirt, and she shivered. If she'd known she was going to be abducted and forced on a plane, she would have dressed more sensibly. Shane had only shoved her suitcase and a winter jacket that she didn't even know she owned into her hands and bid her farewell. "Yeah. It's gorgeous...." She couldn't keep the sarcasm out of her voice. A brisk rush of cold air blew at her again. Spotting a man in a parka on the dock, she stiffened and held a hand to her head to keep her Stetson in place. "Who is that?"

"Your escort to the lodge."

"Thank you." Tugging her short skirt down, she moved through the snow as the man met her halfway and took her suitcase from the pilot. She noted the gold stitching on his jacket. *Castillo Lodge.*

"Hello, Ms. McCormick. I hope you enjoyed your flight."

She nodded even though dread and anger tore up her insides, and all she wanted to do was go home. How could her parents allow this audacity to take place? Wouldn't they wonder where she'd gone? No doubt Shane had it planned. *Jerk.*

The man gestured for her to follow. She trudged behind on the walkway staring at the structure ahead, magnificent with its many windows and wooden beams. Shivering from the cold, she held her jacket closer.

The walk to the lodge wasn't too far. Once inside, she met the soft melody of Christmas carols and a welcoming blast of heat. Her toes were frozen in her boots. Laughter and chatter surrounded her but the huge Christmas tree reaching toward the ceiling drew her attention. Lights and ornaments decorated the massive beauty and a surge of homesickness struck her, reminding her of the two winters she'd spent in New York with Rafe missing her own family in Texas. Her ex-husband had left her alone in their high-rise apartment while he'd gone to prosecute criminals or work on some case that needed his personal attention. Now she had no one for the holidays again.

"This way, please." Her escort smiled and led her to the counter behind the tree.

The check-in clerk glanced up with a welcoming grin. "Hello, Ms. McCormick. We've been expecting you."

Lily just nodded. She didn't want to be here, didn't want to meet her mystery man, or even bother with the opposite sex, period.

The clerk handed her a key card and envelope. "Here is a list of our amenities and various activities offered during your stay. Should you need anything, please let us know. Enjoy."

Lily hesitated. She couldn't help but wonder if her date would be sharing the same room, but she refrained from asking and followed the bellhop up the stairs. They climbed to the second floor and turned down a well-lit hallway. The mahogany carpet held whirls of gold and green. The tension in her chest rose. Maybe she needed a nap. Or a hot shower to warm her bones.

The boy before her stopped at room 215. "Here you go, miss."

Lily drew a few bills from her purse and gave them to him. He smiled and walked off. Taking a deep breath, she slipped the key card into the slot. The light blinked green and she pushed the wooden door open. Elegance met her gaze as she drew her suitcase in. A king-size bed sat in the center of the room, and she noticed the champagne bottle and two flutes on a stand near the window. Decked in gold and green, the place screamed luxury, but she'd much rather be at home.

Unbuttoning her coat, she walked farther into the room and drew a deep breath, needing to get her emotions intact before being forced to meet the man Madame Eve had set her up with. She shrugged her jacket off and threw it on the bed. Blood-red roses sat on the nightstand, and her heart clenched. Her ex-husband used to buy them for her all the time because she loved them and they reminded her of her mother's roses in the backyard. It'd been over three years since she'd received flowers of any type. Grazing a finger over a silky petal, she bent to sniff the bouquet. The heavenly floral scent washed over her, fueling the memories she'd long buried.

"Hello, darlin'."

The southern drawl so like her own made her freeze. Then she whipped around and seethed. "You!"

Chapter Two

A glare marred her delicate features, and Rafe Martinez couldn't help but grin. His ex-wife was as gorgeous as he remembered in her worn-out boots, denim skirt, pink blouse fitting snugly over her petite frame, and her favorite cowboy hat atop her head. Her blonde curls were long, the ends stopping at her breasts. Heat spiraled through him as it did every time he looked at her.

"What are you doing here?" Lily set her hands on her hips, her piercing blue eyes shooting daggers at him.

Her beauty took his breath away. She was still the little firecracker he loved.

"What are *you* doing here?"

She stumbled back a step. "I-I...."

He hid his grin and stood up. It'd taken some orchestrating to get his brother-in-law to help him, but he knew he could count on Shane to get the deed done, since he'd been the one to give Rafe the idea of 1NightStand. Now the rest depended on him. "Cat got your tongue?"

Lily deepened her glare.

He crossed the room to her. She backed away. An old pain blossomed in his chest, but he refused to show that her action bothered him. "Aren't you a little far from Rover, *mi amor?*"

"Don't call me that. And I'm not here voluntarily."

His brow lifted, but he kept his expression indifferent. He

couldn't let her in on the plan just yet. It didn't take much to irritate his hotheaded and stubborn wife, especially when it came to him. "Then why are you here?"

"I could ask the same about you. Isn't this a little far from New York City?"

He spun around and stalked to the bar on the other side of the bed. "I needed a vacation. A colleague told me about this great service so I had to check it out myself."

A curse erupted into the room. "You came here for a one-night stand?"

The rage in her tone lightened his heart. If she could be angry with him then she must care for him still. Pouring himself a drink, he took his time answering. "Actually, more than that." He turned around. "It's three days before Christmas. I hope to spend the whole time with my date and escort her to the ball on Christmas Eve."

Lily's mouth dropped open then closed. "Well, good for you. But let me ask you, where is your date?"

Rafe frowned. "You know, that's a good question. Why and how are you in my room?"

"This is my room!"

He stilled, praying she wouldn't see through him. "That can't be. I specifically requested a brunette as my date."

Lily sputtered. "You—you cad!"

"This must be a mistake." He went over to the chair he'd occupied earlier and pulled his phone out of his coat pocket. "I'll email Madame Eve and get this straightened out. Worse comes to worst, you can go request a different room."

An outraged gasp sounded behind him. "Why do I have to be the one to leave?"

He whirled around and gave her what he hoped was a convincing bewildered look. "Unless...you're my date?"

She paused. "Hell no."

He tsked. "That potty mouth of yours hasn't changed. Delectable as it is, you shouldn't be cursing."

Lily crossed her arms over her chest. The movement pushed her breasts together. His cock throbbed and an ache in his chest expanded. It'd been so long since he'd made love to her. "There's no way I'm staying here with you, Rafe."

"Don't worry. We'll fix this." Turning his attention to his cell phone, he emailed Madame Eve. The woman had sent him a note earlier confirming his plans, and they'd already talked about worst-case scenarios if they were to happen. He'd put his trust in the matchmaker to fulfill his wishes, not knowing where he'd end up, but then he didn't care as long as he was with Lily.

His wife paced. No matter that they were divorced, she would always be his *esposa*. He watched as she flung her hat onto the bed and ran her hand through her hair. His fingers itched to touch her. Memories of her silken tresses gliding over his skin had him mesmerized until he heard her words. "I can't believe this. It's all Shane's fault. If he hadn't signed me up for this, I wouldn't be here, wouldn't see—"

She didn't have to finish that sentence for him to figure it out. She'd avoided him ever since she'd left him. Rafe picked up his drink and gulped the rest of the whiskey. The burn down his throat felt good. He had to be patient and handle Lily with kid gloves. He couldn't afford to scare her off. Who knew when he'd have another chance to convince his wife to come back to him? He missed her. The years apart hadn't changed his feelings toward her, only made his love for her more profound as he'd return to their lonely apartment and spend restless nights thinking about her.

"Is it so bad to see me?"

Lily stopped and stared at him. Confusion passed over her features. "We're divorced. You're here to sleep with some woman and I—"

"Let's just calm down and see what's going on. There must have been a mix up."

She shook her head. "I don't want to be here. I just want to go home."

His phone buzzed and just as he'd planned, Madame Eve emailed him the name of his date. He focused hard on the screen, even though his heart pounded fiercely and he could feel Lily's gaze on him.

"What is it?" She moved to stand next to him.

He held his phone up to show her.

Her eyes widened. "That can't be." She started pacing again. "How is that possible?" She stilled and looked up. "I need to get out of here."

Fear surged to his throat as she crossed the room and jerked the door open. "Lil—"

The door slammed shut. Rafe shoved a hand through his hair and sat down on the bed.

Damn. He'd never expected her to walk out.

Lily stormed down the hallway to the stairs. A knot formed in the back of her throat, sweat coated her hands, and she could barely think after being in the same room as Rafe. Seeing him, standing so close to him—memories she'd long suppressed rushed at her. His musky, masculine scent had teased her nose, reminding her of the many times they'd touched, kissed, loved.

After three years, she'd hoped her emotions wouldn't get in the way and make her act like a fool, but knowing his reason for being here? And witnessing her own name displayed across that screen? It was too much. She paused at the bottom of the stairs.

Madame Eve had paired her with Rafe. Out of all the people who signed up for the service, what were the chances? Was it fate?

Spotting the bar, she walked over to the table by the window and sat down. What was she supposed to do? No way she could spend three days with Rafe, alone in that room and not beg him to make love to her. Desire teased her every time she heard his name, saw his picture or even his face on TV. She'd been without sex for so long, but no one else made her feel as strongly as he did and she didn't want any other man to touch her. But Rafe.

With a groan, she closed her eyes. An image of him entered her mind. Tall, gorgeous, and absolutely dashing—he still had the same effect on her. Her senses stood on edge in his presence. Her body came alive.

Anger and jealousy ran rampant through her. He planned to sleep with some stranger. Rafe had always been faithful in their marriage, but she recalled the female attention he drew just by walking into a room. He was too devastatingly handsome for his own good. As their ranch's foreman's son, Rafe and she had grown up together, but it wasn't until one summer after he'd returned from law school they'd finally given in to their attraction. They'd been reckless and in love when she ran off to New York City with him, but his success became too much for her.

She'd never fit into his life there. After they'd gotten married, he worked harder; she became more depressed. So she left.

And not once had he contacted her after she'd returned to Rover. Until the divorce.

So why did he have to appear here of all places?

"Miss, would you like something to drink?"

Lily looked up at the waitress. "Vodka cranberry, please."

"I'll have a Heineken."

She stiffened as Rafe appeared behind the woman, who pasted on a seductive smile at his appearance. Lily dug her fingers into the armrest, tempted to reach up and rip the waitress's hair out. She hated the constant emotions that came to life, all because of Rafe.

He slid into the seat across from her, a troubled look on his face.

"What do you want?" She couldn't help sounding irritated. Nothing had gone the way she wanted since she'd divorced him. No dates or love interests, because no man matched up to him. Her parents continuously threw candidates at her and dragged her to various social galas to announce her single status. It was embarrassing. Loving Rafe and being away from him had been hell in the past three years, but she was coming to terms with herself—she was destined to be alone.

He shoved a hand through his hair. A dark lock fell over his perfectly tanned forehead. "Look, I'm sorry this happened. I didn't know you had signed up. I was just hoping to get away, to take a break from work."

At the mention of his job, old hate resurrected. It'd always had been about his job. She came in second. "What else is new? You're always working. I'm surprised the city even let you have time off."

Rafe gave her a sad smile and leaned against his seat. "Actually, I'm between jobs."

She stilled. "What do you mean?"

"I quit couple of months ago. I'm no longer the district attorney."

Confusion rose. "Why not? You loved being the DA." *More than you loved me.*

He shrugged. "It got to be too much. I want to help people who deserve to be helped. I want more out of my life. It's time I married again and started a family."

Her throat closed. She couldn't breathe. He was going to start a family with some other woman, give that other person what she'd always wanted. "Well, then good for you."

The waitress appeared and set their drinks on the table. While the woman stared at Rafe, he continued to watch Lily. She ignored them both as she picked up her drink and stirred it. *Wonder what would happen if I accidentally pour it onto the waitress...* Instead, she looked out the window. People dressed in heavy winter gear carried skis and snowboards onto a trail, some walked around with fishing poles, and others were just standing around, chatting and laughing.

She'd always hated snow. It reminded her of the miserable, lonely winters during their marriage.

"Lily."

She glanced at him, eyebrow raised. The waitress had disappeared and he gave her a smile. Her heart thumped and something melted inside her. He always had that effect on her. One look, one touch, and she was a puddle at his feet. "What?"

"You haven't changed any." The tone of his voice brushed over her like a caress and her body warmed.

Annoyance surged to her throat. Pursing her lips, she set her drink down on the table with a thud. "Why would I? No reason for me to."

"Are you happy?"

She stiffened. "Of course. I'm back at the ranch, riding my horses, helping my father with the business. I wouldn't want to leave my home ever again."

He sighed. "I miss you, *mi amor*."

His words were spoken so softly, she almost didn't hear them. She couldn't keep from asking, "You actually planned on having a one-night stand?"

A blush rose to his cheeks. "It's been a long time since I've slept with a woman."

Anger warred with relief. "Why?"

He chuckled as he took a swig of his beer. "I've found fault with every woman I've dated because...they weren't you."

Her gaze jerked to his face, heart pounding loudly in her ears. "It's long over between us."

"I know, but it doesn't stop me from thinking about you."

Some perverse hope flared in her chest. "I can't say that I've thought of you at all."

A grin spread over his face. "It's all right. I know I'm not your favorite person, but let me tell you this: I'm sorry I didn't treat you better."

Her nails dug into her palms. "You weren't a bad husband. You just chose work over me."

He frowned. "I believed if I didn't work hard, you wouldn't stay with me, but you left anyway."

Shock tore through her. She sat up. "What made you think I cared if you were successful or not? All you needed was your job! You didn't need me." She sank into her seat, noting the curious glances cast in their direction. Picking up her drink, she blew out a frustrated breath and took a sip.

"My pride and honor got in the way. I wanted to show your parents that I could take care of you since we'd basically eloped that summer, and I knew they didn't approve of me because I was my dad's son."

Her chest tightened. Rafe's father was the foreman, but still the hired help in her parents' eyes. Her father's biased comments played in her mind. Even though her parents loved her, they believed no one was worthy of her, and they'd blamed Rafe for taking her away. Her return had been met with relief and it hadn't taken long for her parents to insist upon the divorce, which she'd readily gone along with when her husband hadn't come after her. Exhaustion suddenly wrapped around her. "Rafe, it's been so long."

"No matter what I did, it wasn't enough." His hand clenched around the bottle.

She noted a flicker of anguish in his eyes. Sorrow clawed its way to her throat and her prideful front deteriorated. What difference did it make if he knew how she'd felt? "All I wanted was *you*."

His sharp intake of air drew her attention. "I'm sorry, Lily."

She shrugged. A lightness expanded in her chest as if the tension she'd carried over the years evaporated. It was nice to know he'd hurt as much as she did. Those times she'd avoided him, she'd been a wounded animal insistent on hiding from him. When he had come out to visit his parents, she'd made sure she left the ranch. Now it all seemed silly.

An awkward silence settled over them. Her anger seemed to have dissolved some. What would she do here by herself? Loneliness wrapped around her as she whirled the straw in her drink.

Rafe took another swig of his beer then set the bottle on the table and stood up. "You're probably tired. Maybe you should take a shower and rest up. I'm sure the plane ride was rough on you. I know how you've always hated them."

She swallowed hard and stared at his outstretched hand. "What are we going to do about the...?"

"Well...there are no other rooms and you were supposed to be my date, so I guess you're stuck with me this weekend." He gave her a flimsy smile.

"But—"

"Don't worry, Lil. Nothing is going to happen. You know I wouldn't force you to do anything. Besides, I'm here for a long overdue vacation."

The casualness in his voice bothered her, but she nodded. He'd always been a gentleman no matter what. The old trust remained. Besides, stuck in winter-wonderland-hell with no other place to go, she didn't want to get back on that plane anytime soon. "Fine. Guess it wouldn't hurt."

Chapter Three

Rafe stuck his hands into his pockets. They walked quietly next to each other up the stairs, Lily a good three feet away from him. He wanted nothing more than to wrap his arm around her and pull her against him, but he had to play it slow.

It pained him to hear she was happy without him, but he wasn't giving up. No way in hell. He'd do anything to have her back. He hated deceiving her, but he knew his wife. He just needed the time to make her realize she still loved him.

"So, how are your parents doing?" he asked.

She glanced over at him, but returned her attention to the carpet as they reached the second floor landing. "They're fine. Glad to have me home, of course."

His fingers curled into fists. No matter what he did, he would never be good enough for their daughter. He'd do anything for Lily. Working hard hadn't gotten him anywhere and it'd taken him three years to be aware he'd stopped living. "I'm sure. They love you very much. If I wasn't the foreman's son, things may have been different."

Lily stopped and whirled to face him. "That doesn't have anything to do with us."

He laughed softly. "*Querida*, it had everything to do with us."

"I didn't ask you to work harder or prove anything to my parents. I was just happy being with you, but you loved your job more."

The ease of talking about their past told him Lily wasn't holding onto her anger, but he couldn't help the rage at her parents for keeping them apart. He respected the McCormicks, but they had never approved of him, constantly reminding him of how unworthy he was and how he couldn't take care of their daughter. The only solution had been to work hard to obtain his goals, reach success where he'd get recognition and make a name for himself, but what good had that done him? "If that's what you believe."

He strode off to their room, unease boiling in his chest.

"You know, you never came after me."

He paused, his hand on the doorknob. "You didn't want me to come after you. Your parents told me you hated my guts the numerous times I called and that you never wanted to see me again because I wasn't good enough for you. And you told me often enough whenever you threatened to return to the ranch during our marriage."

Without waiting for a response, he unlocked the door and strode in. A shudder tore through his body. Anguish and fury rolled into one. He went to the bar and poured himself a drink. Control slipped further and further away. The game wasn't playing out as he'd planned. He'd imagined anger, a good fight, and eventually the chance to talk about their past, but it was all coming at him too fast.

"You called me?"

He down his whiskey and whipped around. "Yeah, I did. Many times."

Lily closed the door and came into the room. "I didn't know. Sorry."

His gaze met hers. He'd never expected her to apologize. No, not his Lily. He closed the distance between them. Cupping her cheek, he studied the stubborn jut of her jaw. Her guard was up, but relief speared through him when she didn't move away. "Admit you've been avoiding me the past three years."

She drew a deep breath and nodded. Her admission eased the

tightness in his chest. He'd thought he'd have a bigger battle on his hands, but spotting the vulnerable gleam flash in her eyes, a groan ripped past his lips. He didn't think; he covered her mouth with his. An electric shock rippled through his body. She tasted sweet, decadent, yet so familiar. Aware of Lily melting under his touch, he pulled her flush against him. Her arms slid around his shoulders as she met him with ardor. Heat surrounded him. Need tore through him.

His hand cupped her bottom, drawing her against his erection. He deepened the kiss, Lily's whimper music to his ears. Her response fueled his desire. This was what he'd been missing, what he'd longed for. His body came alive, nerves tingling with each lingering swipe of his tongue over hers. But an alarm sounded in his head. He couldn't risk moving too fast or losing her again.

With reluctance, he broke away and fought to clear his mind. Lily stared at him, a stunned expression on her face. Lips swollen, eyes glazed, and breathing as ragged as his—victory surged through him. He dragged her back into his arms and hugged her.

"I shouldn't have done that." Leaning back, he brushed a kiss over her forehead. "I'll draw you a bath. I'm sure you'd like to rest."

Releasing her, he gave her one last smile and sauntered to the bathroom. Lily's gaze burned a trail down his back.

His wife still wanted him. He was sure of it.

He didn't want her. That was the only explanation she could come up with. She touched her lips as she slid farther into the heated water. The jets of the tub surrounded her, massaging her tense muscles. He'd drawn her a bath as he'd said then left her alone in the bathroom. For some reason, she'd expected him to take her back into his arms and kiss her again or...make love to her.

No. He just smiled at her and closed the door, leaving her with troubled thoughts. Knowing that he'd tried to contact her after she'd left him bothered her. Her parents had lied. The days and nights of crying about her marriage's failure came to mind. *Rafe didn't love her. Rafe didn't care. Rafe only wanted his job.* Her parents' words played havoc on her heart. She believed he had wanted the divorce since he hadn't made any attempts at reconciliation or put up an argument when the lawyer served him the divorce papers.

Tension boiled in her chest. Would their situation be different if she'd stuck it out with him? Would he have been content to settle as the District Attorney or desired more from his career? Questions burned in her head. She'd never know, since she'd just packed and left him with no word, like a coward. She'd lived in fear that one day he'd realize she didn't belong in his world or that she wasn't enough for him. Never did she suspect the reason for his obsession to work so hard. Just to prove himself worthy.

She leaned against the lip of the tub and her eyes drifted closed. Heat ran down her spine at the memory of the kiss just shared. Her body had trembled with each swipe of his tongue. She couldn't get enough of him. Thoughts and reasoning dissolved the moment he touched her. Rafe was a generous lover. Memories of their lovemaking made her nipples harden, core throb. Who was she kidding? She'd always want him, probably to the day she died. No one fit her the way Rafe did. No one could claim her or tame her like her ex-husband—she'd surrender to no one, but him.

She recalled the conversation in the bar. *No one could compare to you. Every woman I've dated, I've found fault because...they weren't you.*

Did he still love her? Or was he using 1NightStand to get over her?

Laying a hand on her breast, she brushed over the erect bud. A whimper escaped her lips. She imagined gripping Rafe's dark hair as he bent to tease her nipple. His hand would glide over her knees, her thigh, seeking her center. He'd draw sensuous circles around her clit, pleasure her, and then bring her over the edge.

Her own fingers fluttered over her stomach. Her body heated.

Sweat formed on her forehead. An ache pulsed between her legs. Her breathing turned shallow.

She swallowed her moan when a knock sounded at the door. Her eyes flew open.

"Lily? Are you hungry? I ordered room service."

She sat up with a frustrated curse.

"You doing okay in there?"

No, I'm far from okay. She let her head drop back against the tub. "Yeah. I'll be right there."

Pressing her hands against the sides of the bathtub, she got out. Water dripped to the floor as she grabbed a towel and dried herself, still sensitized by her recent erotic fantasies. What was wrong with her? Stupid question. Her current state could only be blamed on the man out in the bedroom.

Wrapping the towel around her, she jerked the door open and gasped. The room glowed white. Lit candles sat on every possible flat surface. Vases of red roses lined the stand by the window. The table on the far side of the room held dinner settings for two and Christmas carols blared from the stereo on the bar. Hope and pleasure spurred through her.

"What's all this?" she asked. She faced him and her body warmed to see his heated gaze rake over her from head to toe. She noted the darkening of his eyes before he ran a hand through his hair, the movement pulling his white button-down shirt across his chest. A blush rose to his cheeks.

"I ordered dinner then two guys came in and set up the place. Probably something the service does for their couples."

"Oh." Disappointment crushed her elation. She was reading too much into everything. "That was nice of them. Madame Eve does think of everything. Shane had told me how great 1NightStand is. I signed him up for it not long ago."

"Really?" He turned his back to her and rearranged the silverware on the table, suddenly finding interest in the set-up.

Lily frowned. She looked around for her suitcase. "Do you know where my stuff is?"

"One of the maids came in and unpacked for you." Rafe moved

to the table where the champagne bucket sat and poured two glasses.

"They do do everything here." She drew the closet door open and stilled. A lipstick-red gown glittered under the closet light, so like the dress she'd married him in. Her parents had frowned upon her choice of color, but Rafe had always encouraged her spontaneity. Running a finger over the material, she imagined herself on the dance floor in Rafe's arms. A flood of memories rushed at her. Walking down the aisle, standing before him, his eyes glowing with love, the exchange of vows and rings. Then their long honeymoon in their New York apartment. They had needed only each other. Longing squeezed her heart. It seemed an eternity since he'd held her, kissed her, loved her.

Truth struck. She wanted nothing more than to be Rafe Martinez's woman, once again, even for a few days, especially if he planned to remarry and start a family with another woman.

Breaking out of her reverie, she grabbed a pair of jeans, a white sweater, and some underthings. "I'll change and be right out."

Rafe let out a relieved breath when the bathroom door clicked shut. He quickly rubbed his hand over his cock and adjusted himself. Seeing Lily clad in only a towel had his arousal pulsing against the fly of his pants. Golden skin, probably from working on her father's ranch, long legs that tempted him to explore every sinful inch, and face devoid of make-up—he couldn't believe how much more beautiful she'd become.

Stay cool. Be tough. Pace yourself. Don't scare her away. Let her make the move.

It was killing him. He wanted nothing more than to whip that towel off, throw her on the bed, and have his way with her. But what would that accomplish? He needed her to miss him, want him, and most of all, realize she couldn't live without him.

Slow down, cowboy. This is your last chance.

Carrying the champagne glasses to the table, Rafe set them down and sat in one of the chairs. The smell of steak and lobster teased his nose. He was hungry, but more so hungry for his wife.

The door opened and he stood up. Lily smiled at him as she crossed the room to the table. He came around and held out her seat.

"I'm actually starving." She picked up the napkin and placed it over her lap.

"Good." He whipped the lid off her plate. Steam rose, and Lily bent to get a better sniff. "That does smell heavenly. I don't remember the last time I ate."

"Dig in." He went around the table and slid into his own seat, removing the cover off his own dish.

"It's actually kind of nice to be away from the ranch. Maybe we can go take a walk tomorrow out in the snow."

His eyebrow lifted. She disliked winter, always complaining about the cold. "You hate snow."

She shrugged. "It's something different. Change of scenery. I don't leave the ranch much. There is always something to do."

"I'm sure your parents love that. They'd keep you there forever if they could." He couldn't keep the sarcasm out of his voice.

Lily bit her lip. The motion drew his attention; the slow ache in his groin expanded. His fingers wrapped around the stem of his champagne glass. "They love me and I know everything they've done was what they thought best for me."

He frowned, remembering his many conversations with his brother-in-law. He wanted to argue with her and the words slipped out before he could stop them. "And throwing eligible husbands at you is the answer?"

Lily looked up in shock. "How'd you...?"

Rafe froze, inwardly berating himself for his stupidity and wondering if he'd blown his cover. "I talk to your brother once in a while."

"Oh." She stared at the table.

Relief speared through him when she didn't say more. The tune of *Silent Night* filled the room, reminding him of the one time they'd gone Christmas caroling. It'd been a first in their marriage and he'd hoped to make it a tradition, but his job had taken over their holidays together. Regret poured through him as he recalled the amount of time he'd spent away from her, all because he'd felt the need to work harder.

"So...guess you're stuck with me until Christmas Day."

He glanced up at her. "That's the plan, but I wouldn't call it getting stuck with. I'm really okay with this, Lily."

She drew in a deep breath. "Are you disappointed that it's me and not your '*brunette*' date?"

The smidge of anger in her voice made him grin. Reaching across the table, he covered her hand with his. "Are you jealous?"

"No." She moved her hand out from under his and reached for her fork and knife. He watched as she slowly carved a piece of steak and lifted the tender bite to her mouth. He stifled a groan as her lips closed over the fork. "I'd have to care to be jealous."

Rafe took a sip of his champagne and eyed her over the rim. "I'd be jealous if I saw you in some other man's arms."

Lily swallowed her food and sat up, placing her utensils down. "Then that's your problem. I wouldn't care if I saw some other woman all over you."

She was lying. He could tell by the slight curve of her mouth, hiding her impish smile as she took a sip of her drink. "But then neither of us has a date, so you're actually stuck with *me*."

"It is a shame." A mischievous glint shone from her eyes.

Joy thumped in his chest. He couldn't stop teasing her. "Yeah, it's too bad. I was expecting some voluptuous brunette with long legs, not some fiery little blonde."

Her eyebrow rose as she slowly set her glass down. She frowned. "Really? Are you disappointed?"

The quiver in her lips had him out of his seat and at her side. He knelt down, drawing her to face him. "Lily...."

"Do you regret marrying me?"

The sudden change in her demeanor scared him. His thumb ran over her cheek, wiping away a tear. He waited until she met his gaze. "No. Never."

She sniffled and exhaled a loud breath as if relieved.

The urge to tell her the truth lay on the tip of his tongue. Was it too soon? How would she react? Would she be mad that he'd tricked her here?

Lily gripped his wrists and lowered his hands before she reached for her champagne glass again. She downed the contents in one gulp. His disappointment flared as he stood up and headed back to his seat.

"Rafe."

He tensed and turned around. His heart lurched. Lily had risen from her chair, the hem of her sweater slowly gliding upward baring her flat stomach. The sight of her black lace bra made his mouth water. She drew the material over her head and watched him. Nervousness radiated from her as her fingers rested on the button of her jeans. The snap came undone, zipper drawn down, and she shimmied out of her pants. A small patch of lace covered her feminine curls. His chest tightened. He could remember her sweetness, her exotic taste from the many times they'd made love.

His gaze followed every movement as she kicked her jeans away. She reached up and undid the clip behind her head, shaking her hair out. Her light locks fell around her shoulders, framing her face. He drank in every milky inch of her skin. Beauty took his breath away. He swallowed hard, suddenly aware of his cock throbbing fiercely against his fly.

The melody of *Silent Night* seemed louder, but the calming words didn't do much to soothe the arousal tearing through him. "Lily, what are you doing?"

She closed the distance between them, her hips swaying with each step. Heat jolted down his spine. "Show me you've always wanted me, not some other woman."

He studied her face. A flicker of insecurity flashed over her features. He recalled the times she'd complained about dressing for dinner parties and hating how all the women outshone her even though she'd always been the one who kept his attention. No other woman could compare to his Lily. "*Mi amor*, you're perfect.

And I've never wanted anyone but you."

A slow smile formed and then she bit her bottom lip as she curled a hand behind his nape. Her breasts brushed against his chest. "Show me. Be mine. For now."

Her words struck home. He growled and kissed her. Pent-up passion and ardor rose as he ran his hands over her slender back, undoing the catch of her bra and pulling her against him. His tongue tangled with hers, drinking in her sweetness. He slid his palms over her bottom and hoisted her up, her legs circling his waist as he pivoted toward the bed. Reaching the mattress, he laid her down, unwilling to break contact with her as he drew the lace over her arms and off. He trailed his lips over her jaw, nipped the sensitive spot under her ear, and worked his way down her throat, finally stopping at her breasts.

His thumb flicked over the erect nipple and Lily moaned, the sound encouraging him to do more. He closed his mouth over the bud, and pleasure speared through him at her response. Her body arched off the sheets, and she gripped his hair as his hands continued their exploration. She was silk everywhere. Like a kid in the candy store, he felt overwhelmed. He wanted to taste every inch of her skin.

Moving to her other breast, he lavished it with the same attention, his tongue swirling around the taut nub, nipping and teasing it until the areole deepened in color. His fingers fluttered over her hips, her stomach and grazed her lace-clad secrets. He slipped in under the material, his nails sifting through the curls before a digit found her wetness. He growled and sucked harder on her nipple as he pushed another finger in her tight heat. Lily cried out at the invasion. Her inner muscles clamped around him, and he kissed his way down her abdomen. His one hand drew her panties down as she lifted her hips, all the while his other continued thrusting slowly in her heat.

He drew a deep breath, the scent of her arousal—musky and sweet—filling his senses. His cock pulsed, aching to trade places with his fingers. He worked his mouth over her mound before parting her folds. His tongue darted out, teasing the berry. Lily cried out again, her grip in his hair tightening and guiding him to where she wanted his touch as he drew circles around her clit. He closed his lips over the bundle of nerves, alternating pressure as he teased her relentlessly and the tempo of his fingers moving faster, in and out of her. Intense need built in his stomach. Desire to see her fly apart kept his control intact.

It didn't take Lily long to fall apart. Her hips thrust upward, pushing herself against him. He sucked harder as shudders rippled through her body and then she became a limp mass. Crawling over her, he pressed his lips against hers, sharing her decadent essence and then he rose above her, caging her between his arms. Pride thudded against his chest at her blissful expression.

Lily smiled at him then reached for his shirt, and he helped her tear it off before her hand found the button of his pants. He allowed her to undo it and draw the zipper down. His cock sprang free and relief tore through him the moment her fingers wrapped around him. He groaned when she gave him a stroke for good measure and then pushed him onto his back. Eager to oblige, he thumped his head against the headboard and Lily laughed, tugging a pillow behind him.

"My turn."

His cock jumped at her words. He fisted the sheets, wanting to grab her and impale her on his shaft. A mischievous glint entered her eyes as she slid down. Hovering over his groin, she threw him a wicked grin.

"Baby, I'm not going to last long."

Her eyebrow rose. "Don't lie, Rafe Martinez. You and I both know how much you can endure."

He closed his eyes. Their lovemaking had always been hot, playful, painful yet pleasurable. The first swipe of her tongue had him arching off the bed.

"Down, cowboy."

He growled as she tentatively worked the root of his cock, nipping, tasting. Pure torture. Her lips closed over the head. A wave of bliss rolled through him. His balls tightened as she sucked more of his length into her mouth.

Control slid further away. He tensed, reveling in each jolt of pleasure from her delectable ministrations until she teased the slit. "Dammit, Lily," he ground through clenched teeth.

Her wicked chuckle reached his ears. She crawled over him, her breasts blazing a trail across his abs to his chest, and the brush of her hair gave his body new sensitivities he never knew he had.

"I'm usually the impatient one.... This must be something new." She flicked her tongue over his nipple and grinned. His hellcat was playing with fire. He jerked her forward and smothered her laughter. Her arms circled his shoulders as he kissed her feverishly. He tasted himself on her; his arousal heightened to the breaking point.

Lily reached over to the nightstand, and he didn't notice what she had until he heard the ripping of foil. His heart thumped. He didn't want the barrier between them, but it was for the best. He continued to kiss her while she sheathed him, his nails digging into her waist.

Lifting her until his cock touched her entrance, he leaned back to study her eyes. Molten heat burned in the depths as she poised over him and slowly sank onto his shaft. Her lashes fluttered to her cheeks as he held her close. They both groaned aloud, the movement intense yet profound. The desire to push her down until he impaled her fully had his hips twitching to surge upward. He reveled in each inch of her wetness wrapping around him.

"Oh, Rafe. I miss this. I miss you."

His heart lurched. Restraint dissolved. He thrust all the way into her, using his arm for leverage. Lily cried out. Her hips rose and met him with each hammering blow. He couldn't get enough of her. He wanted to imprint himself in her passage, make her realize she needed this, needed him. Forever.

He cupped her breast, giving it a firm squeeze before closing his mouth over the taut bud and sucking hard. Her movements became frantic, rhythm uneven as she pounded down on his cock. She was a ball of fire in his arms, magical yet wildly untamable with her response.

Letting go of her nipple, he pistoned into her faster, his body demanding release with each glide and pull through her heat. He reached between them and found her clit. He pinched. Lily screamed, her inner muscles convulsing around him. Her shriek rang in his ears as he pushed her onto her back and thrust uncontrollably, groping for the end. The sweat coating their bodies made their skin slick. Rafe slid against her with each rocking motion of his hips. His body tensed, tremors wracked through him as he spilled into her. Release swamped his entire being as his strength escaped him and he collapsed against her.

A sense of homecoming rushed over him. He marveled in the moment a bit longer before he slid out of her and lay on his side, gathering her into his arms.

Their lovemaking was better than he'd remembered.

Her soft, contented sigh brushed against his skin as she cuddled closer, her breathing evening out. He glanced down to see her eyes closed and lips parted as she blew out another breath. Exhaustion claimed him. He pressed a kiss to her forehead and allowed himself to relax.

He'd won one battle, but surely there would be many more. *One step at a time, Martinez.*

And he had two days left to convince her she still loved him.

Chapter Four

Lily eyed Rafe warily as they made their way down the snow-covered trail. She'd been disappointed to find herself in bed alone when she woke up. After her shower, Rafe had returned from downstairs and they'd gone to breakfast together as if last night had never occurred. She'd recommended a walk just to get out of the lodge, and he'd been acting weird all morning. Surely, *he* couldn't regret what had happened.

She frowned. "What's wrong with you?"

He glanced at her as he tugged his coat closer around him. "What do you mean?"

"You're being stupid." Somehow they'd fallen into the camaraderie they'd shared before life had gotten complicated with their marriage and then their divorce.

His brow lifted. "You're the one who wanted to go on this walk. You hate snow."

Lily looked up at the white sky. Flurries fluttered around them. For once, she didn't mind being out in the cold. She'd found a pair of snow boots, a scarf, and gloves in the closet. Her brother must have had someone pack for her knowing full well what she needed. "I actually don't mind it as much as I thought I would."

"You complained about it the whole time in New York."

She frowned again. The city seemed so far away at the moment as did life before their divorce. Whenever a blizzard struck, people were in near panic with the weather. She hated the aftereffects—crowded sidewalks, mounds of snow with no place to go, and grumpy pedestrians who couldn't stand the cold. Her gaze circled the white around them. Her winter-wonderland-hell didn't seem so bad after all. Their lovemaking had touched something in her, filled something she hadn't known missing. It scared yet excited her. The knowledge that she only had these next few days with him before she returned to the ranch and he the city pounded in her heart. She was determined to make their time together count before he pushed her out of his life forever and replaced her with another woman. "I don't know. It looks pretty here. Can you imagine snow in Texas?"

He shrugged. "I'm sure there are parts of Texas that do get snow."

"Not in Rover. I don't think I'd ever seen snow until we married. But then what would I know, since I wasn't there long enough and you only cared about working." She couldn't help it. She wanted some sort of reaction from him other than the indifference she'd met all morning.

Rafe glanced at her and shrugged again, never once breaking from his walk.

A growl worked up her throat. She moved ahead two steps and whirled around to face him, blocking his path. "What is your problem?"

Startled, he stopped. "What do you mean?"

"You!"

He gave her a blank look, which fueled her annoyance further. "Me...?"

She let out a frustrated grunt. "Last night...are you...do you...?"

His eyebrow rose. "What?"

She spun around and stalked off. Tears burned her eyes. Her emotions became chaotic. She didn't know what she wanted or why she would want anything beyond what had occurred. She'd had enough time to absorb what he'd admitted to her about her parents and have found fault with her own actions, but what they'd shared last night along with his nonchalant behavior this morning struck a nerve. Maybe he'd signed up for 1NightStand because any woman would do. Maybe he hated that she'd been the one to seduce him last night. Maybe all the words he'd spoken since she got here were lies.

"Lily!" Rafe's fingers wrapped around her wrist and jerked her around. She could barely make out his features as tears blurred her vision and a sob rose to her throat. "Where are you going?"

"Nowhere!" She tried to tug her hand away, but his grip tightened.

"What's going on?"

"Leave me alone!" She finally pulled free. His arm dropped to his side.

"Okay." He pivoted and headed back to the lodge.

Her mouth fell open as he disappeared down the path. Her heart tightened, pain expanding in her chest. He was leaving her just like that? The old Rafe would have coddled her, held her until she told him what was wrong because he knew her so well and would give her everything before she asked for it. Until she had withdrawn from him during their marriage. She froze. With a flustered cry, she ran after him.

Maybe *she* wasn't worthy of *him*.

Rafe drew in a deep breath. He'd woken this morning, heart heavy with the knowledge that their time together dwindled and last night should have marked a breaking point, but he wasn't so sure.

His behavior bothered her somewhat, which showed she still cared for him, but was caring enough? No. He wanted everything from her, mostly a second chance to prove he could be the best husband, her soul mate, and the father to their children—he'd do just about anything to convince her of that. Control slipped further away each waking moment, and he'd just about reached the point of begging her to give him a chance, but he had his pride. How long before she broke down and realized what they could have was precious and binding? Knowing how rebellious his Lily was, she'd quickly do the opposite because of her stubbornness and he'd lose her before he knew it.

His body burned with tension, his chest ached, and doubts continued to fill his mind.

Lily's outburst on the trail had scared him. She'd sought comfort and solace for what had happened last night, but he couldn't give it to her, not until she sorted out her own feelings for him. He played a risky game, but he was certain she still loved him. If only she would give them an opportunity to start over and stop seeing this weekend as a mini-vacation.

He reached their room and unlocked the door. Shoving his hand through his hair, he let himself in and went straight to the bar. Something to soothe his anxiety and fear of losing Lily. Getting her here had been the easy part, but making her see the truth about them was a battle he refused to lose. His fingers shook as he pulled the cork out of the decanter and poured himself a good-sized whiskey shot.

Taking the drink in one gulp, he appreciated the burn of the liquid down his throat when the door flung open and he whirled around to see Lily. The anguish in her eyes tore at his insides. Her body shook as she wrapped her arms around herself. His insides softened at the despair cloaked around her. He didn't think. Striding across the room, he pulled her into his arms and kissed her. Need claimed him. Desire clawed its way out.

He pushed the door closed and pressed Lily against it. Her fervor matched his as she dug her hands into his hair and kissed him back. He worked the button of her jeans and slid the zipper down. His cock ached uncontrollably. One look, one touch and he was hard whenever she was near. He needed to test her wetness, feel her inner muscles close around him, just be *in* her. Lily cried out the minute his finger breached her heat. She was definitely wet and ready.

She kicked her boots off as he tore at her clothes. She did the same to him as they made their way across the room to the bed, a trail of clothing following in their wake. He pulled her into his arms and covered her lips again. His hands roamed freely, grabbing, pinching, caressing every part of her body he could reach. Control seemed lost.

Breaking from their kiss, he flipped her onto her stomach,

curling a hand under her pelvis and lifting her until she kneeled. Lily glanced over her shoulder at him, eyes laden with heat, mouth swollen.

"Hurry," she murmured.

It was all he needed. He grabbed a condom from the nightstand and sheathed himself in two seconds. The first thrust tore an animalistic scream from his throat. He moved once he'd felt the tight clamp of her inner muscles, the action encouraging him not to hold back. Hammering into her, he reveled in each pull and push through her wetness. Each jolt of pleasure through his body gripped his heart.

He reached around her, his fingers finding the taut bundle of nerves between her legs as he continued rocking into her. Lily buried her face into the pillow, her cries muffled and breasts rubbing against the sheets with each fierce thrust. He shoved harder, needing to brand her, claim her.

The thought of another man claiming his woman sent his head into a spin, and his movements became more frenzied and intense. He couldn't lose her, couldn't live without her. His fingers danced over her clit, circling, teasing the engorged bud as he trailed kisses and nips over her shoulders. Lily's body tensed. Her sex wrapped around his shaft and each shudder, tremor drew him closer to his own release as she thrashed against the sheets.

"Rafe...no more," she cried out.

He needed to see her come again before he finished. Her beauty enthralled him. The wildness of her hair around her face, the whimpers slipping past her lips touched every nerve in his body.

"Baby, you can take more, can't you?" He thrust harder. His balls tightened, making the desire to come in her all the more profound. The thought that this would be the last time he made love to his Lily broke his heart. He couldn't let go. Leaning over her, he slid his hands along her stomach and cupped her breasts, his fingers tweaking her hard nipples. His mouth watered to kiss them, tease them with his tongue. With a growl, he pulled out just to flip her over and entered her once again. Lily cried out at the change in position. He drew a nub in his mouth and sucked hard. His fingers reached between them and circled her clit, this time tugging and pinching. Her legs wrapped around his waist, her hips arching up to meet each push into her wetness.

Tension rose as he neared his release. His movements became wild, out of control. He slid his arms under her knees and held her open. The sight of his member plowing into her heat sent him over the edge. Lily came again, her muscles milking him as he shot into her. With one last thrust, he collapsed on top of her, trying to catch his breath.

He didn't know how much time had passed before he opened his eyes. *Silent Night* played in the background from the radio as Lily hummed it into his ear and rubbed his back. Contentment enveloped him but he knew their troubles were far from over. When he tried to pull out of her, she held onto him tighter.

"Not yet," she said.

He propped his elbows on each side of her head and looked down at her. Her eyes were slightly troubled and he frowned. Running a finger along her cheek, he asked, "What's wrong? Did I hurt you?"

She gave him a watery smile. "I'm sorry," she murmured. "I'm so sorry."

Fear rose to his throat. "For what?"

"Just because." Her gaze trailed over his features. "I realized something when you walked away."

He paused, hope flaming in his chest. "What?"

She sniffled. "You thought you weren't worthy of me, but you know what? Maybe I'm the one who isn't cut out to be your wife. Maybe I'm the one who destroyed our marriage and the best thing was for me to leave. I blamed you because it was easier."

Rafe pushed away from the bed, hating the feel of leaving her warmth. Stripping the condom off his cock, he spun around to face her and threw the hated baby barrier in the trash can next to the night stand. "Lily—"

"No." She rose to sit and held up her hand. "Hear me out. No matter what my parents did to keep us apart, it was really my fault. I was jealous of your job and more of a burden than anything to you. Say you forgive me."

He shook his head. Another side of Lily that he didn't expect. He wanted her to realize that she loved him and wanted to be with him once again, not that she'd made mistakes in the past.

Lily bit her lip. Tears appeared in her eyes. "Oh."

"Lily, it's not that. You were everything I had ever wanted...and you still are everything I want."

She gasped and grappled for the bed sheet to cover up her nakedness. "Then why were you so cold to me earlier? One second you're unreachable, then you're hot as fire. Why are you doing this to me? What game are you playing?"

Her pained questions tore at his insides. How could he answer her? His gaze trailed over her features. The aftermath of their lovemaking glowed around her. Her loveliness still took his breath away. Days and nights of dreaming and plotting how to win her back had kept him going in life. Then truth struck him. A laugh surged to his throat. All the while he'd been planning on how to get her back, he'd miscalculated how much his own pride would keep them apart.

She hugged the sheet to her chest. "You think this is funny?"

The disgruntled quirk of her lips made him laugh out loud.

"Rafe Martinez, I hate you." She said it so calmly that he sobered up quickly and sat on the edge of the bed. Her shoulders hunched in defeat, and his heart clenched. Tenderness claimed him as he moved forward and cupped her cheek.

"I love you. Always have and always will."

Her lips parted as a soft exhale of air rumbled out. "Don't lie."

"I almost died when you left. But I refuse to lose you again. Come back to me. Give me a second chance. I want forever, *mi corazón*."

A sob slipped out before she answered him. "We're divorced."

"Marry me again."

She gasped then indifference encompassed her features. "You just wanted to have a weekend fling with some woman."

"I wanted a fling with *my* woman."

Lily jerked backward. She covered her mouth with her hand as if to hold in a sob. He pried her fingers away and laid her palm against his thigh, noting the slenderness of her bones and smoothness of her skin.

"You know that building next to the library?"

"No."

He looked up. The blatant confusion on her face was adorable. He leaned in and gave her a quick, hard kiss. "The place that we used to go to for ice cream in Rover?"

She tugged her hand back. "What about it? It's closed. Someone bought it a few weeks ago and it's getting renovated."

He drew in a deep breath. If this didn't work, then he had nothing else. "I bought the building."

She frowned. "For what?"

"I'm opening up my own law firm, once I pass the Texas Bar Exam."

"Why?" Her question came out barely audible.

He waited till her gaze met his. "Because my home is wherever you are. And I want to live wherever you want to be."

As if dumbfounded, she just stared at him. He didn't know what to think. Fear, anxiety, nausea rose to his throat. He'd screwed up. Once again.

Standing up, he blinked back his own tears. He'd gambled and lost.

"Rafe."

He paused until he felt her hands circle his chest from behind and her breasts pressed against his back. "I don't want you to give up anything because of me."

Whipping around, he caught her face in his palms. "But I wouldn't be. I'd have my law firm and your parents may never approve of me, but I'd be with you. That's all that matters."

A slow smile spread across her lips. She lifted a hand and caressed his taut jaw. "I love you. And I don't ever want to live without you."

Relief soared through him as he pulled her into arms, and Lily kissed him with passion, lust, and most importantly, love.

He couldn't count his lucky stars, but he sent a silent thank you to Madame Eve for making his *Silent Night* wish come true.

Chapter Five

Lily hummed *Silent Night* as she stroked a lock of Rafe's hair off his forehead. They'd bathed together and made love again before retiring to bed where they'd talked about their hopes for the future. His admission of love came as a surprise, as did his move back to Rover. The gesture made her love him more, even though a part of her worried that she was ripping his dreams away from him. He continued to assure her that *she* was all he wanted. And they'd start new with this second chance Madame Eve granted them.

Her parents were probably going to have a heart attack once she announced that she and Rafe were back together, but she didn't care. To live without her man was worse than surviving day to day without love. And that's what she'd been doing for the past three years, moving through life in a haze.

He made her whole, and Lily would never let anything come between them again.

A buzzing caught her attention and she realized it was Rafe's phone. Leaning over the bed, she reached in his pant's pocket, intending to turn the device off when the name on the screen caught her attention.

Hope everything went well. I'm scared when my sister returns. Pray my efforts helped your and Lily's happiness ~ Shane.

She turned and shook Rafe's shoulder. He grumbled something unintelligent and tried to wrap his arms around her, but she punched him in the chest and knocked his hands away. Rafe's eyes flew open and he frowned.

"What's this?" She held his phone to his face.

He cursed.

"Well?"

He reached for her but Lily slid out of bed before he could touch her. "I can explain."

Picking up the robe on the chair, she slid her arms through the sleeves and tied the sash around her waist. A part of her encouraged her temper to flare, but the happiness overwhelming her in the past few hours kept her rage at bay. Rafe and her brother had tricked her into coming here. They'd used Madame Eve. Kidnapped her and thrown her on the plane, all because Rafe had planned this.

"*Mi amor....*"

She settled her hands on her hips. His unease brought out her mischievous side. After the hell he'd put her through—lying about wanting to marry another woman, seeking a one-night stand, and teasing her with his words since she'd arrived—it was payback time. "What is Shane talking about?"

His face turned red as he drew in a deep breath. "I figured...I figured you wouldn't see me so Shane recommended 1NightStand and I worked it out with Madame Eve. Shane helped me get you on the plane and all."

She chucked the phone at him and it struck his bare chest. Rafe winced. "And it hadn't occurred to you that all you had to do was show up at my front door?"

He shoved a hand through his hair; his eyebrow rose in disbelief. "Would you have seen me?"

Crossing her arms over her chest, she kept her expression serious. "Maybe."

A slow smile spread over his face as he slid his legs over the bed, grabbed at her robe, and drew her up to him. "Don't lie. I know you. You'd probably kick my ass first before you forgive me for anything. Tell me. If I had told you that I loved you and wanted you back the moment I saw you, what would you have done?"

Lily frowned, but the answer was clear. She would have run

and avoided him as she'd done all those times he'd visited his parents. Knowing herself, she usually wasn't as forgiving, but her husband had known her well enough to act cautiously. "Why do you even want me back if I'm so horrible?"

He nuzzled her robe, drawing the folds apart with his teeth until his lips touched the swells of her breasts. "Because you belong to me, *mi esposa.*"

Her heart melted. She wanted nothing more than to be his wife once again. Gripping his head in her hands, she pulled him up for a kiss.

"Are you going to kill Shane for helping me?"

She grinned. "We'll see how well you convince me *not* to."

Rafe laughed and drew her robe off. "Then I better hope I do a good enough job or he'll hate having me for a brother-in-law again."

"We'll see, lawman. You only have one full day left before we go home."

"Time's wasting, then." He picked her up and threw her onto the bed before he covered her body with his and settled his mouth over hers.

She couldn't have asked for a better way to spend her holiday vacation.

❧

~About the Author~

Contemporary Romance Author, Clarissa Yip, leads a life of adventures and mischief. Constantly on the run, she's forever seeking the next best story. Her dreams involve finding the ultimate way of sharing her world with yours. From the Hawaiian island of Oahu to the beautiful season-changing New York, you'll never know where to find her. Find Clarissa on Facebook and Twitter or drop her a note at clarissayip@gmail.com.

www.clarissayip.com

Happy Holidays

...from Madame Evangeline

and Decadent Publishing...

Made in the USA
Charleston, SC
19 January 2012